EMBER AND STONE

ENA OF ILBREA, BOOK ONE

MEGAN O'RUSSELL

Ink Worlds Press

For the ones who have survived the flames.
You are strong enough to topple kingdoms.

EMBER AND STONE

The crack of the whip sent the birds scattering into the sky. They cawed their displeasure at the violence of the men below as they flew over the village and to the mountains beyond.

The whip cracked again.

Aaron did well. He didn't start to moan until the fourth lash. By the seventh, he screamed in earnest.

No one had given him a belt to bite down on. There hadn't been time when the soldiers hauled him from his house and tied him to the post in the square.

I clutched the little wooden box of salve hidden in my pocket, letting the corners bite deep into my palm.

The soldier passed forty lashes, not caring that Aaron's back had already turned to pulp.

I squeezed my way to the back of the crowd, unwilling to watch Aaron's blood stain the packed dirt.

Behind the rest of the villagers, children cowered in their mother's skirts, hiding from the horrors the Guilds' soldiers brought with them.

I didn't know how many strokes Aaron had been sentenced

to. I didn't want to know. I made myself stop counting how many times the whip sliced his back.

Bida, Aaron's wife, wept on the edge of the crowd. When his screams stopped, hers grew louder.

The women around Bida held her back, keeping her out of reach of the soldiers.

My stomach stung with the urge to offer comfort as she watched her husband being beaten by the men in black uniforms. But, with the salve tucked in my pocket, hiding in the back was safest.

I couldn't give Bida the box unless Aaron survived. Spring hadn't fully arrived, and the plants Lily needed to make more salves still hadn't bloomed. The tiny portion of the stuff hidden in my pocket was worth more than someone's life, especially if that person wasn't going to survive even with Lily's help.

Lily's orders had been clear—wait and see if Aaron made it through. Give Bida the salve if he did. If he didn't, come back home and hide the wooden box under the floorboards for the next poor soul who might need it.

Aaron fell to the ground. Blood leaked from a gash under his arm.

The soldier raised his whip again.

I sank farther into the shadows, trying to comfort myself with the beautiful lie that I could never be tied to the post in the village square, though I knew the salve clutched in my hand would see me whipped at the post as quickly as whatever offense the soldiers had decided Aaron had committed.

When my fingers had gone numb from gripping the box, the soldier stopped brandishing his whip and turned to face the crowd.

"We did not come here to torment you," the soldier said. "We came here to protect Ilbrea. We came here to protect the Guilds. We are here to provide peace to all the people of this great country.

This man committed a crime, and he has been punished. Do not think me cruel for upholding the law." He wrapped the bloody whip around his hand and led the other nine soldiers out of the square.

Ten soldiers. It had only taken ten of them to walk into our village and drag Aaron from his home. Ten men to tie him to the post and leave us all helpless as they beat a man who'd lived among us all his life.

The soldiers disappeared, and the crowd shifted in toward Aaron. I couldn't hear him crying or moaning over the angry mutters of the crowd.

His wife knelt by his side, wailing.

I wound my way forward, ignoring the stench of fear that surrounded the villagers.

Aaron lay on the ground, his hands still tied around the post. His back had been flayed open by the whip. His flesh looked more like something for a butcher to deal with than an illegal healer like me.

I knelt by his side, pressing my fingers to his neck to feel for a pulse.

Nothing.

I wiped my fingers on the cleanest part of Aaron's shirt I could find and weaved my way back out of the crowd, still clutching the box of salve in my hand.

Carrion birds gathered on the rooftops near the square, scenting the fresh blood in the air. They didn't know Aaron wouldn't be food for them. The villagers of Harane had yet to fall so low as to leave our own out as a feast for the birds.

There was no joy in the spring sun as I walked toward Lily's house on the eastern edge of the village.

I passed by the tavern, which had already filled with men who didn't mind we hadn't reached midday. I didn't blame them for hiding in there. If they could find somewhere away from the torment of the soldiers, better on them for seizing it. I only hoped there weren't any soldiers laughing inside the tavern's walls.

I followed the familiar path home. Along our one, wide dirt road, past the few shops Harane had to offer, to the edge of the village where only fields and pastures stood between us and the forest that reached up the eastern mountains' slopes.

It didn't take long to reach the worn wooden house with the one giant tree towering out front. It didn't take long to reach anywhere in the tiny village of Harane.

Part of me hated knowing every person who lived nearby. Part of me wished the village were smaller. Then maybe we'd fall off the Guilds' maps entirely.

As it was, the Guilds only came when they wanted to collect our taxes, to steal our men to fight their wars, or to find some other sick pleasure in inflicting agony on people who wanted nothing more than to survive. Or if their business brought them far enough south on the mountain road they had to pass through our home on their way to torment someone else.

I allowed myself a moment to breathe before facing Lily. I blinked away the images of Aaron covered in blood and shoved them into a dark corner with the rest of the wretched things it was better not to ponder.

Lily barely glanced up as I swung open the gate and stepped into the back garden. Dirt covered her hands and skirt. Her shoulders were hunched from the hours spent planting our summer garden. She never allowed me to help with the task. Everything had to be carefully planned, keeping the vegetables toward the outermost edges. Hiding the plants she could be hanged for in the center, where soldiers were less likely to spot the things she grew to protect the people of our village. The people the soldiers were so eager to hurt.

"Did he make it?" Lily stretched her shoulders back and brushed the dirt off her weathered hands.

I held the wooden box out as my response. Blood stained the

corners. It wasn't Aaron's blood. It was mine. Cuts marked my hand where I'd squeezed the box too tightly.

Lily glared at my palm. "You'd better go in and wrap your hand. If you let it get infected, I'll have to treat you with the salve, and you know we're running out."

I tucked the box back into my pocket and went inside, not bothering to argue that I could heal from a tiny cut. I didn't want to look into Lily's wrinkled face and see the glimmer of pity in her eyes.

The inside of the house smelled of herbs and dried flowers. Their familiar scent did nothing to drive the stench of blood and fear from my nose.

A pot hung over the stove, waiting with whatever Lily had made for breakfast.

My stomach churned at the thought of eating. I needed to get out. Out of the village, away from the soldiers.

I pulled up the loose floorboard by the stove and tucked the salve in between the other boxes, tins, and vials. I grabbed my bag off the long, wooden table and shoved a piece of bread and a waterskin into it for later. I didn't bother grabbing a coat or shawl. I didn't care about getting cold.

I have to get out.

I was back through the door and in the garden a minute later. Lily didn't even look up from her work. "If you're running into the forest, you had better come back with something good."

"I will," I said. "I'll bring you back all sorts of wonderful things. Just make sure you save some dinner for me."

I didn't need to ask her to save me food. In all the years I'd lived with her, Lily had never let me go hungry. But she was afraid I would run away into the forest and never return. Or maybe it was me that feared I might disappear into the trees and never come back. Either way, I felt myself relax as I stepped out of the garden and turned my feet toward the forest.

2

The mountains rose up beyond the edge of the trees, fierce towers I could never hope to climb. No one else from the village would ever even dream of trying such a thing.

The soldiers wouldn't enter the woods. The villagers rarely dared to go near them. The forest was where darkness and solitude lay. A quiet place where the violence of the village couldn't follow me.

I skirted farmers' fields and picked my way through the pastures. No one bothered me as I climbed over the fences they built to keep in their scarce amounts of sheep and cows.

No one kept much livestock. They couldn't afford it in the first place. And besides, if the soldiers saw that one farmer had too many animals, they would take the beasts as taxes. Safer to be poor. Better for your belly to go empty than for the soldiers to think you had something to give.

I moved faster as I got past the last of the farmhouses and beyond the reach of the stench of animal dung.

When I was a very little girl, my brother had told me that the woods were ruled by ghosts. That none of the villagers dared to cut down the trees or venture into their shelter for fear of being taken by the dead and given a worse fate than even the Guilds could provide.

I'd never been afraid of ghosts, and I'd wandered through the woods often enough to be certain that no spirits roamed the eastern mountains.

When I first started going into the forest, I convinced myself I was braver than everyone else in Harane. I was an adventurer, and they were cowards.

Maybe I just knew better. Maybe I knew that no matter what ghosts did, they could never match the horrors men inflict on each other. What I'd seen them do to each other.

By the time I was a hundred feet into the trees, I could no longer see the village behind me. I couldn't smell anything but the fresh scent of damp earth as the little plants fought for survival in the fertile spring ground. I knew my way through the woods well enough I didn't need to bother worrying about which direction to go. It was more a question of which direction I wanted to chase the gentle wind.

I could go and find fungi for Lily to make into something useful, or I could climb. If I went quickly, I would have time to climb and still be able to find something worth Lily getting herself hanged for.

Smiling to myself, I headed due east toward the steepest part of the mountains near our village. Dirt soon covered the hem of my skirt, and mud squelched beneath my shoes, creeping in through the cracked leather of the soles. I didn't mind so much. What the cold could do to me was nothing more than a refreshing chance to prove I was still alive. Life existed outside the village, and there was beauty beyond our battered walls.

Bits of green peeked through the brown of the trees as new buds forced their way out of the branches.

I stopped, staring up at the sky, marveling at the beauty hidden within our woods.

Birds chirped overhead. Not the angry cawing of birds of

death, but the beautiful songs of lovebirds who had nothing more to worry about than tipping their wings up toward the sky.

A gray and blue bird burst from a tree, carrying his song deeper into the forest.

A stream gurgled to one side of me. The snap of breaking branches came from the other. I didn't change my pace as the crackling came closer.

I headed south to a steeper slope where I had to use my hands to pull myself up the rocks.

I moved faster, outpacing the one who lumbered through the trees behind me. A rock face cut through the forest, blocking my path. I dug my fingers into the cracks in the stone, pulling myself up. Careful to keep my legs from being tangled in my skirt, I found purchase on the rock with the soft toes of my boots. In a few quick movements, I pushed myself up over the top of the ledge. I leapt to my feet and ran to the nearest tree, climbing up to the highest thick branch.

I sat silently on my perch, waiting to see what sounds would come from below.

A rustle came from the base of the rock, followed by a long string of inventive curses.

I bit my lips together, not allowing myself to call out.

The cursing came again.

"Of all the slitching, vile—" the voice from below growled.

I leaned back against the tree, closing my eyes, reveling in my last few moments of solitude. Those hints of freedom were what I loved most about being able to climb. Going up a tree, out of reach of the things that would catch me.

"Ena," the voice called. "Ena."

I didn't answer.

"Ena, are you going to leave me down here?"

My lips curved into a smile as I bit back my laughter. "I didn't ask you to follow me. You can just go back the way you came."

"I don't want to go back," he said. "Let me come up. At least show me how you did it."

"If you want to chase me, you'd better learn to climb."

I let him struggle for a few more minutes until he threatened to find a pick and crack through the rock wall. I glanced down to find him three feet off the ground, his face bright red as he tried to climb.

"Jump down," I said, not wanting him to fall and break something. I could have hauled him back to the village, but I didn't fancy the effort.

"Help me get up," he said.

"Go south a bit. You'll find an easier path."

I listened to the sounds of him stomping off through the trees, enjoying the bark against my skin as I waited for him to find the way up.

It only took him a few minutes to loop back around to stand under my perch.

Looking at Cal stole my will to flee. His blond hair glistened in the sun. He shaded his bright blue eyes as he gazed up at me.

"Are you happy now?" he said. "I'm covered in dirt."

"If you wanted to be clean, you shouldn't have come into the woods. I never ask you to follow me."

"It would have been wrong of me not to. You shouldn't be coming out here by yourself."

I didn't let it bother me that he thought it was too dangerous for me to be alone in the woods. It was nice to have someone worry about me. Even if he was worried about ghosts that didn't exist.

"What do you think you'd be able to do to help me anyway?" I said.

He stared up at me, hurt twisting his perfect brow.

Cal looked like a god, or something made at the will of the Guilds themselves. His chiseled jaw held an allure to it, the rough stubble on his cheeks luring my fingers to touch its texture.

I twisted around on my seat and dropped down to the ground, reveling in his gasp as I fell.

"You really need to get more used to the woods," I said. "It's a good place to hide."

"What would I have to hide from?" Cal's eyes twinkled, offering a hint of teasing that drew me toward him.

I touched the stubble on his chin, tracing the line of his jaw.

"There are plenty of things to hide from, fool." I turned to tramp farther into the woods.

"Ena," he called after me, "you shouldn't be going so far from home."

"Then don't follow me. Go back." I knew he would follow.

I had known when I passed by his window in the tavern on my way through the village. He always wanted to be near me. That was the beauty of Cal.

I veered closer to the stream.

Cal kept up, though he despised getting his boots muddy.

I always chose the more difficult path to make sure he knew I could outpace him. It was part of our game on those trips into the forest.

I leapt across the stream to a patch of fresh moss just beginning to take advantage of spring.

"Ena." Cal jumped the water and sank down onto the moss I had sought.

I shoved him off of the green and into the dirt.

He growled.

I didn't bother trying to hide my smile. I pulled out tufts of the green moss, tucking them into my bag for Lily.

"If you don't want me to follow you," Cal said, "you can tell me not to whenever you like."

"The forest doesn't belong to me, Cal. You can go where you choose."

He grabbed both my hands and tugged me toward him. I tipped onto him and he shifted, letting me fall onto my back. I caught a glimpse of the sun peering down through the new buds of emerald leaves, and then he was kissing me.

His taste of honey and something a bit deeper filled me. And I forgot about whips and Lily and men bleeding and soldiers coming to kill us.

There was nothing but Cal and me. And the day became beautiful.

3

I let Cal follow me up and down the mountain for hours. Cal filled the silence with news of everyone in the village. His family owned the tavern, so all news, both the happy and the terrible, passed through the walls of his home. He didn't know what the people were saying about Aaron yet. He'd followed me before anyone had grown drunk enough to loose their tongue.

"Les had better be careful, or he's going to be on the hunt for a new wife," Cal laughed.

I forced a chuckle. I hadn't been paying close enough attention to hear what Les had done this time.

I cut through a dense patch of bushes, trying to find where treasures would grow when summer neared. I didn't mind the twigs clawing at me or the mud clinging to my clothes.

Cal didn't mention his displeasure at being dirty. He was too content being with me.

I let him hold my hand, savoring the feel of his skin against mine. His warmth burned away the rest of the fear the soldiers had left lodged near my lungs.

Cal pulled me close to his side, winding his arm around my waist.

"I can't go home without proper goodies for Lily." I wriggled free from Cal's grasp.

I followed a game trail farther up the mountain, searching for evergreens whose new buds could help cure the stomach ills that always floated around the village in the spring. By the time the peak of the afternoon passed, I had enough in my bag to please Lily and had spent enough time climbing to give myself a hope of sleeping that night. I turned west, beginning the long trek home.

"We don't have to go back." Cal laced his fingers through mine.

"You think you'd survive in the woods?"

"With you by my side?" His hands moved to my waist. He held me close, swaying in time to music neither of us could hear. He pressed his lips to my forehead. "I think we could stay out here forever." He kissed my nose and cheeks before his lips finally found mine.

My heart raced as he pulled me closer, pressing my body against his.

"Cal"—I pulled an inch away, letting the cool air blow between us—"we have to get back. Lily won't be happy if I'm out too long."

"What'll she do? Scowl at you?"

"Kick me out, more like." I started back down the mountainside. "I don't fancy sleeping in the mud."

I'd lived with Lily for more than half my life, but that didn't make the old healer obligated to keep me a day longer than she wanted to.

Cal caught me in his arms, twisted me toward him, and held me tighter. He brushed his lips against mine. His tongue teased my mouth, luring me deeper into the kiss.

I sank into his arms, reveling in the feel of his hard muscles against me.

He ran his fingers along my sides, sending shivers up my spine.

I sighed as his lips found my neck and trailed out to my shoulder.

"We have to go," I murmured.

Cal wound his fingers through mine. "Let's hide in the wood forever."

"Cal—"

"I love you, Ena." A glimmer of pure bliss lit his eyes.

"I'm going," I said. "Come with me or find your own way back."

Cal pressed his lips to my forehead. "Lead the way."

If I hadn't known him so well, I might not have heard the hint of hurt in his voice.

I didn't want to hurt Cal, but I didn't have anything of myself to offer him. It was easy for Cal to declare his love. He had a solid roof, a business to inherit, a family who cared for him. I was nothing but an orphan inker kept from sleeping in the mud by the goodwill of an ornery old woman.

Cal followed me silently down the slope of the mountain.

I stopped by a fallen tree. The stench of its rot cut through the scent of spring.

"You're the best part of the village." The words tumbled out of my mouth before I'd thought through them.

"I guess that's something. Better than anyone else has gotten out of you."

"Better than they ever will."

His boots thumped on the ground as he ran a few steps to catch up to me. I didn't fight him as he laced his fingers through mine and pressed his lips to my temple. I didn't slow my pace as I started walking again either.

I hadn't been lying—we needed to be heading back to the village. As much as I loved the woods, I didn't fancy being in the trees at night.

The villagers and soldiers might have avoided the forest and mountains because of ghost stories, but their foolishness didn't make the woods entirely safe. I could hear the howls of the wolves at night from Lily's loft where I slept. And farm animals had been lost to creatures far larger than wolves. I didn't fancy having to hide up a tree, shivering as I waited for the dawn. I didn't know if Cal would be able to make it high enough in a tree to be safe.

I let my mind wander as we reached the gentler slopes toward the base of the mountain, wondering over all the terrifying animals that could be hiding just out of sight. Dug into a den that reached below our feet. Hiding in the brush where I couldn't spot them.

A shiver of something ran up my spine.

"You should have brought something warmer." Cal let go of my hand to take off his coat.

"I'm fine." I searched the shadows, trying to find whatever trick of the forest had set my nerves on edge.

Trees rustled to the south, the sound too large to be a bird and too gentle to be death speeding toward us.

I stopped, tugging on Cal's hand to keep him beside me, and reached for the thin knife I kept tucked in my bag.

Cal stepped in front of me as the rustling came closer.

My breath hitched in my chest. I wanted to climb the nearest tree but couldn't leave Cal alone on the ground. My hand trembled as I gripped the hilt of my blade tighter.

"Are you going to try and stab me?" a voice called out. "I don't think it would do you much good."

I would have known that voice after a hundred years.

I gripped my knife tighter, fighting the urge to throw it at my brother's face as he stepped out from between the trees.

"Emmet." Cal stretched a hand toward my brother as a man with black hair and dark eyes stepped out of the shadows beside Emmet.

I took Cal's arm, keeping him close to me.

"Ena"—my brother gave a nod—"Cal."

"What are you doing here?" I asked before Cal could say something more polite.

My brother shrugged. His shoulders were wide from his work as a blacksmith. The familiarity of his face—his bright blue eyes, deep brown hair, and pale skin—tugged at my heart. He looked so much like my mother had. She'd given the same coloring to both of us.

But the hard line of his jaw, which became more defined as he turned to the other man, that Emmet had inherited from our father.

The black-haired man gave my brother a nod.

"I found out you'd gone to the woods, and I decided to check on you," Emmet said.

"How did you find me?" I asked at the same moment Cal said, "We were just heading back."

"You should go then," Emmet said. "I can make sure Ena gets home safe."

"I'd rather—" Cal began.

"I think you've spent enough time in the woods with my little sister." Emmet pointed down the slope. "Keep heading that way, you'll find the village soon enough."

The man next to my brother bit back a smile.

Pink crept up Cal's neck.

"It's fine." I laid a hand on his arm. "Go."

Cal turned to me, locking eyes with me for a moment before kissing the back of my hand. "I'll see you tomorrow." He didn't look back at my brother before striding away.

I glared at Emmet as Cal's footsteps faded.

A new scar marred Emmet's left cheek. His hands had taken more damage since the last time I'd seen him as well.

"You shouldn't be alone with him in the woods," Emmet said when the sounds of Cal's footsteps had vanished.

"And you shouldn't be following me."

"I wanted to be sure you were safe," Emmet said. "A man was killed in the village today, did you not hear?"

"I saw it." I tucked my knife into my bag. "I watched the soldiers whip Aaron to death. But I don't see any soldiers around here, so I think I'll be just fine."

The man gave a low laugh.

"Who are you?" I asked.

"A friend," he said. He looked to be the same as age as my brother, only a couple of years older than Cal and me. If I hadn't been so angry, I might have thought him handsome, but there was something in the way he stood so still while I glared daggers at him that made me wish I hadn't put my knife back into my bag.

"You should get back to the village," Emmet said. "The mountains aren't a safe place to wander."

I turned and climbed farther up the mountain, not caring that he was right.

"Ena." Emmet's footfalls thundered up behind me. "You should get back to Lily." He grabbed my arm, whipping me around.

"Don't tell me where I should be." I wrenched my arm free.

"Then don't be a fool. Get yourself home. You don't belong out here."

"I had Cal with me."

"Being alone with him in the woods is a fool of a choice, too. You've got to think, Ena."

"Don't pretend you care!"

A bird screeched his anger at my shout.

"Ena—"

"You don't get to show up here, follow me into the woods, and try to tell me what to do." My voice shook as I fought to keep from scratching my brother's damned eyes out. "Once a year—once a gods' forsaken year—you show up in Harane. You don't get to pretend to care where I go or who I'm with."

Emmet's brow creased. "I do care. I make it back as often as I'm allowed."

"Liar." The word rumbled in my throat. "The only reason you haven't come back is because you don't want to."

A stick cracked as the black-haired man stepped closer.

"Where have you been, brother?" I'd been saving the question for nearly a year. Holding it in, saying it over and over again in my head as I imagined myself screaming it at Emmet. In all the times I'd thought through it, I'd never pictured him drawing his shoulders defiantly back.

"I've got to work for the blacksmith," Emmet said. "I've finished my apprenticeship, but I've got to pay—"

"You're a damned chivving liar."

"What would I be lying about?" Emmet asked.

"I went to Nantic," I said, "caught a ride in a cart to get to you."

"What?" Emmet said.

"Found the smith where you were supposed to be." I stepped forward, shoving Emmet in the chest. "Two years? Two years since you ran from the blacksmith's, and you've been lying to me."

Emmet's face paled.

"I went to find you, and you weren't there! I was lucky Lily even took me back after I left like that."

Emmet caught my hands. "Why did you go looking for me?"

"You don't get to care. You don't get to lie to me and pretend to care."

Emmet's stone face faltered for the first time. "I do care, Ena. I've come to visit because I care."

"Stopping in once a year doesn't make you a decent brother." I tore my hands free, feeling the bruises growing where he'd gripped my fingers. "You left me here. I didn't even know how to find you. I didn't know if you'd ever come back."

"I had to. I'm sorry, but what I'm doing is more important than being a blacksmith."

"How?"

Emmet looked up to the sky. "It is. You just have to believe that it is."

"And it's more important than I am?" I stared at my brother, waiting for him to crack and tell me there was nothing in all of Ilbrea more important than his only living blood relation.

"It's more important than all of us," Emmet said. "I'm sorry if I can't be the brother you need me to be, but my work has to be done."

"Why?"

"Because there has to be more to this chivving mess of a world than waiting for the Guilds to kill us." Wrinkles creased Emmet's brow. "I can't spend my life waiting to die."

The black-haired man placed a hand on my brother's shoulder. "She should get back to the village."

"Right." Emmet nodded.

I stared at the dark-haired man, wishing he would fade back into the shadows and disappear.

"Then let me help you," I said.

"What?"

"If you have work that's so important, let me help you. I'm not the little girl you left behind in Harane. Wherever it is you've been hiding, take me with you. We're blood, Emmet. I should be with you."

"No." Emmet shook his head. His hair flung around his face. "You belong here."

"I belong with the only family I have." I stepped forward, tipping my chin up to meet his gaze. "I'm not a child. I can help. Let me come with you."

"You can't." Emmet stepped away from me. "You've got to stay with Lily. You're safer here, Ena."

"You're a chivving fool if you believe that."

"It's true. You have to stay in Harane. I have to keep you safe."

"See you next year, brother." I stormed past him and back down the mountain.

He didn't follow.

I've never believed in peaceful lives and beautiful tales. Those are no truer than ghost stories. Both are lies we tell ourselves to make the pain we suffer a little less real.

Happiness doesn't swoop in and save us when everything turns dark and bloody. And men do far worse to each other than monsters could ever manage.

Even the men who aren't demons, the ones you should be able to trust when the worst storm comes, they'll hurt you as well.

At the end of the tale, there is nothing left but pain and forcing yourself to survive.

The ink stained my fingers, leaving them a bright blue. The color was pretty, I'd done my job well, but against the dull brown of the workshop, the hue seemed obscene. There was nothing in Harane to match the pigment's brightness.

But Lily had asked me to make the color, preparing for the merchants who would come all the way down from the capital, Ilara, seeking inks as summer neared.

It should have been Lily inside grinding up leaves and berries to make the inks that were her living, but she was too busy with her other work. Work that would see her hanged by the soldiers.

A cough had swept through the village, and no one in Harane could afford the gold demanded by the Guilds' healer. It was left to Lily to see to the children so far gone with fever they couldn't hold their heads up anymore.

She'd sneak her herbs into the houses of the desperate, treating the ill with whatever she could grow in her garden and the things I could forage in the woods. Lily rarely brought me with her when she tended to the sick and wounded. Only when there was something she wanted me to learn, or too many desperate people for her to handle on her own. I don't know if she kept me away out of fear or mercy, but either way, it ended up the same.

Lily would leave a written list of inks for me to blend and give spoken orders of what tonics and salves she needed made. I'd sit in the house, letting it fill with enough steam to clog my lungs as I made vials of ink in one set of bowls and healing things in another, all on the one worn, wooden table. I think Lily believed any Guilded soldier sent to her home wouldn't have the sense to know which flowers had been chosen for their ability to fight fever and which had been selected for their pigment. She was probably right.

Whatever her reasoning might have been, the rains hadn't stopped in the three days since I'd left my brother in the forest, and I was trapped with a mortar and pestle, grinding sweet smelling leaves until I couldn't move my fingers anymore as the storm finally drifted east over the mountains.

I left the pulpy mixture of the ink to sit. It would be hours before the stuff would be ready to be carefully strained and then poured into a glass jar to be sold.

Sun peeked in through the windows as I moved on to grinding roots for Lily's remedies. The pungent smell tickled my nose as I worked my way through one knot and then another.

A tap on the door, so light I almost thought the rain had come back, pulled me out of the monotonous motion. I froze with the pestle still in my hand, listening for sounds outside.

The tapping came again.

I gave a quiet curse before calling, "Lily's out, but I'll be with you in one moment," as I pulled down the tray that hid under the tabletop. I set the roots, leaves, mortar and pestle, and vial of oil on the tray and fixed it back under the table as quickly as I could without risking any noise.

I untied the top of my bodice, shaking the laces loose and grabbing both strings in one hand as I opened the door.

"So sorry." I tied my bodice closed over my shift. "I must have drifted off."

I looked up to find, not a soldier come to drag me out for whipping, but Karin, who gave me a scathing look as she slipped past into the workshop.

"Fell asleep?" Karin circled the long table where I'd hidden the tray before peeping through the curtain that blocked off the bit of the first floor where Lily slept.

"The storm made me sleepy." I ran my fingers through my hair, leaving smudges of blue behind that would drive me mad trying to wash out later.

"And there's no one else here?" Karin's eyes twinkled as she stopped at the ladder that led to the loft where I slept. "No one who might make you forget to work?"

If I hadn't known Karin since before either of us could walk, I would have grabbed her skirts and torn her from the ladder as she climbed up like she owned the chivving shop. But Karin meant no harm, and stopping her search would only make the rumors that I'd had a man in the house keeping me from answering the door fly through the village faster.

I could have told her the truth. I had been busy working on illegal remedies for Lily and was afraid a soldier had come to the door. And I'd rather be accused of sleeping on the job than hanged for helping an unguilded healer offer remedies. But then Karin would be obligated to turn me in or risk punishment from the soldiers herself.

I leaned against the table, tracing the outline of a purple ink stain, listening to the sounds of Karin checking under my cot and opening my trunk that wouldn't have been large enough to hide Cal anyway.

"You really are the most boring person who's ever lived." Karin carefully lifted her skirts to come back down the ladder.

"I'm sure I am." I took a box of charcoal and dumped a few

bits into a fresh mortar. "So you might as well scoot back to more interesting company and leave me to my work."

"Don't you dare start on something that's going to make so much of a mess." Karin snatched the charcoal-filled mortar out of my reach. She stared at me, a glimmer of delight playing in the corners of her eyes.

I knew she wanted me to ask why she'd come and what I'd need clean hands for. The bit of obstinance that curled in my stomach wasn't as strong as the part of me that wanted something interesting to be happening after all the rain. Even if it was only Handor and Shilv fighting over whose sheep were harassing whose again.

"What is it, you fairy of a biddy?"

"Only the best, most delightful news." Karin took my shoulders, steering me to the pump sink in the corner. She worked the handle while she spoke. "Well, after word came south on the road that the map makers with a load of their soldiers were coming our way—"

"What?" I froze, a brick of harsh soap clutched in my hand.

"There's a whole pack of Guilded heading our way. How have you not heard?"

"I've been inside working." I scrubbed at the blue and black on my hands. "Some of us have things we actually have to get done."

"You should admit the real problem is you never bothering to talk to people besides Cal and Lily. You should try making friends, Ena. It would be good for you."

"Yes, fine." I snatched the pot of oily cream from the shelf. "What about the soldiers?"

"Right." Karin leaned in. "So, word comes down the road that there's a whole caravan of paun Guilded headed our way. Cal's parents are head over heels planning to have all the fancy folks at the tavern, the farmers have started trying to hide their stock so it can't be counted, and"—she paused, near shuddering with glee—"Henry Tilly took his horse and disappeared for two days."

"What?" I wiped the cream and the rest of the color from my fingers with a rag. "Did the soldiers get him?"

"No." Karin laughed. "He rode north, all the way to Nantic."

"Toward the paun caravan? Who in their right mind would do such a thing?"

Karin took my elbow and led me to a seat at the table. She pushed aside the curtain to Lily's room and snatched up Lily's hairbrush.

"Nantic is a much bigger place than Harane." Karin shook my hair free from its braid. "So many things to offer that we don't have in our tiny little village."

"Like people who tell stories that actually make sense?"

Karin dragged the brush roughly through my hair in retaliation. "Like a scribe."

"What?"

"A Guilded scribe. One who can offer all the official forms the Guilds force us to use for every little thing we do. Like buying land, being buried...getting married."

"Henry is getting married?" I spun around wide-eyed. "To you?"

"Oh gods no, not me!" Karin screwed up her face. "I'd never marry him. His left eye's bigger than his right."

"Who is he marrying then?" I knelt on the chair, gripping the back.

"Malda!" Karin clapped a hand over her mouth.

"What?"

"Henry found out the soldiers, and map makers, and entire fleet of paun were on their way and raced through the night all thirty miles up to Nantic to get marriage papers from the Guilds' scribe." Karin twirled the brush through the air. "And do you know why?"

"Love, I suppose."

"She's pregnant. That little mouse Malda is pregnant and

more than just a little. Gods, now that I know, it's impossible not to see how her belly's grown."

"Henry's a slitching fool." I dragged my fingers through my hair.

Karin grabbed my shoulders, making me face front in the chair again.

"A fool he is," Karin said, "but at least he cares for Malda enough not to risk the paun catching her pregnant without a husband. If those soldiers found her out, she'd be taken and sent to give birth on Ian Ayres in the middle of the sea. No one ever comes back from that place."

A chill shook my spine, but Karin kept talking.

"Henry brought coin to Nantic to pay the scribe, but the scribe told him he'd have to wait seven months for marriage papers."

"Seven months?" I tried to turn again, but Karin whacked me on the head with the brush.

"By which time there will be a new little screaming Henry or Malda in this world. Henry had to give the scribe his horse to get the papers and spent the last two days trudging back through the rain."

"Is he all right?" My eyes darted toward the tray hidden under the table. That long in the cold rain, and it was only a matter of time before Lily had to darken his door.

"He's in the tavern right now having a warm frie to cheer him for his wedding this afternoon." Karin twisted my hair. "They're laying hay out in the square to make a space for it. The whole thing will be done long before the sun sets, so Malda will be a married woman before the Guilds can set eyes on her ever-expanding belly."

"This afternoon? Today?" I asked.

"Yes, Ena. That is how days usually go. The whole village will be turning up for this wedding, so you need to look like a proper lady, and I need just a little bit of your magic to give me a wonderful spring blush." Karin scraped my scalp with pins.

"What for? Even if they put down enough hay to feed the horses for a season, we'll all still end up covered in mud."

"Because," Karin said, stepping in front of me and pointing a finger at my nose, "nothing makes a man consider the fact that marriage is inevitable more than a wedding. Henry panicking could be our chance to snatch a prize worth having."

Heat shot up to my cheeks.

"No." I stood, not meeting Karin's eyes as I stalked to the corner where the few small tubs of powders and paints for women's faces were kept. "You dab as much pink on your cheeks as you like, but I'll have none of it on me. I'm too young to be worrying about marriage."

"But is Cal?" That awful twinkle sprang back into Karin's eyes.

"Paint your face, you wretch." I tossed her a tin.

6

It took more than an hour for Karin to paint her face to a marriageable hue, riffle through the few clothes I owned to choose what she wanted me to wear, and give up on the idea of her painting my cheeks as well.

She'd just finished tightening the laces on my bodice to display enough of my breasts to be considered obscene, when Lily stepped in through the garden door, basket over her arm and mud clinging to her boots.

Lily stared from Karin to me. "So, you've already heard the joyous news."

"I told her." Karin gave my bodice laces one more tug. "Had to get her ready for the wedding, didn't I?"

"What's to be gotten ready for?" Lily set her basket on the table. "Put your breasts away, Ena. You're pretty enough to get into plenty of trouble without two beacons poking out the front of your dress."

"They're not poking out." I glanced down, making sure there wasn't more showing than I'd thought.

Lily unloaded the goods from her basket. "There is a fine line between the kind of beauty gods bless you with, and the kind given by the shadows to bring trouble into your life. You, Ena Ryeland, are balancing on the edge of beauty becoming a curse. So, tuck your tits back in your top before someone you don't fancy decides they have a right to the body you were born with."

"Yes, Lily." My face burned red.

Karin slapped my hands away as I tried to loosen my bodice. She grabbed the pale blue fabric of my shift instead, giving it a tug to cover more of my chest.

"Help me get these things put away so we don't miss the wedding." Lily went to her bedroom, leaving a trail of muddy boot prints behind. "We need to bring something for the bride and groom. I would say they should be gifted a lick of common sense, but it seems they threw that away five months ago when a roll in the hay seemed worth risking a life for."

Karin turned to me, her eyebrows creeping up her forehead. "I'll see you there," she mouthed before dodging out the door.

"Is that girl gone?" Lily asked.

"Yes, Lily." I examined the goods Lily had brought home with her. A fair number of eggs, two loaves of seed bread, a bottle of chamb, and a skein of thick spun wool. "You saw that many today?"

"Bad stomach, an awful cough, and had to stitch up the side of Les's head."

"What happened to Les's head?" I tucked the eggs into the shallow basket by the iron stove and wrapped the bread in a cloth.

"If you ask Les, he knocked his head in the barn." Lily stalked back out of her bedroom, a clean dress on, mud still clinging to her boots. "If you look at the manic glint in his wife's eyes, she finally got sick of the slitch and smacked him upside the head hard enough to draw blood."

"What did Les do to make her so mad?"

"Damned if I know what he's done this time." Lily pumped the sink to scrub her hands. "That boy was born stupid, and he didn't get much better once he learned to talk."

"Fair enough." I took over pumping the giant metal handle. Lily methodically washed the skin around her nails in the cold water. "The map maker's party is coming through. Should be here tomorrow from the sounds of it."

"Karin said as much."

"Map makers always come with a pack of soldiers. Who knows how big the company will be?"

"Either way, they should be through pretty quick." I passed Lily a cloth to dry her hands on. "They aren't coming to Harane on purpose. They're only taking the mountain road to get someplace else."

Lily nodded silently for a moment. "I don't want you in the village tomorrow. Head out to the mountains in the morning."

"It's been raining for days. There won't be anything for me to bring back but mud."

"Then bring back some mud." Lily took my face in her hands. "I don't want you around when the paun come through. I won't have it on my head when that pretty face of yours becomes a curse."

A knot of something like dread closed around my stomach. "I'll just stay inside and out of sight."

"You'll get to the mountains and thank me for it." She squeezed my face tighter.

I stared into her steel gray eyes.

"Do you hear me, girl?"

"Yes, ma'am."

"Good." She let go of my face. "Now, what in this chivving mess should we give the idiots getting married this afternoon?"

"Something for a chest rattle." I pulled up the loose floorboard that housed all of Lily's illegal goods. "If Karin is right, Henry will need it in a few days if he doesn't already."

"Fine. Give it to his mother so the fool doesn't go losing it."

"Yes, Lily." I pulled out one of the little wooden boxes that held the thick paste.

"Out you get then." Lily grabbed the broom from near the woodstove. "Go celebrate the panic caused by young lust."

I managed to pull my coat on before she spoke again.

"And let this be a lesson to you, Ena. Give yourself to a man with no sense, and you'll end up getting married on a godsforsaken muddy day to a fool who no longer owns a horse."

I darted out the door before Lily could say anything else. I cared for the old lady, even if she was harsh and a little strange. She swore worse than a Guilded sailor just as easily as she whispered comfort to the dying.

No one in Harane could blame Lily for her rough edges. Nigh on all of us owed our lives to her for something or other, and the few who'd been lucky enough never to need Lily's help would have been awfully lonely living at the foot of the mountains with the rest of us dead.

Mud soaked my boots before I'd made it through the garden and to the road. I lifted my hem as I leapt over the worst of the puddles, though I knew there was no hope of my skirt making it through the day unscathed.

The air in the village tasted different than it had a few days ago, and not just from the rain. The stink of despair had fled, replaced by a dancing breeze of hope.

It was true enough that Henry and Malda were only getting married to escape the wrath of the Guilds. If the lords far away in Ilara hadn't passed a law banning children being born outside marriage, then Shilv wouldn't have been carrying hay to the square.

Malda wouldn't have had to fear being snatched up by soldiers, loaded onto a ship, and sent out to the isle of Ian Ayres to give birth. Henry wouldn't have had to give up his horse. I wouldn't have been dodging puddles with salve in my coat pocket. And the whole village would have had endless hours of entertainment for the next few months wondering if Malda was carrying a child or had only taken too strongly to sweet summer cakes.

But the Guilds ruled Ilbrea with their shining, golden fist. If they said women carrying babies out of wedlock were to be taken, there was nothing we could do to fight the paun. Just like we couldn't stop them from whipping Aaron to death. In the whole land of Ilbrea, there was nothing unguilded rotta like us could do but try and avoid the Guilds' notice and hope they weren't bored enough to come after us anyway.

I'd gotten so lost in wondering what would have happened to Malda and her baby if Henry hadn't had a horse to offer, I walked right past the tavern.

"Ena!" Cal called out the kitchen window, waving a flour-covered rag, which left a puff of white floating in the air.

"Don't hang out the window," Cal's father shouted. "If you want to talk to the girl, bring her inside like a civilized man."

Cal bit back his smile. "Miss Ryeland, would you grace us with your presence in our humble kitchen."

"Why thank you." I gave as deep a curtsy as I could manage without sinking my hem deep into the mud and headed back up the street to the tavern door.

Harane didn't have many businesses that would interest travelers, and everything that might appeal, aside from Lily's ink shop, had been packed into the very center of the village. The tavern, cobbler, stables, tannery, and smith had all been built close together with narrow alleys running between them, as though whoever had laid the foundations had thought Harane would become a town or even a city someday.

That person had been wrong.

Harane was nothing but a tract of fertile farmland situated thirty miles south of Nantic and twenty-nine miles north of Hareford on the Guild-approved road that ran as close to the mountains as travelers dared to get. The only reason the tavern managed to fill its aged, wooden tables every night was the travelers who needed a place to stop between Nantic and Hareford, and the village men, like Les, who were too afraid of their wives to go home.

The tables in the tavern only had a smattering of people since the travelers hadn't arrived for the night and the village folk were getting ready for the surprise wedding.

"Ena." Cal waved me in through the kitchen door.

The scent of baking pastries, roasting meat, and fresh poured frie warmed my face before I even neared the wide fireplace and big iron oven.

"I take it you heard?" Cal raised an eyebrow at my hair.

I ran my fingers along the delicate twists Karin promised would win me a husband, blushing to the roots of my hair as I met Cal's gaze. "Karin insisted."

"Careful of the hot." Cal's mother pulled a tray of sweet rolls from the oven. The tops had been crusted to a shining brown.

"Those are beautiful." I leaned in to sniff. "I didn't think you'd spend the time on a last minute wedding."

Cal's mother tsked. "I'm making three loaves of bread for the wedding. One for each of them."

I coughed a laugh.

"The rolls are for the Guilded coming through," she said. "I only hope it's true they're coming tomorrow. If not, the lot will go stale. But if I wait to start until they arrive, I won't be able to make enough to sell." She worried her wrinkled lips together. "I've already had the rooms upstairs cleaned, and Cal's pulled fresh barrels of frie and chamb. I only hope it's enough."

"Does it matter?" I leaned against the edge of the table. "It's a caravan of paun. If you don't have enough for them, they'll just have to stay in their camp where they belong and move on south all the faster."

"We need their business," Cal's father said. "A day with the caravan will be more coin than we'll see for the rest of the summer. The gods smiled on us when they sent the map makers down the mountain road."

"Right." I felt my mouth curve into a smile even as a horrible cold tingled down my neck and surrounded the dread in my stomach. "I'm very happy for you."

"Is there anything else you need me for?" Cal asked.

"Go." Cal's mother shooed him toward the door. "But if anyone dares say something snide about your father and me not coming to the square, tell them not to darken the tavern door for a month. I don't care how thirsty they are for frie."

"Yes, mother." Cal kissed his mother's cheek and took a basket from near the stove.

"Someday soon, there will be a wedding worth leaving work undone for," Cal's mother said. "This is not that day."

I bit my lips together and let Cal put a hand on my waist, guiding me back out into the main room of the tavern.

"Honestly," Cal said in a low voice as soon as the kitchen door shut behind us, "it's probably better my parents not come."

"Why?" I whispered.

"Poor Henry has to stand in front of everyone, with the whole village knowing full well what a slitch he was to let Malda hang for so long. Imagine adding my mother's glare to that weight."

I laughed, and the cold and dread around my stomach vanished with a tiny pop of joy.

7

I'll never know how they managed to find enough hay to coat the mud in the square. Not that the square was large, or even properly a square.

On the northern end of the village, someone, a very long time ago, had surrounded a square of land with heavy stones. No one had moved the stones or stolen them to build for fear of angering some unknown spirit. So, the rocks as big as my torso lay undisturbed, and the people of Harane gathered within them whenever the need arose.

Most often, the need came from the soldiers issuing Guild decrees or doling out punishment. But we used the square for things like weddings and summer celebrations as well. I don't know if people thought there was some good to be gained from gathering within the stones, or if it was pure stubbornness in not letting the Guilds steal the square and make it an awful place where none of the villagers dared tread.

Either way ended with Henry and Malda standing side by side in front of a horde of people.

Tomin had become the eldest in the village after a lung infection took a few of the older folks during the winter, so it was his place to stand with Henry and Malda to perform the wedding.

"And in the bonds of marriage, do you swear to protect your other half?" Tomin said. "Through winter and drought? Through flood and famine?"

"I do," Henry and Malda said together.

Henry's face was pale, whether from fright of being married or exhaustion from walking back from Nantic, I couldn't tell.

Tomin reached into his pocket and pulled out a filthy rag. "Hands please."

Malda and Henry both held up their right palms.

Tomin unfolded the rag and patted the clump of dirt within it flat. "Hard to find anything dry."

The villagers chuckled, and Tomin gave a gap-toothed grin.

"From the dirt we all have come." Tomin sprinkled dirt onto Malda's palm. "And to the dirt we all must go." He sprinkled dirt onto Henry's palm. "May your journey in between be sweeter for standing by each other's side."

Together, Henry and Malda tipped their hands, letting the dirt tumble onto the muddy hay at their feet.

"Your lives are one," Tomin said. "Live them well!"

The crowd cheered.

Malda threw her arms around Henry's neck and kissed him.

The children winced and whined—the rest of us clapped and hollered.

Before Malda had stopped kissing Henry, someone began playing a fiddle. A drum joined a moment later, and Henry took Malda's hands, dragging her to the center of the square to dance.

I laughed at the look of pure horror on Malda's face. An arm snaked around my waist.

"Are you going to look as petrified when I make you dance?" Cal whispered in my ear.

"I don't think you could make me do anything." I twisted out of his grip and darted toward the center of the square where everyone had picked up on the dance.

Cal raced to my side, taking me in his arms before anyone else could have the chance. We spun and bounced in time with the music as the hay beneath our feet was eaten entirely by the mud. Cal lifted me and twirled me under his arm until my heart beat so fast I thought it might race out of my chest. His laughter rang in my ears. The bright joy that lit his eyes sent my soul soaring up high above the clouds.

Then Henry's father wheeled out a barrel of frie. The crowd shifted toward the drink.

And the whipping post was there, waiting at the back of the celebration.

There was no blood on the ground, the rain had washed it all away, but dark stains mottled the post. The wood had been worn down in places where the soldiers' victims had strained against their bonds.

My feet lost the feel of the dance, and I swayed, staring at the bloody monument to all the damage the Guilds had done.

"Ena?" Cal took my waist in his hands. "Are you all right?"

"Tired." I nodded. "I'm just tired."

"Come on." He led me to the side of the square where Henry's father doled out frie in borrowed cups. I stood on the edge of the crowd while Cal dove between people to snatch each of us a drink. He emerged a moment later, his hair rumpled, but clasping a cup in each hand. "Here."

I took the cup and sipped the frie. The drink burned a path down my throat, past my lungs, and into my stomach, but didn't make me feel any better.

Cal laced his fingers through mine and led me to the south side of the square. We sat on one of the largest of the boundary stones, watching the dancers spin round and round.

"It's a nice wedding," Cal said. "And Henry's family seems happy to be getting Malda."

"They do." I took another sip of frie, trying to burn away the taste of sick in my mouth.

"Malda grew up on a farm, so she won't have trouble getting used to the labor Henry's land will require."

"She's a strong girl," I said. "They'll do well together."

"We'd do well together." Cal leaned in close. "Better than them. I could provide for you better than Henry ever—"

"I have my own work." I tightened my grip on my cup.

"And you could work with Lily if you wanted," Cal said. "But you wouldn't have to. I'm going to inherit the tavern. It's a good income, Ena."

"Don't, Cal. Please don't."

"I know we're young." Cal knelt in the mud front of me, making it impossible for me to look away from his beautiful eyes. "And I'm not saying we should get married soon. We could wait until next summer, give Lily some time to get used to the idea of you moving to the tavern."

"I couldn't." The truth of the words tore at my chest. "I can't."

"She'll make do on her own."

"I can't live in the tavern. I can't be married to a man who makes his coin from soldiers."

"Ena—"

"The soldiers coming is good for your family, but to me it only means death. I couldn't smile at them and serve them. They are monsters. Your family makes their living feeding the monsters who slaughter us."

The glimmer of light in Cal's eyes faded. I could still see the post over his shoulder, coming in and out of view as the people danced where they had stood to watch Aaron murdered only a few days before.

"You are everything bright and wonderful, Cal. But I could never be your wife."

I stood up, set my cup down on the rock, and walked out of the square. I didn't look back. Cal didn't follow.

The night is pitch black, and I am racing down the road.

The thundering of the horse's hooves doesn't cover the pounding of my heart. I search for a glimmer of light up ahead, but there's nothing.

Only endless night.

I keep riding until fear finally wakes me.

I left for the woods at dawn the next morning. I'd heard Lily come in after the wedding but stayed silently huddled under my blankets. I didn't want to talk to her. Didn't want her to stare at me with her steel gray eyes and know she felt sorry for me—even though she'd never say it.

After a night spent trapped in a horrible dream, I still didn't want to see her. I slipped out of the house when the sun finally rose and fled for the safety of the forest.

The trees didn't ask what kind of a foolish girl would turn down the best marriage Harane had to offer. The birds didn't call me a hypocrite for making inks to be sent to Ilara where only the gods knew if Guilded paun would be using them. The rotting leaves squishing under my feet didn't say there could be no hope of joy for an orphan girl incapable of loving anyone.

I made it higher in the mountains that day than I ever had before. I stuffed every chivving leaf and lichen into my bag that had a chance of making Lily happy and took pleasure in the pain its growing weight caused me.

Better now than later. I tried to comfort myself. *Better for Cal to know you could never live in his tavern now, before Karin chooses a husband.*

The thought of Karin lying in Cal's arms made me scream loud enough to send a flock of birds scattering to the sky. But it didn't change anything. Cal belonged in the tavern with his family. I could never live with being glad the Guilds were coming.

Simple as that.

When I'd finally gotten tired enough that climbing back down the mountain would be painful, I turned around and headed home.

By the time I made it out of the forest, my legs shook so badly I wasn't sure I would be able to climb over the fences to get back to Lily's. I took a deep breath to steady myself. There was something more in the wind than the usual scent of animal dung and trees.

I took another breath, trying to find what the stench might be. My gaze caught on something on the horizon, a pillar of smoke rising from the northern side of the village.

Taking off at a run, I headed toward the flames, ignoring the trembling in my legs that threatened to send me face first into the dirt.

The smoke wasn't from the very northern edge of the village, and it was back from the main road, off toward the farms on the western side of Harane. I scrambled over fences, dodging around terrified livestock that had scented the fire and knew they had no chance of escaping their pens.

I didn't hear the screams until I neared the road.

A man crying out in agony.

I stopped behind Shilv's house, teetering between running to get Lily to help whoever had been hurt badly enough to make that sort of noise, and being afraid of leaving someone to die alone.

The man screamed again, and I ran forward, toward the sound.

"What..." My question faded away as I saw why Shilv had been screaming.

Five Guilded soldiers in black uniforms stood in a line, staring down at Shilv who clutched the bloody stump of his arm to his chest. Shilv's wife Ester knelt ten feet away, sobbing as she stared at her husband.

I stood frozen for a moment before instinct took over.

And I ran.

Around the side of the house, leaping over the fence and tearing through the pasture without looking to see if any of the soldiers had followed me.

My breath hitched in my chest as I ran. Shilv had been toying with the Guilds for years, hiding his livestock when the scribes came to do their tax accounting.

A hand for the money Shilv owed. If Lily could take care of the wound and make sure no infection set in, Shilv wouldn't be too bad off. His wife was strong. They'd find a way to make do.

I looped back out to the road, heading toward the fire. I pressed my back to a house to peer down the road before venturing into the open.

Shilv's screams had faded, and there was no blood here. But there were soldiers. A pack of soldiers moving down the road with some purpose I didn't understand. They kicked in the door of a house. I ran across the street while they weren't looking and dove into the shadows of a stable.

The horse kicked against the wall, fighting to break free. The banging shook my ears as I ran to the western end of the stable.

I didn't have to go farther than that.

Flames shot up from the Tillys' house. The whole place had been eaten by the inferno. Two figures lay bloody and bare across the walkway. Henry's unmoving back bore the marks of a terrible whipping. His father's chest had been cut open by something sharper. Both of them were dead.

I bit my lips together until they bled as I swallowed my scream.

I didn't know where Malda was. If they'd left her in the house, there was nothing I could do for her. Nothing even Lily could do for her.

"Lily."

A fear like I hadn't known in nine years seized my lungs, choking the air out of me. I ran south, along the backs of the houses, racing toward home.

Lily was smart. She hid the things the Guilds had banned. She only treated people she knew she could trust. The villagers loved her. They would sooner let themselves be whipped than turn Lily in to the Guilds.

Soldiers had gathered behind Les's house. I ducked between buildings and toward the main road before I could see what might have become of Les and his angry wife.

I made it all the way to the side of the tannery.

If I cut between the tavern and the public stables, then looped behind the houses, I'd reach home in a few minutes. I had to warn Lily, make sure she had everything hidden.

I leaned out to check up and down the street. Pain cut through my head as someone grabbed my hair and tossed me to the ground.

The dirt flying into my mouth cut off my scream.

"Who is this sneaking around?" a man said.

I pushed myself to my knees. A kick to the ribs sent me back to the ground.

"Get her up," a second voice said.

A hand grabbed the back of my coat, hauling me to my feet.

Screams came from the south end of the village as a new pillar of smoke drifted toward the sky.

"What's your name?" A soldier leaned close to my face.

I wanted to scratch his leering eyes out, but another soldier had pinned my arms behind my back.

"Your name." The soldier took my chin in his hand.

"Ena." I spat the dirt out of my mouth, letting it land on his fingers. "Ena Ryeland."

"Ryeland isn't a land owner here." A man in white scribes robes stepped forward.

"I don't own land," I said. "I'm a worker, that's all. Now let me go."

Laughter came from behind me.

I glanced back. There were six other men in black uniforms. I tried to yank my arms free.

"What kind of work would a pretty little thing like you be doing?" The soldier trailed a finger down my neck.

"Don't touch me." I kicked back, catching the man who held me in the shin.

The soldier stepped closer to me, pinning me between him and the one I'd kicked.

"You have attacked a soldier of the Guilds of Ilbrea." He wrapped a hand around my throat, cutting off my air. "You just made a terrible mistake."

"Gentlemen!" Cal's voice shouted from across the road. "Come have a drink!"

"We're busy here." The man behind me pressed his hips to my back.

I coughed as I tried to pull in air past the pain squeezing my throat.

"I can promise each of you, you'd rather have some frie and roasted lamb than mess with that." Cal laughed. "Come in. Drinks are on the house, and you can forget that little street scum ever bothered you."

None of the soldiers moved.

"You're here to uphold the laws of our great country." Cal beckoned them toward the door. "You are doing all of us a service by clearing the law breakers out of our village. Come, let me give you a good meal as a token of thanks. I promise the frie we have is the best you'll find south of Ilara."

The soldier in front of me stepped away. He let go of my throat, and the world swayed as I gulped down air. "One this pretty must be diseased anyway. Let's go, lads."

The man holding my arms threw me back down into the dirt.

"I have chamb, too, if any of you prefer," Cal said. "Six years old. I'm told the grape harvest was perfect that season."

Cal led the soldiers into the tavern.

I pushed myself to my feet before the last of them disappeared and ran back between the buildings. I'd made it past the smith's when footsteps pounded up behind me and a hand slammed me into the rough clapboard.

"Do you think I'm that much of an idiot, girl?" The man's breath touched my neck. He leaned into me, pressing his stiffness against my back. "I will not be disrespected by a filthy little rotta."

"Please don't." I tried to reach into my bag, for the knife tucked under the layers of foraged things.

He grabbed my wrist, twisting my arm with one hand and snaking my skirt up my leg with the other.

"Don't do this." I wanted to scream for help, but helping me would be a death sentence.

"Rotta need to learn their—"

A grunt, a rasp, and a gurgle cut through the man's words.

I turned in time to see a spray of red fly from the soldier's throat as he toppled to the ground.

"We need to go." A hand seized mine, dragging me away from the dying soldier.

I looked to the one who had saved me. Black curling hair and deep brown eyes—the man who'd been with my brother in the woods dragged me away.

10

"Emmet." That was the first word I managed to say. "Where's Emmet?"

"South. Far away from here." The black-haired man kept my hand held tightly in his.

His skin was clean. His hand hadn't been covered in the blood that had sprayed the dirt alley.

"Why are you here?" I asked.

"Are you angry I saved you?" He pressed me into the shadows as he peered around the side of Handor's shed.

"No."

"Then it should be enough that I'm here. We need to get to the woods."

"I can't." I yanked my hand from his grasp.

"If you stay here, they'll kill you. The soldiers watched that man follow you, and now that man is dead."

"I can't just leave. I have to get to Lily. If the soldiers are going after people, I have to warn her."

The man closed his eyes for a moment. "Where's her home?"

"Southeast end of the village," I said. "I can get there on my own."

"You're not leaving my sight." He grabbed my elbow, steering me to the trees between homes. "Is Lily fit enough to travel?"

"She's old but she's not decrepit."

"It'll be easier for us to stay alive if I don't have to carry anyone." He didn't offer any explanation as he took off running behind the houses.

I didn't ask for one.

"It's across from the next house," I said as the towering tree that stood in front of Lily's worn, wooden home came into view. Smoke rose from behind the barren branches.

I ran faster, outpacing the black-haired man.

My heart thundered in my ears. The pounding of faraway hooves rattled away all reasonable thought.

The man caught me around the waist, keeping me in the cover of the shadows. I didn't need to go any closer.

The soldiers had displayed her out front by the road. Her gray hair drifted with the breeze as the rope around her neck twisted. Flames cut through the roof of Lily's home, their brightness outlining her shape, as though her death would set the whole world to blazing.

11

The man kept his grip around my waist as we ran away from Lily's house. He darted between buildings and sprinted for long stretches. I made it up and over the fences on my own. I don't know how. I couldn't feel anything. Not the pain in my limbs. Not the terrible, silent scream that echoed in my chest.

I had gone numb. Completely and totally numb.

The man spoke words. Instructions for when to run, and when to lie down in the grass and hide.

I must've done as he said. We made it to the cover of the trees alive.

The stench of the smoke had broken through the scent of the forest. Or maybe it only clung to me.

"We need to keep moving." He grabbed my arm again, steering me farther into the woods.

"Moving?" The word felt heavy in my mouth.

"I can't be sure the soldiers didn't see us coming this way," he said. "The farther we get from Harane, the better off we'll be."

"But I can't just leave." I shook free of his grip. "I'll hide here until they all move on."

"And then what?" He had a cut on his forehead. I didn't know how he had gotten it. "You can't go back there. I killed that soldier—the soldier who left his friends to follow you. They'll blame his murder on you. Harane isn't safe for you, not now, not ever again. We have to keep moving."

"But I can't just leave. The soldiers might not"—a sharp pain pummeled my chest—"the soldiers can't have killed everyone."

"Probably not." He grabbed my arm, dragging me into the forest.

"What does that mean?"

"If people cooperated and didn't fight back, they might still be alive." He stopped at a thick patch of brambles.

"Karin might need help," I said. "Cal is still back there."

He dug a heavy pack out of the brambles, swinging it onto his back before turning to me. "Cal is the boy from the woods?"

I nodded.

He looked up into the trees. "Will he follow you?"

"What?"

"If we wait until dark, I can try to go back for him. If I tell him you're waiting in the woods, will he come?"

"I..." I wasn't sure if Cal would come. If he would hear I had lost the little shred of a life I had been clinging to for so long and come running to my side, ready to abandon everything he had ever known. "I don't want him to. He has a family and a home in the village."

A wrinkle formed between the man's dark eyebrows. "Then there's nothing for us to do but leave. You can't go back to Harane. I'm sorry."

"But where am I supposed to go?" I said. "I could go to Nantic or Hareford, but I don't have any coin. I can work—"

"You can't go anywhere along the mountain road." He reached toward me. "It'll be the same soldiers patrolling."

The trees twisted and swayed around me.

He took my hand, and somehow I managed to make my feet move.

To get farther away than Nantic or Hareford would take days. To get anywhere off the mountain road I would need a map, and food, and money.

"Where am I supposed to go?" A hollow, childish fear settled in my chest.

"I'll take you to your brother."

"South?"

"No." He paused for a moment, staring up at the steep mountain ahead of us. "I'll take you where he's supposed to meet me. You'll be safe there until you can figure out where you want to go."

The light faded from the sky, but he kept moving farther up the mountain. My legs screamed their protest at being asked to climb even more. Part of me wanted to lie down and wait for the forest to eat me whole. More of me wanted to run as far away as the land reached, beyond even the power of the Guilds.

"Why?" I asked when I couldn't bear to swallow the question any longer.

It took a moment for the man to speak. "Why what?"

"Why Harane? Why did the soldiers decide to come after our village? Weren't they satisfied with the damage they'd already done?"

"I don't know if a Guilded soldier is capable of feeling satisfied until a town and all its people are nothing more than ash." He stopped next to a wide boulder. Moss covered the stone, hiding most of its rough texture. He trailed his fingers along the bare patches of rock. "The whisper I heard on the wind said some fool traded a horse for marriage papers. No reason but hiding a baby to be that desperate for a scribe's help. Even the paun scum from Ilara were smart enough to know that. Made them wonder who else might be breaking the laws in Harane."

"Henry." I dug my fingers into my hair. The grit of dirt and soot covered my scalp. "All of this happened because of Henry."

"That's not true." He patted the boulder and started climbing again. "He might have been wrong not to take better care of the girl carrying his child, he might have been a slitching fool for trading his horse and thinking the scribe wouldn't know why, but the death, the blood—that's on the Guilds. They're the ones who are determined to destroy us. Everything else is just reasons the Guilds tell themselves they have a right to slaughter the tilk."

Tilk.

I hadn't even thought the word in forever. The Guilded never used the kind term for common folk. They called us rotta instead. I'd started thinking it, too. Like I believed we were disposable rodents who deserved to be exterminated for contaminating the Guilds' perfect kingdom.

"Do you think they'll leave any of the village standing?" I asked.

"Maybe. It would be a long ride from Nantic to Hareford otherwise."

I had more questions, but I couldn't bring myself to ask them. My soul had grown too heavy to bear another word of pain.

The twilight chill tickled the back of my neck. The sounds of the forest waking up for the night carried through the shadows.

I wanted to say we needed to stop, climb high in a tree and hope we made it until morning. But he kept walking, and I didn't know if letting the animals kill me would be the kinder fate.

He took my hand as he cut sideways along the edge of a rise, as though he were afraid I would tumble off the slope or run back to the village if given the chance.

I ducked my head as bats chittered above us. A gaping darkness grew from the mountainside, blocking our path.

I took a quick step to walk nearer to him. My free hand fumbled, digging into my bag for my knife.

"It's all right." He let go of my hand and stepped into the darkness in the mountain.

I held my breath, waiting for the sounds of some animal tearing him apart.

A tiny spark broke through the black. Then a deep blue light glowed in the cave.

He stood in the middle of the hollow, holding a blue light in his hand, searching each of the stone corners.

"Nothing's been sleeping here for a while." He waved me toward him. "We'll be safe here for the night."

Giving one last glance to the woods behind me, I stepped into the shelter of the cave.

It wasn't large—it only cut about ten feet back—and wasn't wide enough for me to spread my arms out. There were no loose stones on the ground, though aging sticks had been piled in the back where something had once made its bed.

He set the blue light down in the center of the cave before shrugging out of his pack. "You should eat something before you sleep."

"I'm not hungry." I knelt next to the blue light.

It wasn't a lantern with colored glass as I'd thought, but a stone formed of bright blue crystals that seemed to have trapped the spark of a fire deep within itself.

"What is this?" I reached out to poke the stone, expecting him to tell me to stop. But he only watched as my finger grazed the cool surface of the rock.

"A lae stone." He pulled a set of six black rocks from his bag.

"Won't the soldiers be able to see all that light?" I trailed my fingers over the sharp ridges of the lae stone.

"These don't light up." He laid the six stones out along the mouth of the cave.

"Then what are they for?"

"Protecting us." He eyed the line of stones before turning back to his pack.

"What do you mean?"

He didn't speak until he'd unfastened the bedroll from his bag, pulled out a packet of dried meat, and forced a piece into my hand.

"Do you know the ghost stories that keep people out of the mountains?" He leaned against the wall of the cave.

"Sure." I shivered. The cold of the night seeped into my bones now that the heat of the climb had left me. "Everyone knows the stories, even the paun."

"Well, the ghosts that haunt these mountains aren't dead," he said. "I should know. I'm one of them."

I sat against the cave wall opposite him, pressing my back to the cold, damp rock.

"There's magic in these mountains, Ena." He pointed to the stones. "These hold a tiny piece of it."

"You're mad."

"No. I'm a Black Blood."

"No." I shook head. "No. Black Bloods are a legend. Magic doesn't exist outside the Guilds' control. The sorcerers in Ilara hoard all the magic in Ilbrea."

"Your brother said almost exactly the same thing." A hint of a smile caught in the corners of his eyes.

"My brother does not have a speck of magic in him."

"He doesn't. But he saved my life, and he's joined my family. Which makes you my family as well."

"I don't understand." I looked toward the night beyond the opening of the cave. I had trapped myself in the forest with a madman.

I have nowhere else to go.

"You don't have to understand," he said. "I owe your brother a debt. I heard the Guilds had decided to raid Harane and there was no way Emmet could have gotten to you in time. So I came for you myself."

"You came to the village for me?" The weight of his words sank into my stomach, pulling my gaze back from the open air.

"I promised your brother you would be protected." A hint of worry flitted through his dark eyes. A wrinkle that had no place on the face of one so young creased his brow. "I'm sorry I made it so you can't go back. It wasn't my intention."

"You saved me. I can't be anything but grateful for that." I wrapped my arms around myself, trying to stop my shivering.

"Here." He untied the bedroll, laying the thin pad and heavy wool blanket out on the ground. "You should get some sleep."

"You've just said there's magic outside the Guilds' control and you want me to sleep? With a fancy, glowing, blue stone and six rocks as protection?"

"We've got a long journey ahead of us. You'll have plenty of time to figure out if you think the Black Bloods are real."

I didn't move. "Where are we going to meet my brother?"

"Farther into the mountains. No point in telling you where, you'd never be able to find it."

"Right." I crawled over to the bedroll. The cold ached in my hands. "Can we start a fire?"

"Not safe." He leaned his head back against the stone wall. "Not with the chance of soldiers trying to find us."

"Are you keeping watch?" I untied my dirt-caked boots.

"No need. The stones will protect us."

"Do you have another set of blankets?" I crawled under the heavy wool, grateful for the weight of it even though the air had left the material chilled.

"I was supposed to be traveling alone."

"You should share with me." I pulled the blanket up to my chin.

"I'll be fine."

"If you die of cold, I won't be able to find my brother."

He gave a smile that only moved one corner of his mouth. "I'm not sure which Emmet will do first," he said as he untied his boots, "thank me for saving you, or murder me for dragging you through the mountains."

"I've no idea. I don't really know him."

I turned away as he crawled under the blanket. Even through

my coat, I could feel the heat of him. It made the cave seem less like a tomb.

The blue light blinked out, leaving us in darkness.

I took a shuddering breath. "I don't know your name."

"Liam." His breath whispered on the back of my neck.

"I have nightmares, Liam. I'm sorry if they wake you."

12

The night stretched in front of me. Endless blackness I would never be strong enough to defeat. The pounding of hooves battered my ears, but there was a new sound.

Screaming.

A terrible, painful shriek.

I knew someone was dying. I could hear it. The awful resigned fear of a horrible end to a tortured life. I strained my eyes, trying to see into the darkness, searching for the one whose life would soon end. I couldn't let them die alone. I couldn't let their legacy be nothing more than ashes and blood.

But the blackness surrounded me, and the racing horse carried me onward, deeper into the dark.

The screams fell silent.

"Ena," a voice called. "Ena, wake up."

I opened my eyes to a darkness that was not pitch black. Faint hints of the moon and stars peered into the cave.

"Ena?" Liam had a hand on my shoulder. He'd shaken me awake. "Are you all right?"

I blinked up at him, needing to be sure this wasn't just a

horrible new trick the years old nightmare had learned. I took a deep breath. The blanket that covered me stank of damp and dirt. "I'm fine," I said. "I told you I have nightmares."

"You did." Liam laid his head down on his arm. "You're safe here. I won't let anyone hurt you."

I turned back toward the stone wall and stared at the cracks, trying to memorize as much of the pattern as the dim light would allow me to see. I dug my nails into my palms, trying to keep myself awake.

But the world had asked too much of me that day, and sleep swallowed me.

The nightmare didn't come again.

13

We woke at the first hint of dawn. I rolled the blankets back up while Liam packed his stones away. In the early morning sun, there was nothing remarkable about the rocks. They were all dark stone, so black they almost looked like the obsidian I'd seen in some of the fancy traders' carts. There were no markings on their surfaces, no spark glowing within like the lae stone.

When the few things were packed up, Liam stood outside the cave, staring east toward Harane for a long time.

I followed his gaze.

Even as high as we'd climbed, the trees still blocked our view of the land beyond the forest.

I knew Harane was down there somewhere. Whether it was still on fire, already reduced to ash, or if the ones who had survived the soldiers' terror were waking up to another day as though nothing had happened, I didn't know. I would never know.

I hoped some of them were still alive. I hoped someone would be kind to Lily and give her a proper funeral in thanks for all she had done for the villagers. But they were a part of a life I could never return to.

I said a silent thanks and farewell to Lily, who had scooped a crying child out of the mud and given her a home.

I sent a wish to Karin that she would survive and find a husband who would protect her.

I asked for forgiveness from Cal. The boy who made me laugh and forget the darkness. The boy I'd very nearly loved. The boy who would grieve for me.

I held them all close to my heart and tossed their memories into the wind, where they could fly free and far away from whatever journey lay ahead of me.

Liam turned and started up the mountain.

I followed him without looking back.

We climbed in silence for a long while. Liam would stop every so often and look back as though wanting to be sure I could keep up. I'd stare back at him, munching on the dried meat I was finally hungry enough to eat, then he'd climb again.

I picked through my bag as we went, tossing the things I'd gathered for Lily away from our trail.

"What are you doing?" Liam asked after a root clump I'd pitched hit the ground hard enough to make a sound.

"Lightening my bag." I tossed another root ball onto a mound of rocks that had slid down the mountainside. "I don't think the soldiers will follow our trail because of it, do you?"

"I don't think any of them would be brave enough to climb this far into the eastern mountains, no matter whose throat I slit."

"Then keep going." I shooed him onward. "If this journey is going to take as long as you said, it's best for us to make good time."

I pitched a clump of lichen aside.

"You use that in ink making?" Liam crossed his arms, decidedly not climbing the mountain.

"No, for Lily's other business."

He stared at me for a moment.

"Healing," I said.

"Healing?" Liam wrinkled his brow. "Emmet never mentioned Lily being a healer."

"I'm not sure he knew. Since he only showed up once a year, it was hard to be sure I told him all the good stories about learning how to stitch skin back together, being vomited on by half the village, and hoping I didn't get hanged by the Guilds for it." I clenched my jaw, refusing to let my mind slip back to seeing Lily hanging from the tree. "Lily helped everyone in Harane who couldn't afford to pay the Guilded healer or was too sick to make it all the way to Nantic. I gathered this lot for her from the woods, but"—I pulled a handful of moss from my bag and tossed it aside—"no point in lugging all this through the mountains."

Liam started up the slope again, moving more slowly, as though inviting me to walk by his side.

I kept my pace even, not catching up to him until we'd reached a new twist in the rise.

"She shouldn't have gotten you involved in healing," Liam said without looking at me.

"I lived in her house. If a soldier had lifted the wrong floorboard, they would have executed me whether I had ever been useful or not. If the Guilds are going to murder me, I'd rather have it be for something worth dying for."

It took me a few minutes' walking to notice Liam had shortened his steps to match my own, smaller stride. I wanted to run up the mountain out of spite, but my muscles ached with every step.

"You should have told him," Liam said. "If Emmet had known Lily was getting you involved in something dangerous—"

"He'd have found another place to abandon me?" I took a deep breath, willing the scent of the forest to bring the comfort it always had. "Lily was closer to family than my brother. I wouldn't have left her to go to some stranger's house if he'd bothered to try and make me."

A stranger's house was where I'd have to go. If I could find someone to take me. An inker or a healer who needed an extra hand. I could clean, too, cook a bit, though nothing wonderful. I'd have to find work, find something useful to do. If I couldn't, I'd have to find a man to marry who could pay my way. I was young, but I'd seen girls wed well before my age. It was either that or end up a whore.

"Emmet will find a place for you," Liam said, like he'd read the fears in my mind. For all I knew, he could have. "He's been to plenty of places off the mountain road. He'll help get you settled someplace safe."

"I don't want my brother's help. I don't need him."

"I never said you did." Liam looked sideways at me, a hint of pity playing in his dark eyes.

"And I don't feel bad for not telling him about Lily." A fist of anger wrapped around my gut. "It's none of his business to begin with. And if we're worrying about keeping secrets, my brother running around with a man who keeps magic rocks in his pack is a bit worse than me shoving lichen in some wounds."

Liam's face turned to stone. For a moment I thought he'd shout. I wanted him to.

"Of course, maybe my brother's plain lost his mind. He ran from a fine life as a smith to follow a madman with a bag full of rocks through the mountains." I untied my rag of evergreen buds and scattered them across our path.

"You're following the same man through the mountains," Liam said.

"I didn't have much of a choice."

"And the *rocks* in my bag protected us last night."

"Because of your magic?" I tossed a mushroom at his boot. "Magic the Guilds haven't claimed?"

The muscles on the sides of his neck finally started to tense. "The Guilds can't use the kind of magic that runs in my blood."

"I really have followed a madman."

"Worse, you've followed a Black Blood." He stopped and turned to face me.

"A children's story." I stepped nearer to him, tipping my chin up so I could glare into his eyes.

"Tilk whisper of my people, but that doesn't make us any less real."

"Ghosts of bandits rampaging through the mountains, slaughtering anyone fool enough to cross them? We have enough monsters in Ilbrea without scary stories coming true."

"I'm not a monster. And my people are not bandits." He stepped forward, leaving only enough space between us for my bag on my hip. "There is plenty of blood on my hands. I've killed more men than I care to count, but it's either that or hide in the woods and wait for the Guilds to slaughter every last tilk. If fighting for an Ilbrea free from the Guilds makes you think I'm a monster, so be it."

"Fighting against the Guilds." All the air had left the mountainside. The echo of his words muffled the birdcalls in my ears. "That's where my brother has been? Not whoring his way through the countryside or being a back alley thief?"

"He found out what the Black Bloods are working toward. He chose to join our cause."

"Cause?" Sound and air popped back into existence as I shouted at him. "Like you think you could do any good? Like you're actually going to rebel against the Guilds."

"We are. We are standing at the dawn of a new age of freedom. Our rebellion—"

"Rebellion is not possible!" I paced in angry circles between the trees. "Fighting the Guilds isn't possible. How many thousands of soldiers do they have? How many sorcerers? All standing against the Guilds does is make you a volunteer for execution."

"Freedom is only impossible until someone has won it."

"So you and my brother are just going to march into Ilara and demand the Guilds stop tormenting us?"

"Eventually, yes." Blazing determination shone in his eyes.

He meant it.

It was the most terrifying thing I'd ever seen. Not because I was afraid of him. It was the idea of hope that scared me down to my very soul.

I laughed loudly, dimming the fierceness in his eyes.

"I suppose that's what you've been using my brother for, making you swords for your battle." I clapped a hand to my chest. "My apologies, Lord Black Blood, you don't need a sword. You've got magic rocks to guard you."

He stayed silent for a moment, then picked up the mushroom I'd chucked at his feet. "We do have stones to guard us. We have people and plans, weapons, and the will to bring down the Guilds forever. You don't have to believe me, not about the Black Bloods, or the magic, or the end of Ilbrea as we know it.

"But I'd have thought better of you, Ena. A girl who climbs into mountains known to kill and comes out alive with the means to save others—if she can't believe in the hope for a better tomorrow, then maybe we are all damned to burn." He tucked the mushroom back into my bag. "You should hold onto that. People outside of Harane get sick. Someone might need this where we're going."

"And where would that be?" I ran to catch up to him as he strode up the mountain. "Further into your fairytale?"

"We're going to a place guarded by stone, where the people who fight against the Guilds have made their home."

"What if I say no?" I dodged in front of him, blocking his path. "What if I refuse to indulge a lunatic in his madness?"

Liam stared at me. I waited for him to shout. He pointed behind me. "The mountain road is that way. If you want to avoid soldiers who might recognize you, I'd head north, away from the map makers' party. Get as close to the coast as you can, and hope fate favors you and allows you to stay hidden. Having to explain to your brother that you walked away from me in the woods won't be pleasant, but I won't force you to come with me."

Part of me wanted to turn and head west. Forge out into the mountains, and if an animal decided to eat me, so be it.

Part of me still wishes I'd turned and walked away.

But I didn't.

Liam nodded and started climbing the damned mountain again.

I followed him.

I tied the flap of my bag shut to keep the rest of the things I'd collected for Lily safe.

I stared at the mound of lumps in the bottom of his pack where he'd stowed the stones. I pictured myself slitting the bag open, stealing the stones, and pelting Liam's head with them. Safer to imagine that than to even begin to let myself think he could be telling the truth.

The top of the rise peeked through the trees with a wonderful glimmer of sunlight promising my legs flat ground to walk on. Gritting my teeth against the pain, I sprinted up the last bit of the mountain. Rocks took over the very edge of the slope, marking the end of the forest's reign. I burst out of the trees and into the sunshine.

There was no glorious meadow waiting for us at the top of the mountain. Only more mountains reaching as far as the land would allow me to see.

The beast we'd climbed was nothing more than a foothill to its fearsome brothers, who soared so high, trees stopped growing far before their summits. I thought I knew how deep the mountains ran, but I had never seen a full view of them, never once understood the terrifying vastness of the land.

Liam stopped next to me, scanned the mountains, took a deep breath, and headed north.

Toward a place the Guilds' map makers had never laid out for the world to know.

I stepped forward as far as I could on the eastern edge of the rise. The ground crackled beneath my feet like it might give way and toss me over the side of the mountain. I leapt back from the rocks, onto the ground softened by the dirt of the forest.

Liam stood a hundred feet away, waiting at the curve where one ridge descended to the next. He watched me as I looked back out over the mountains I'd never seen on any map. The enormity of it threatened to swallow me whole.

For a moment, I was a little girl staring into the endless black, terrified she'd be lost forever.

I felt Liam staring at me.

I turned away from the cliff to follow him.

He waited while I caught up to him, gave me a nod, and kept walking.

14

A long time ago, before the Guilds came to power in Ilbrea, there was a mother and a baby and a terrible storm.

The wind raged and howled. The rain came down so hard, no man could see the path in front of him. But the mother had been gifted with magic. She could form her own lightning, burn with her own fire—she had no reason to fear what the ungifted hid from. She ventured out into the storm with her baby, refusing to let the skies dictate her path.

The gods saw the mother and knew she thought herself stronger than the might of their storm. So they brought more rain, flooding valleys and upending forests until the mother's magic began to wane.

Exhausted and afraid, she lost her way, and had no hope of finding a safe haven from the storm. She clutched her baby in her arms, and begged the gods for forgiveness.

The gods do not forgive, and the storm raged on.

She scaled the summit at the heart of the mountains, climbing ever upward as strength abandoned her limbs, searching for a place she could shelter her child. A wide boulder was the slim hope the mountain granted, offering relief from the wind but not the pounding rain.

Lightning split the sky, and her baby wailed in her arms. The gods would not grant her child mercy, so the mother begged the mountain itself. Offered everything she had, everything she was, if the mountain would shield her child from the wrath of the gods.

She lay her hand on the great boulder, and poured out every ounce of magic she had, filling the black rocks far below with a power never meant to live in stone.

The eastern mountains are one, and separate. A vast range ruled over by one mighty summit no mortal could conquer. But the magic stirred the great one, and she bade the smaller peaks obey her. The mountain opened, granting the child shelter, as the mother was washed away by the gods' storm.

The child grew within the mountain, raised by the magic its mother had infused into the stone.

The child became a part of the mountain, and the mountain a part of the child. The mountain had bargained for the safety of the babe to gain magic. The mountain didn't know the mother's magic would change the shape of its stones, and make the mountain feel. For the heart of the mountain, where the baby found shelter, grew to love the child. To cherish each beat of its heart that echoed through the caverns and rocks.

But even young raised by magic grow up.

When the child was grown, the mountain opened its gates and let the person it loved walk out into world. But the mountain gave the one it had raised a promise—those who shared the child's blood would be marked as beloved of the mountain, and would always find safety in its embrace.

The child found a partner and had children. And those children had children. And each of those children carried the mark of the mountain in their blood.

And then the child raised in stone died.

The mountain mourned, and feared it would never again have anyone to love.

So the mountain sent a cry out on the wind, calling all the children who carried its mark in their blood home.

The generations of children felt the cry, felt the black stone in their blood calling them back to the heart of the mountain. So they ventured deep into the mountains where no one else dared go.

The mountain sheltered them from the outside world, killing all who would threaten the ones who carry the black stone in their blood. And the beloved children only left their sanctuary to slaughter those who dared to threaten the mountains they'd claimed as their own.

The day after the Guilds murdered Lily, I followed the madman Liam through the mountains, heading toward a place where impossible people believed in impossible things.

We didn't speak much the rest of that day, only an offer of food, and a warning of slippery ground. He found another cave for us to sleep in and surrounded the opening with his black stones. He crawled under the blanket beside me without protest.

The nightmare came. The endless black and the pounding of hooves. A gentle voice pulled me from the dream before the screaming began.

I woke to the weight of Liam's arm draped over me. I fell back asleep before I could wonder if he was awake.

My legs had never been so sore in my life.

We started the morning climbing up and over the ridge of a mountain. I looked at the long downhill waiting for us and felt a foolish sense of relief. Then I started down and realized what an idiot I'd been.

Liam kept to a pace I could match. I tried to tell myself his legs were dying, too, but I knew he was probably trying to be kind.

I had things I wanted to know—how exactly my brother had saved Liam and gotten involved in this fool's rebellion, what the hell kind of good he thought he was going to be able to do throwing stones against a giant like the Guilds, how much longer we'd have to walk—but I was too stubborn to break the silence. I didn't know if he was too stubborn to speak or just enjoyed hearing only our footsteps for hours on end.

It didn't matter much either way. I just kept tromping up and down mountains, refusing to hint at the pain that made my legs tremble.

The sun had moved past midday when Liam finally spoke more than five words at a time.

"We should get some more water." He didn't actually address me, or look at me. For all it mattered, he could have been speaking to the stones in his pack.

"We need water and more food," I said. "Unless you've got more dried meat stashed in your pack, or we'll be getting wherever we're going soon."

"I'll get us some fish."

"Fish from..." The sounds of flowing water stole my will to speak.

We rounded the corner, and a wide, shallow river blocked our path.

I opened my mouth to ask how he'd known we were close to water, before swallowing the question.

Liam shrugged out of his pack by the side of the river.

I fished the empty waterskin from my bag and knelt by the bank. I hadn't realized how thirsty I was until water was within reach. I uncorked the skin and dipped it into the wonderfully cold river.

The chill of it raised goose bumps on my flesh. I downed half the skin before sitting and unlacing my boots.

"We're not crossing through," Liam said as I set my boots aside.

"I didn't say we were." I stripped off my stockings. Deep purple bruises marked my feet and legs. I laid my stockings out next to my boots.

"Then what are you doing?"

"Catching fish between my toes."

His brow furrowed as I rolled my skirt up past my knees.

I dipped my feet into the freezing water and didn't bother biting back my moan of joy as the cold dulled my pain. A fish twice the size of my hand swam past my ankles.

"Hmm, too big for my toes. I guess you'll have to use your magic on the fish."

Liam pulled out each of his three waterskins and began filling them one by one.

"I don't know much about magic. We've never had a sorcerer visit Harane." I kicked my feet through the river. "Maybe you could form a spear of water to skewer us a meal. Or make the river solid and trap the fish where they swim."

He splashed water on his face.

"You could tell them about your rebellion and see if they'll jump up on land," I offered. "See if they're willing to sacrifice themselves to a worthy cause."

He crouched down next to the stream, running his fingers through the dirt as though searching for something.

"If you can't catch a fish, I'll find us something to eat." I scanned the plants around us—some trees, a few low-lying bushes, plenty of scrub and grass growing along the ground. "I can't promise it'll taste very nice, but—"

A sharp buzz cut through my words as a stone streaked out of Liam's hand and shot into the water. A moment later, a fish bobbed to the surface.

Liam leaned over the river and snatched the fish out of the current. He held the lifeless fish up, flipping it one way and then the other before laying it on the ground.

"What was that?" I dug my fingers into the dirt.

"Fishing." He shot another stone toward the river.

I pulled my feet from the water and dragged my stockings back on, not caring that my feet weren't dry.

Liam lifted another slain fish from the river.

"How did you do that?" I yanked on my boots.

He gave a half smile and laid the second fish next to the first.

"Was that magic?" I asked.

"Of course not." Liam pulled the knife from his belt. "I have it on good authority that magic only exists under the control of the Sorcerers Guild."

"Well, clearly I was wrong." I stood and inched my way

toward him. "Unless you are from the Sorcerers Guild and are wasting a massive amount of effort tormenting me."

He started to clean the fish, like he hadn't done anything strange.

"You can't clean them with magic?" I asked.

"Some could. But that's not the sort of gift I was given."

He didn't look up. I desperately wanted him to. I wanted to look into his dark eyes and search for something I hadn't noticed before, any hint that he belonged to a world so different from the one in which I'd lived my life.

"What sort of gift were you given?" I asked.

"I'm a trueborn Black Blood."

"So you've said."

"That is my gift." With a flick of his finger, the killing stones flew out of both the fish and landed in the water with a plop, plop.

"What does *trueborn Black Blood* mean?" I knelt beside him.

"I'm a keeper of the pact." He looked up at the mountains. "I work with stone magic."

"So flying stones and the rocks that guard us?"

"Close enough."

"And that's all?"

His gaze met mine. There was no hint of magic in his dark eyes, just a touch of laughter. "I wasn't given the sort of gifts the Sorcerers Guild prizes."

"It doesn't matter. They'd still take you, lock you in their tower in Ilara and make you move stones for them."

"I know." He started cleaning the second fish. "They've taken some of the Black Bloods before, tried to take even more. The beasts hoard magic, and what's not under their control, they'll stop at nothing to destroy. We save as many as we can, get them out of reach of the Guilds."

"Aren't we already out of reach of the Guilds? All of Ilbrea could have fallen into the sea and we'd have no way of knowing."

"We keep the Black Blood children with strong magic hidden from the Guilds," Liam said. "It's the tilk children we have to rescue. Show one hint of magic, and the Guilds will snatch a child from their mother's arms to lock them in the Sorcerers Tower in Ilara."

A shiver shot up my spine.

"Some want to go," Liam said. "Safety, prestige—the Guilds paint a beautiful picture of what they offer. We don't fight that. They can go if they like. But the children who see joining the Sorcerers Guild for what it really is—captivity, being forced to fight against your own people if the order comes down from the Guilds. The ones who would rather die than be taken to the stone tower, we get as many of them out as we can find."

"How?"

"Carefully." He rinsed his hands in the water. "I'll go get some wood for a fire."

He walked off into the trees, leaving me sitting next to the two dead fish.

"Magic," I whispered to the river. I'd seen it. I couldn't deny it. "I'm following a madman with magic."

I dug into the very bottom of my bag, pulled out the bits of moss that were left behind, and made a little bundle by the riverbank. I searched the ground near the fish for twigs and sticks to start a fire.

"Magic." I leaned the twigs against the moss. "What has my chivving slitch of a brother gotten himself into?"

I waited until I heard his footsteps coming back to strike the flint and light the fire.

"Hungry?" Liam laid his armful of wood by the flames.

"I've been tromping up and down mountains. Yes, I'm hungry."

A laugh rumbled in Liam's chest. Not a bursting laugh, or a true cough of joy, but I liked the sound. It was good to know someone could laugh after slitting a monster's throat.

I built the fire up while he skewered the fish. Birds I didn't recognize circled overhead as we ate our meal. They were larger than the kinds that searched for carrion on the western edge of the mountains. I ate my fish as quickly as I could without risking swallowing bones.

"We'll have to find shelter earlier tonight," Liam said.

I rinsed my hands in the river, and took one last, long drink.

"I can walk as far as you can," I said.

"It's not that." Liam pointed northeast along the edge of the river. "Shelter is hard to find in some parts of the mountains, and there are things I'll not risk meeting after dark."

"But you're a Black Blood." I slung my bag across my shoulder. "The mountains will protect you."

"Some myths really are myths." He reached down and took my hand, helping me to my feet. "And some myths are too real for my liking."

"What's that supposed to mean?" I stayed close to his side as he headed north, suddenly afraid one of the birds high above would swoop down and try to carry me away in its great talons.

"Nothing. It doesn't mean anything at all." The tension in his shoulders told a different tale.

"Did you grow up here?" I asked. "In the mountains?"

He didn't answer until we'd cut around a bow in the river. "I was raised like a Black Blood."

"I don't know what that means."

"Does it matter?" He climbed to the top of a mound of rocks and reached down to help me follow.

I ignored his hand as I climbed. "It matters to me."

"Why?"

"Because if a fool like you managed to survive childhood in these mountains, I'd be less afraid of birds swooping down to carry me off." I jumped down on the far side of the rocks. My legs screamed their hatred of me.

"I grew up in the mountains farther east than where we're

going." He stood on top of the rocks, gazing east. "There are beasts that will carry off children if you give them the chance, but it's still safer than being near the soldiers."

"So"—I looked up to the birds still circling above us—"you're saying one of those beasts could come down and snatch me?"

"If they got hungry enough." He jumped down from the rocks and landed next to me with a thump that shook my nerves. "But they prefer their food to be decaying before they taste it. Don't die and they'll probably leave you well enough alone."

He gave me another of his half smiles and strode off up the river.

"I hope he knows he's not funny," I muttered to myself.

One of the great birds cawed overhead, and I ran to catch up to Liam, hating myself for acting like such a coward.

We followed the stream for hours. I gathered berries and edible sprouts, tucking them into my bag for later. There were plants I'd never seen before. I wanted to stop and examine them, see what use they could be, but Liam's constant plodding forward kept me from pausing. The way he moved, the way his gaze darted between the peaks on either side of us, made me afraid to linger.

When the sun had started to drop toward the west, the path ahead of us opened up into a wide valley. Scrub bushes and grass covered the flat terrain. The mountains to the east and west of the valley were formed of steep rock with no hint of plants clinging to their sides.

I turned to the path behind us. There weren't the towering woods of the slopes near Harane, but there were proper trees. Then the valley began, and it was like the trees were too frightened to grow on the open ground.

"Where are the trees?"

Liam gnawed on the insides of his lips. "They don't grow in the Blood Valley."

"I can see that."

"We could wait here for the night," he said.

"And if we do?"

"We'll be stuck sleeping in the valley tomorrow night. It takes more than a day to cross. I hate taking you on this path."

"Probably could have avoided it if you hadn't come south to help me."

"There are easier paths to where we're going." Liam looked up to the graying sky.

The birds that had been following us for hours had abandoned their chase.

"Bit late to go back now." I walked past him, out into the valley. A chill nipped at the base of my neck, like a frozen noose ready to tighten.

I waited for him to pull me back or for the ground to swallow me whole.

"We should be able to get a mile or two in before we have to stop for the night." He stepped past me and into the scrubland.

The sharp snap of thin branches came with every step. The flatness of the valley was a relief, but I'd never been so glad to be wearing a long skirt in my life. At least the thick folds of the material offered a bit of protection from the twigs constantly jabbing at my legs. And at least the pain of the poking distracted me from the valley.

There was nothing truly frightening about the valley. The ground held firm, the wind smelled of new spring growth. But I couldn't get rid of the chill on my neck.

As the sun crept farther down, Liam began gathering wood as we walked, picking up the thickest of the branches that had fallen from the low bushes.

"Does this mean we'll get to have a fire tonight?" I gathered a handful of twigs and tucked them into my bag.

"We'll need one." He pointed east to a boulder that stuck out of the mountainside. "Ena, you're very brave."

"Am I?" I snatched up every twig I could find as we headed toward the boulder.

"You know you are. If you weren't, you wouldn't still be alive." He shook his head.

I wanted so badly to know what thoughts were rattling around in his head hard enough he had to shake them into order, to hold his face in my hands and stare into his eyes until I'd gotten one complete truth out of him.

"What's coming tonight," he said, "I'm sorry you have to witness it, and I swear I will keep you safe."

"Safe from what?"

He stopped in front of the boulder. The brush had been pulled up along the face of the rock, as though some other travelers had sought the same, poor refuge.

"The Blood Valley isn't a pleasant place." Liam laid down his firewood and took off his pack.

"I figured as much from the name." I added my wood to his pile.

He pulled out the stones and surrounded us, making a wide circle with the boulder at our backs.

"Are monsters going to come for us when night falls?" I forced out a laugh.

Liam looked up toward me. There was no smile playing on the corner of his lips. "The monsters don't come until well after dark."

"Huh." I knelt beside the firewood. "We've got some time then."

"Most don't mean any harm." Liam sat beside me, sorting through the wood as though rationing our supply. "I'm not even sure they can think."

"Does it matter if they can think if they're trying to kill us?" I pulled the flint from my bag.

"Don't light the fire yet. Better to save the wood."

"For when the monsters come." I set the stones down next to the frame of twigs he'd built.

He leaned against the boulder, staring out over the valley. "If you believe the legends, this place used to be the most beautiful land in the eastern mountains. A valley of flowers and trees, some even say a stream ran through the center."

"What happened?" I sat by his side, watching the light around us fade.

"People settled here."

"And they tore up the trees and trampled the flowers?"

"No. They lived peacefully, until they were attacked. One dark night, strangers came into the valley from the north and the south, trapping the valley folk."

"The Guilds?"

"I don't think so, but I can't say for certain. The invaders brought true monsters, things I don't think exist outside the mountains."

I pulled my coat closer around me.

"The valley folk were penned in. They had no chance of escaping," Liam said. "When morning came, the valley floor had been stained red with blood. They say the trees and flowers died before the next sunset."

"That's a terrible story."

"It's not a story," Liam said. "All of it's true."

"How do you know?"

"I've seen it." He untied the bedroll from his bag, shook the blanket free, and handed it to me. "I need you to trust me, Ena. Whatever you see, whatever comes for us, you have to stay here."

"Is this meant to be a joke?" I knew it wasn't, but I couldn't give up that last sliver of hope.

Liam touched my cheek. His fingers were warm against my chill skin. And despite their calluses, and the blood he'd spilt, there was tenderness as he brushed back the hair that had fallen free from my braid. "I won't let them hurt you. I need you to believe that."

My heart thundered in my chest, but I only nodded.

He stayed looking into my eyes for one more breath before turning away and picking up my flint to start the fire.

A tiny pang sliced through my lungs, and the chill of the night tripled without his touch.

As the last of the sun faded from the valley, our fire crackled to life.

A shiver shook me to my teeth.

"You should wrap up," Liam said.

I tucked half the blanket around me, and held up the rest for him.

"I'll be fine," he said.

I didn't move.

He poked at the fire, keeping the wood from tumbling apart, then sat beside me and took his half of the blanket.

We sat in silence as the darkness came in full. I hadn't realized how much comfort the caves had offered. Sitting with the boulder at our backs and the stones in front of us seemed like a fool's way of begging to die.

The first sound that carried on the night wind was laughter, a cheerful chorus of it, as though someone had just told an excellent joke on their way out of a tavern.

I would have wondered what the joke was if Liam hadn't tensed beside me.

The hum of distant music filled the air as a fiddler struck up a fresh tune.

I leaned close to Liam's ear to whisper, "Are there people out there?"

"Not anymore."

Voices spoke not twenty feet away.

I squinted, peering into the darkness toward the noise, but I couldn't see anyone.

"Mama, mama!" The child's voice traveled in front of us as though he were running to his mother's arms.

I glanced to Liam. Pained lines creased his brow.

"How often have you come through the Blood Valley?" I asked.

"Twice," Liam said, "but I sheltered farther on. I've never heard these echoes before."

"I'll not stay in the dark with you," a female giggled. "I don't care if you're handsome. That only makes you more of a rogue."

"If you don't want to sneak away with me, I'll find someone who does," a man said.

"You wouldn't dare." The laughter left the woman's voice. "How could you even threaten such a thing?"

A wisp of a shadow fluttered through the darkness.

"Tamin," the woman shouted. "Don't you dare walk away from me. Tamin!"

The music changed, and voices joined the tune. The happy song settled a stone of dread in the pit of my stomach.

I gasped as a figure appeared in the distance, walking briskly as though following a long lost road. The man wore a light shirt with no coat to protect him against the night chill. The feeble light of the lantern he held in front of him flickered with a wind I could not feel.

"What is he?" I whispered.

"A ghost," Liam said, "or maybe he's only the valley remembering."

The man weaved across the valley and faded from view.

More voices came from distant wisps of shadow, patches of the night that seemed to solidify, swirling around a life that was meant to be led. They moved about in a group near where the music seemed to play. The way they shifted in the night changed with each new song, as though the darkness danced to the long dead tune.

It wasn't until my hands began to cramp from clutching the blanket that another solid form appeared—a girl my age leading a boy away from the other shadows.

They ran silently through the night until he caught her around the middle and pressed his lips to her neck. She twisted in his arms and kissed him, twining her fingers through his dark hair.

It seemed like an intrusion to stay so near them as his fingers found the edge of her blouse and traveled up the bare skin of her back.

A crack cut through the air.

The sound wasn't loud or terrifying, no worse than a branch breaking off a tree, but Liam sat up straight as though preparing to run.

"They're coming."

My breath hitched in my chest. The young pair were still kissing, unaware of the danger preparing to end their lives.

"They need to run," my words came out as a strangled whisper. "We have to tell them to run."

I let go of the blanket, but Liam took my hand before I could try to stand.

"It's too late," Liam said.

Another, louder crack cut through the night.

The young couple finally noticed something was wrong. The boy stepped in front of the girl as though trying to shield her, but there was no way for him to know from which direction the danger came.

A scream carried from the southern side of the valley.

Before I could try to see if the one screaming had taken form, a wail sounded from the north.

"We have to get inside." The boy grabbed the girl's hand, dragging her toward the center of the valley to some safety I couldn't see.

A third crack shook the ground beneath us. I held tightly to Liam's hand.

"I won't let them hurt you." Liam spoke over the terrible screams that rent the night.

A great blackness tore up from the ground, sweeping through

the fleeing wisps, seizing them and dragging them below the earth.

"What kind of a monster lives below the ground?" I asked.

"I don't know."

A band of solid figures charged into view, their shining weapons raised. For a moment, I thought they had come to slay the beasts that attacked from below. Then one of the men buried his blade in a shadow. The shadow screamed and became a woman with blood dripping down her chest.

My muscles tensed, ready to run out into the darkness to help the woman. The man stabbed again, and she fell to the ground and lay still as deep red stained the dirt around her.

"Please no!" a man shouted. He ran not thirty feet in front of us, fleeing from two men chasing after him, swords ready to kill.

A tentacle of darkness writhed up from the ground and seized the fleeing man around the stomach. His cry of pain and terror echoed in my ears.

"Run! Everyone run!" a fool called into the night.

Dozens of people took shape, fleeing from their attackers. An arrow caught an old man in the back before he had taken two steps.

"Run," I whispered. "Please run."

Liam laced his fingers through mine, offering the only comfort he could.

The boy and girl who had cared for nothing but each other's flesh such a short while before were both slain by swords. He was stabbed through the chest. Her head was taken clean off.

Bile shot up into my throat.

A shriek carried from high overhead, and the pitch of the terror on the valley floor changed. A great bird soared through the darkness, picking up people and tossing them aside, grabbing a woman in its sharp beak and cracking through her spine before swallowing her whole.

The high scream of a child cut through the ringing in my ears.

The bird heard the noise as well and dove toward the sound.

"No!" I leapt to my feet, desperate to save the child from the vicious beast.

"Ena!"

I stepped forward, and the night around me changed. The stench of blood and fear filled the air. There weren't dozens of shapes running through the slaughter, but hundreds.

"Leave them alone!"

The attackers turned toward my shout.

Liam seized me around the waist, dragging me back.

"No." I fought against his grip as the scent of blood disappeared. "I have to help them!"

"It's too late, Ena." He kept his arms wrapped tightly around me. "They're already dead."

A tendril of darkness lashed up from the earth, snaking closer, swaying back and forth as though scenting the air.

"Can it see us?" I asked.

"You stepped outside the stones," Liam said. "They all can."

The great bird spiraled through the sky and dove straight toward us.

A scream tore from my throat as the bird opened its talons, reaching for us. But the shouts of the attackers and the shriek of the bird drowned out the sound.

I tried to think of a way to escape, but Liam kept me pinned to his side, one arm wrapped around my waist, the other shielding my head as the talons stretched toward us.

A hum that shook my bones and a blazing blue light burst from the six stones Liam had laid on the ground. The bird's talons scraped against the glow but could not reach our flesh.

The men attacked our sanctuary, but the stones blocked their swords. The tendrils of shadow whipped through the darkness, cracking up from the ground as though determined to swallow our barrier.

"I'm sorry," I said. I don't know if Liam heard me.

A scream in the distance dragged the bird's attention from us. It soared up and over the valley. Cries of terror echoed in the monster's wake.

The men turned their backs on us, ready to slaughter the innocents who didn't have magic to protect them.

Liam didn't let me go. I think he was afraid I would run

toward the ones screaming in pain. I wanted to. Every bit of me ached to. But he held me tight, and what chance did I have fighting against a giant beast?

The screams of the dying valley folk dimmed as time wore on. There were fewer of them left to cry, and their defiance had abandoned them.

The fire at our feet flickered feebly.

I looked to our pile of unburnt wood. I didn't want the fire to die, but I didn't know if I could keep from running if Liam loosened his grip on me.

"Let me in," a voice whispered from the darkness. A little girl crouched in front of the rocks. Tears and blood stained her face. "Please let me in before they find me."

"We can't," Liam said.

"We can't leave her out there." I broke free of his grip.

"Ena, she's not real. She hasn't been for a very long time."

I knelt next to the stones, inches from the girl.

"Please," the girl said, staring into my eyes, "I don't want to be alone."

"You can't go out there." Liam knelt beside me, locking his arm around my waist. "The monsters would add you to the tally of their dead, but you won't be able to save her."

A ball of grief pressed into my throat. "It's all right, littleling. You're not alone, I'm right here with you."

"They're coming." A sob shook the child's chest.

"I know," I said, "but you are brave, and you are strong."

"Don't let them find me."

"I..." I had no words of comfort to offer.

The clang of swords came closer.

"I'm right here," I said. "I will not leave you."

Liam took my hand, anchoring me to a world away from ghosts as the men found the child.

"No!" She tried to run, but the men were too quick.

One caught her by the arm and spun her around, shoving his blade into her stomach as though her death meant nothing.

The world tilted.

He dragged her back and dropped her next to the safety of our stones. He laughed as he walked away.

The child lay gasping on the ground, fighting for air that would only prolong her pain.

"It's all right," I said. "Just close your eyes and everything will be better. No one can hurt you, not anymore."

My whole body shook as I watched the little girl take her last few breaths.

Her eyes fluttered closed, and she faded into darkness.

Liam lifted me away from the stones, back to the boulder. He laid more wood on the embers of our fire.

"When will it end?" I asked.

"Not for a while." He draped the blanket over me and sat next to me.

A fresh wave of screams came from farther north in the valley.

He wrapped his arms around me, and I leaned into his warmth, waiting for the battle to end.

I don't know how long it took for the valley to finally fall silent. The human screams stopped first, then the bird vanished, and then the ground stopped shaking. Sometime before dawn, I drifted to sleep.

The sun on my face woke me the next morning. I kept my eyes shut.

If Liam had been wrong, if it wasn't ghosts we had been forced to witness being murdered, but real, living people, then I'd sat in safety and let them all be killed. If hundreds of people had been slaughtered right in front of us, then the valley floor would be coated in blood.

The weight of Liam's arm around my shoulder changed. I could tell from the pace of his breathing that he was awake.

This is the world, Ena. Bloody or not, it's all there is.

I took a deep breath and opened my eyes.

A vast valley of low scrubland shone gold and green in the dawn light. I gave a shaky exhale, burying the fear and grief down far enough they couldn't break me.

"Are you all right?" Liam asked.

"Yes." I pulled the string from the bottom of my braid and shook my hair free. "We'll be out of here before dark?"

"Unless disaster hits." Liam's gaze kept darting back to me as he rolled up the blanket. "I'm sorry you had to see that. I didn't—"

"I'm fine." I ran my fingers through my hair and wove it into a fresh braid. "I just don't understand why. Of all the terrible things that have happened in this world, why does this keep coming back? Why should these people continue to suffer in death?"

"The mountains have magic all their own. Some even say the mountains have a heart that feels and loves." Liam picked up the stones that had protected us from the monsters, both men and beasts. "Maybe the mountains don't want us to forget how evil the world can be."

"I didn't know that was a thing people forgot."

"Ena, I..." His voice trailed away. He slung his pack onto his back. "I only wanted to help you. I'm sorry if any of this makes your nightmares worse."

I stomped out the last embers of our fire. "Don't worry. The nightmare came long before I met you."

He waited while I draped my bag over my shoulder. Then we walked to the center of the valley and headed north.

There wasn't a trace of blood on the ground.

We found shelter under an outcropping of rocks that night. I was so tired I fell asleep before Liam climbed under the blanket behind me.

I slept through the whole night without a single dream. I woke in the morning to find I'd turned in my sleep. My cheek rested on Liam's chest, and he held me tight, as though even in sleep he wanted to protect me from the ghosts of long ago torment.

"This place we're going," I said as I trailed my fingers along the bark of the trees, "what sort of place is it?"

"What do you mean?" There was a hint of a smile in Liam's voice.

I wanted to dash in front of him to see if the smile had actually made it all the way to his face. Instead, I tipped my head back to stare at the treetops. We'd left the scrublands behind, and trees had taken over the mountainside again.

The forest we'd spent the afternoon trudging through wasn't made of the harsh sort of trees that had clung to the other slopes we'd traveled. These trunks were thick and healthy, with hordes of bright green buds waiting to burst through. The soil beneath our boots held a strong scent of fertility, as though the mountain herself bade the plants to grow.

"Are we going to a village?" I asked. "Is that where we're meeting my brother?"

"There aren't villages in the mountains. Villages need roads for people to reach them."

"A settlement then?" I stopped beside a low patch of berries, kneeling down to touch the waxy leaves.

"I suppose?" Liam leaned against a tree. "It's our encampment for the warm months."

"Encampment?" I picked one of the nubs that would become a berry, crushing the hard knot between my fingers. "Right."

"What were you hoping for? A grand set of caves?"

I heard the smile again and glanced up to find a beautiful glimmer in his dark eyes.

"If you want to know the truth, I was hoping for someplace I might be able to take a bath and wash my clothes." I wiped the sour-scented pulp from my fingers onto a tree. "There's enough mud on my skirts to plant a thriving garden."

Liam stepped forward, raising his hand.

I froze, not even remembering how to breathe, as he wiped his thumb across my cheek. "I'll make sure you get the chance to wash your face, too."

Heat rose up my neck and flared into my cheeks. Days in the mountains, of course I looked like a child come in from playing in the mud.

He brushed something away from my other cheek and stepped back.

I missed the warmth of his hand on my skin. An odd knot twisted the place where my lungs and stomach met.

"We'll find you a new pair of boots as well," Liam said. "A dozen more miles in yours and you might as well be barefoot."

I swallowed the sound I had meant to be a laugh.

"You'll be comfortable enough. I promise." He turned and started weaving through the trees again, heading east.

You're a filthy little waif he saved because he made your brother a promise, Ena Ryeland.

Yelling at myself in my mind didn't lessen my want for him to turn around and touch me again.

Don't be a chivving fool.

I ripped the knot from between my lungs and stomach, and packed it away with all the other things I refused to feel.

The dark space where I shoved the things I didn't want to face was bottomless. Like the sacks of the demons who come to steal naughty children in the dead of winter. A massive void that could fit all the horrors I wished to shove inside it. The seams never tore. The fabric never protested the weight.

So I shoved more and more darkness inside, hiding from the danger, one cast away thought at a time.

"Will my brother be there already?" I quickened my pace to catch up.

"I doubt it. Even with our having to take the long way, and even if his work had gone better than we'd hoped, I can't imagine he'll have beat us back."

"Long way? Did you say *long way?*"

Liam stopped and rubbed his hands over the dark scruff that had grown on his chin. "I couldn't keep you close to the mountain road. Not with the chance of Guilded soldiers wanting to see you in a noose. We had to go into the mountains, and once you dive that deep into the range, there are few paths men can survive."

"But you're a trueborn Black Blood. You can use stone magic."

"How do you think I know which ways a man can survive? We'll be to the encampment soon, and once Emmet arrives and we figure out where the best place for you is, I'll do what I can to make sure the journey out of the mountains is an easier one."

I bit my lips together for a moment, letting the things I wanted to say fade away.

"I needed new boots anyway," I said.

Liam shook his head. When he started to walk, he didn't move as quickly as before. Not like he wanted to be sure I could catch up, more as though he were searching for something.

I scanned the forest around us, trying to spot whatever it was he might be looking for.

Birds filled the trees in greater numbers than we'd seen farther east in the mountains. Small animals scurried through the woods as well, rustling the decay of last autumn's leaves in their wake. Moss clung to the northern side of the trees, though none that I saw would be useful in healing. Lichen grew in a patch by the side of a great boulder made of dark stone.

It struck me as strange that the moss and such hadn't seen fit to grow on the stone's surface.

The base of the boulder dug into the ground, hiding its edge from view. I pictured the stone reaching all the way down to the root of the mountains, touching the heart that had cared for the ill-fated woman and her stone-raised babe.

"Ena"—Liam stepped back to walk by my side—"I think you should take my arm."

"What for?" I asked even as I rested my hand on his elbow. "You think after our days of climbing, this gentle stroll will drop me?"

"No." Liam slowed his pace again. "But the first time feeling it can be shocking to some."

I didn't have the chance to open my mouth to ask what under the sky he was talking about.

It started like a bright flash of heat in the front of my ribs and tip of my nose. I flinched, shying away from the unnatural warmth, but Liam placed his hand on mine, guiding me forward.

"Trust me, Ena."

I let my body lean farther into the heat and found the warmth didn't burn. The feeling was less like a fire trying to sear my skin away and more like the bright burning of wanting something with my whole being. The utter joy and pain of longing filling my entire soul, and knowing that desire might burn away everything I was, and not having enough thought left beyond the wanting to care.

Liam led me forward, and the feeling ate me whole. I gasped and swayed on the spot.

"Just a little farther and you're through." Liam wrapped his arm around my waist, holding me close to his side.

We took two more steps, and the feeling faded, leaving me bereft and empty.

"Are you all right?" A hint of worry wrinkled Liam's brow.

"What was that?" I said, thankful my voice came out strong and not as hollow as I felt.

"A much larger version of the stones that protected us on our journey." He pointed back over my shoulder.

A second black boulder, free of moss and lichen, hid between the trees. If I squinted through the forest, I could see another stone poking up in the distance.

"Liam?" a voice called.

The shock of it sent me reaching for the knife in my bag.

"It's all right," Liam said softly before raising his voice. "It's me."

The branches of a tree to our left rustled and groaned as a man climbed down from a perch high above.

"You're late." The man beamed at Liam, striding over to give him a clap on the back before even bothering to look toward me. "And you've found a stray."

I tipped my chin up and met the man's laughing gaze without a hint of mirth.

"This is Ena Ryeland." Liam stepped away from me, giving a little nod in my direction. "Emmet's sister."

The man looked from Liam to me as though trying to see what part of the joke he'd missed out on. "She's not." He shook his head, sending his sandy brown hair flying around his face. "She can't be."

"I am." I shot the man a glare. He wasn't much taller than me, and though I'm sure he was cleaner than I was, the only reasons I could see for being the slightest bit polite to the man were the two long knives dangling from his belt. I crossed my arms and stepped toward him. "Is my brother here?"

"No," the man said, "haven't heard a chirp of him. Oh, Emmet's not going to like this."

"There weren't any other options," Liam said. "Sal, run on to camp and have them toss up a tent for Ena. Get Cati on finding her some fresh clothes and a bath."

Sal nodded, narrowing his eyes at me. "Emmet is not going to like this." He turned and ran into the trees.

"Sal," Liam called after him.

Sal turned, his face brightening as though Liam might tell him my existence had actually been a joke.

"Put her tent next to mine."

Sal shook his head, flattening his mouth into one long line. "Whatever you say, Liam."

"I'll make sure you get a good meal, too." Liam gave me a nod.

"Right, thanks."

I followed him through the trees in the direction Sal had fled.

The air beyond the stones tasted different than it had on the outside of whatever magic the boulders created.

It was something beyond the scent of smoking meat that drifted through the trees. More like a tang of vibrancy. Like the flavor of that one precious day when spring is done with its hard labor and decides to flourish into full summer bloom had been bottled, and the perfume of it had been misted through the trees.

Voices carried through the woods, more than just Sal and Cati. Dozens of voices.

My shoulders tensed as a cluster of tents came into view. All of the tents were large, big enough to fit an entire shop. Behind a cook fire, one wide tent had the flaps tied open, so the five people sitting inside laboring over food at a long table could stare at me as Liam led me past.

The number of actual living people in the camp sent my heart skipping at an irregular beat, ricocheting against my ribs, though I wasn't sure why.

Liam nodded and waved to the people we passed, but he didn't stop to answer their questions.

Where had he been, had he been attacked...who was I?

No one seemed angry their questions weren't being answered. They just turned back to their business while staring at me out of the corners of their eyes.

"Are you in charge?" I whispered as Liam led me past the last tent.

"How do you mean?" Liam turned down a worn path toward a clearing in the trees.

"You know damn well what I mean."

"Then yes."

The dirt in the clearing had been packed down as though trampled by hundreds of angry feet. Halved logs and carved stumps surrounded the space, as though spectators had enjoyed whatever sport had driven even the slightest hint of growth from the ground.

We passed by a chair wide enough to fit two, with a soaring bird carved into the back. I wondered for a moment how they had found a tree large enough to create such a thing.

Magic.

Prickles tingled the back of my neck.

On the far side of the clearing waited another batch of tents, larger than the first. A path cut through the center of them, with smaller trails leading off to the back rows where the tents seemed barely large enough to fit a cot.

A few men and women poked their heads out to gape at me as we passed.

I tucked the hair that had pulled free from my braid behind my ears and kept my head held high. I couldn't stop them from worrying that Emmet's sister had been brought to the camp, but I wouldn't have them murmuring that she had shown up looking like a filthy, chivving coward.

We stopped in front of the largest tent in this area.

A girl waited next to it, her arms crossed as she stared between Liam and me. Her hair was cut short so it rested above her shoulders. She wore a shirt and bodice, and pants like a man.

The hilt of a knife poked out of the top of her boot. But it was the way she watched us, like she wasn't staring at the filth on my clothes but instead thinking of how best to gut me, that made me like the girl.

"Cati." Liam nodded.

"You've been gone a while." Cati tipped her head as she examined me. "She does look like him."

"Makes sense, I suppose," I said.

"Speaks like him, too," Cati said.

I started to say she was wrong before swallowing the words for fear my speaking might prove her right.

"I'll get her cleaned up," Cati said. "Rothford wants to meet with you, and I'm sure there's a dozen other things need doing. If you get started now, you might get to sleep tonight."

Liam shut his eyes for a moment before nodding and shrugging out of his pack. "Thanks, Cati."

"This way." Cati started down another path, leading me away from the tents. I followed her, not giving in to the temptation to look back at Liam. "We'll get you washed and work on some decent clothes for you."

"Thanks."

"Glad to," Cati said. "What kind of terrible would we be if we weren't kind to someone who came up the mountain road to get to us?"

"We didn't come up the road," I said. "We cut east and came north through the mountains."

"What?" Cati whipped around and studied me again, taking in everything from my worn boots to my filthy face.

"It's a bit of a story." I shrugged. "Liam thinks the soldiers might want me hanged."

Cati stayed silent for a moment before tipping her head back and laughing. "I think I might like you."

She beckoned me on through the trees to a mound of rocks sticking out of a cliff.

"Honestly," Cati said, "I've told Emmet he should bring you here more than once. Gods, he'll be furious. I can't wait till he gets back."

She stepped between the stones and out of sight. I took a deep breath before following her, expecting the burning to flare in my chest again, but a humid warmth and the sound of flowing water greeted me instead.

Two lae stones hung from the ceiling of the cave, casting their glow on the pool beneath. A crack in the rock wall fed water into the bath. The overflow from the current surged over the edge and into the darkness on the far side.

Cati fished in one of the dozen alcoves carved into the wall and pulled out a basket of soap that smelled as fresh as summer flowers. "Give yourself a good scrub, and I'll be back with some clean clothes."

She pressed the soap into my hand and left me alone in the cave.

I lay in the pool, trying not to wonder at how the water had been heated. It might have come from a fire burning far beneath the ground. Or, there was the far more terrifying option—I was sitting in a bath warmed by magic. In a camp protected by magic. After following a man whose blood held magic.

I scrubbed my hair with the sweet-smelling soap, digging my fingers into my scalp hard enough to hurt.

If Karin had been here, she'd have been positively giddy at being surrounded by magic.

Karin wouldn't have made it through the mountains.

It wasn't a pretty thought, but I couldn't come up with a way to tell myself it wasn't true.

My eyes stung with missing Harane and all the people there. Or who had once been there.

I ducked beneath the water, rinsing the suds out of my hair. I stayed under for a moment, letting the faint rumble of the water entering and leaving the pool drown out the thoughts of wounds I couldn't mend.

Warmed by magic or not, I couldn't help but be grateful for the bath. I scrubbed my face hard before coming up for air.

"You all right?" Cati stood at the edge of the pool, looking down at me.

I brushed aside the instinct to cover my nakedness and met her gaze. "I'm halfway to clean, so things are looking up."

"Good." She stared at me for another moment before moving to a pile of clothes set at the side of the cave. "We don't usually get unexpected guests in the camp, so we don't keep many extra clothes on hand. Lucky for you, when I said I needed things for Emmet's sister, a few of the women volunteered their wardrobe."

"Is Emmet that well liked?" I scrubbed my arms, getting rid of the last layer of mountain dirt.

"I don't know how many people like him, but we all owe him, and that's worth even more." Cati knelt by the clothes. "We've got three choices for boots, so we'll see which fits best. All of them are worn, but they're in better shape than the tatters you climbed here in." She rummaged through the pile and pulled out a slightly worn, deep blue skirt. "It'll be a bit short at the ankles on you, but honestly that's for the best up here."

"It doesn't matter to me. If it's clean, I'll take it."

Cati flashed me a quick smile. "Good. I truly don't know how the southern runners manage to get clothes onto all the sorcis they save."

"Sorcis?" I climbed out of the pool, wrapping myself in the cloth she'd laid out for me.

"Sorcerers we save from being trapped by the Guilds." Cati held a shift up to the light of the lae stones. "We don't bring the sorcis here, though. We funnel them south as quick as we can. The farther from Ilara they are, the safer they are."

"Is that what my brother is doing? Bringing children with magic south to keep them away from the Guilds?"

"No." Cati held a bodice up to my torso, tossed it aside and picked up another, which would fit tighter than Lily would have ever allowed. She scowled at it for a moment, then pressed it into my hands. "That'll look nice."

"What is Emmet doing?" I held out my arms for her to drape the shift and skirt across.

"Things that are better not spoken about."

I didn't like the sound of that.

I didn't know Emmet, not as he was. My understanding of my brother was a strange mix of what I remembered of him from when I was little and we still lived together in our parents' home, and the Emmet I'd created in my head over the years of him being gone.

For so long, the Emmet in my mind had been brave and strong, a warrior I could depend on if the Guilds ever came for my blood. When I found out he'd abandoned Nantic and me, I'd decided he was a chivving coward who didn't care for anyone but himself. Now, with Cati holding boots up to the bottom of my foot, I realized I didn't know Emmet at all. I probably never had.

I'd been a little girl when Emmet and I had shared the loft in our parents' home. I'd still thought the fairy stories he'd told me to get me to go to sleep were real.

Then I learned that nothing as beautiful as a happily ever after existed in this world, but he was already gone. Taken far away where I could pretend I still knew my brother.

"This should work for now." Cati left a pair of brown boots by my feet. "Get dressed, and we'll find you something to eat."

She walked out of the cave, leaving me alone.

I tried not to think of who the clothes actually belonged to as I pulled them on. Liam had already saved my life. I didn't like the idea of being beholden to so many people at once. But the feeling of being genuinely clean was enough of a comfort to make me forget how many times I might have to say thank you to strangers.

I picked up my old clothes to take them with me. The dull stink of them sent heat to my cheeks. I'd shared blankets with Liam in these mud-packed clothes.

My face flushed even hotter at the idea of him thinking of me as the filthy little sister of the great Emmet Ryeland. Then I realized he had probably already stopped thinking of me at all, and hurt nibbled at the edges of my stomach.

After days spent with only Liam, it seemed strange to be without him.

But he'd trudged back to his home, a place where he was in charge and had tasks to tend to and decisions to make. I'd left the ruins of my home behind. I had no ink to blend, no chores from Lily to accomplish. I was wearing other girls' clothes in a strange place where the only certainty about my future was how livid my brother would be to find me here.

"Ena?" Cati called in.

"Coming." I stepped out into the late afternoon sun. The wind chilled my neck under my wet hair.

"That's better." Cati gave a nod. "There'll be a comb waiting in your tent. At least there will be if Marta did as I asked."

"Thanks," I said, "for the clothes and all of it."

"Think nothing of it. You just came through the mountains to get here. The fact that you survived the journey makes you worthy of clean clothes and a comb in my book."

"Right." I followed her back toward the cluster of little tents. "Thanks though."

"Sure." She stopped next to the largest tent at the head of the path. A small tent had been set up right beside it. "This'll be for you."

She pulled aside the flap of the small tent and bowed me in. A cot, a stump for a chair, and a taller one for a table had been set up inside. A carved wooden comb lay on top of the thick blankets on the bed.

"It's not much," Cati said, "but this is about all we have to offer here."

"It's all I need." I pushed a little smile onto my face, hoping I looked thankful without having to say it again.

"I'll have someone bring food in a bit." Cati gave a nod, let go of the tent's flap, and I was alone.

For the first time since I'd smelled the smoke in the woods near Harane, there was nothing for me to do. No one for me to try and save, no soldiers to flee from, no mountains to climb.

I stood in the tent for a long while. The chatter of voices cut through the fabric, but the stillness in my little shelter smothered me. I lay down on the bed and shut my eyes, wishing there were something familiar left in the world.

22

Music dragged me from the blackness of my dream. I woke to find myself still surrounded by darkness.

For one terrible moment, I thought the nightmare had learned another new trick, a way to keep me pinned in its grasp by not letting me know if I was awake.

Then I saw the glimmers of light fighting through the fabric of my tent and remembered where I was. I lay on top of my blankets for a few minutes, listening.

Someone plucked at an instrument. A few voices sang along, though not all of them very well. Chatter weaved in and out of the music. Laughter, too. The steady thumping of feet striking the ground kept time with the tune.

Dancing.

Old stories of ghosts reveling in the woods, luring in living men and making them dance until they died, shot a shiver through my shoulders.

"You ran into the mountains with a Black Blood, Ena. You can't afford to become a coward now."

I sat up on my cot and combed my hair. The normality of the motion soothed my nerves. I didn't have a string to tie the end of a braid with, so I let my hair lie loose around my shoulders in a way that would have driven Lily mad.

Remembering her scowling face carved another tiny hole in my chest.

One day, there might be nothing left of me but a vast emptiness.

I pressed my hands to my chest and took a deep breath. My heart beat within my ribs, thumping against my hands. That had to be enough. Breathing and living had to be enough. It was all I could manage.

I ran the comb through my hair one last time and stepped out of my tent.

Lae stones hung along the wide path between the tents, making a trail of blue light to the clearing beyond. Squaring my shoulders, I walked toward the music, determined that, if I was going to walk into the middle of a ghost's revel and be made to dance until I died, I would do it with my head held high and not a hint of cowardice about me.

People filled the clearing—sitting on the halved logs and stumps, clustered around a barrel and small fire on the far side, dancing on the packed earth in the center. Two women stood on one of the benches, playing their instruments, switching between songs with barely a nod or word spoken between them.

Lae stones hung from the trees, casting their light on the whole joyous mess.

I stood at the far edge, watching, searching for the reason for the celebration. I didn't see a pair acting like a new bride and groom, or spot anyone preening like the party was being held in their honor.

But they were all smiling and laughing.

"Ena?" A girl my age with hair so blond it was almost white stepped in front of me.

"Yes." I didn't know what else to say.

The girl smiled, and dimples punctured her rosy cheeks. "I

was wondering if you were going to wake up hungry. I tried to bring you some dinner earlier, but you were asleep, and Cati said you'd been through the mountains so I didn't think it would be right to wake you."

I dug my nails into my palms, praying to whatever god could listen so far into the mountains that if this blond girl had seen me sleeping, she at least hadn't found me in the middle of the nightmare.

"Well"—the girl took my hand like we'd been friends since childhood and led me into the clearing—"you're awake now, and you've got to be starving. Bless the stars for Liam, but I'm sure he didn't feed you nearly as well as he should have." The girl gave a bright laugh.

"We managed."

The sounds and movement in the clearing changed as the revelers began to notice me. The whispers started lapping from the far end. One of the women stopped playing, only starting again when the other stomped on her toe.

"Come on." The girl tugged me through the center of the pack.

I kept my face front and my breathing even, refusing to let any hint of pink creep into my cheeks.

"We've got a bit of stew over here," the girl said. "Neil doesn't usually take well to people ferreting for food once he's done feeding the camp for the day, but if you want something more than that, I think he might make an exception for you."

A cluster of men just older than me stopped their whispering as we drew level with them.

"Because I'm Emmet's sister?" I said loud enough for the men to hear.

Three of the four had the good sense to turn their faces from me. One with bright red hair met my gaze and gave me a nod.

"That and you managed to survive being alone with Liam for days." The girl laughed again.

"What's your name?" I asked.

"Oh, sorry." The girl wrinkled her nose as she stopped next to the barrel. "I hardly ever meet new people, so I suppose I forget how it's meant to be done. I'm Marta."

"Nice to meet you," I said, but Marta had stopped listening to me.

"Can I get a stew and ale?" she spoke to the older man who seemed to be in charge of minding the barrel and the fire with the stewpot hanging over it.

The man looked at me with narrowed eyes before nodding.

"We eat pretty well here," Marta said, "at least as far as being in the camp goes. It's not anything compared to what we get in the winter, but I suppose that's the price we pay."

She kept chattering as the older man pressed a wooden bowl of stew into one of my hands and a mug of brown ale into the other. He gave me a nod, and what might have been a smile, as Marta led me away.

"Honestly," Marta said, patting the bench for me to sit next to her, "I think you'll be happy here once you've settled in a bit. Life isn't fancy, but we're safe here, and we're helping, and that makes it all worthwhile. And I am glad to have another girl near my age here. There aren't very many of us, you know, and to have a new person come in, it really is exciting."

"I'm glad." I took a bite of my stew, risking burning my mouth in exchange for a reason not to have to say more.

"I've been telling Emmet he should bring you here for two years now," Marta said. "The look on his face when he finds out you're here will be brilliant. I hope I get to see it. And I hope we get to keep you. Maybe we'll work on convincing him together. Between the two of us, I think we could do quite the job of it."

"Maybe."

Marta kept talking while I ate the thick stew and drank the ale that tasted of pressed flowers. I didn't say much, I just tried to ignore the people pretending not to stare at me, and watched the ones dancing.

There wasn't a hint of fear clouding their joy. People laughed and sang in a way I'd never witnessed in Harane. I hadn't even known enough about what being safe was supposed to mean to realize how much fear had tainted every part of life in the village.

I blinked away images of a dark-stained post, and tamped down the anger even thinking the word *safe* boiled within me.

23

"If you would only let me do something to help," I said for the fifth time that hour as I followed Marta through the camp.

"You need to rest," Marta said. "Don't worry about helping."

"Marta, if—"

She ignored me and ducked into the open kitchen tent, leaving a sheet of paper under a stone on the table and giving Neil a wave before hurrying on toward the makeshift stables near the western side of the camp.

"I could be useful." I spoke through my teeth as I chased Marta through the trees.

I'm not proud of the three days I spent following Marta through the camp.

The first full day I had with the Black Bloods I mostly just slept. The climb through the mountains had taken more out of me than I cared to admit.

After that, the horrible itching ache to be doing something set in. I didn't care if it was climbing through another mountain range, digging for roots, or mucking up after the horses. The idea of sitting still and waiting for my brother to come back set my every nerve on edge.

Marta paused at the fence of the horse paddock. There were only six horses roaming between the trees. Truth be told, I wasn't exactly sure how they'd gotten the horses up the mountain. They certainly wouldn't have made it on the path Liam and I had climbed.

Even thinking his name set a chill on my neck and a stone in my stomach. I hadn't seen him since he'd left me in Cati's care when we'd arrived. From the little people were willing to tell me, he wasn't even in the camp anymore.

"It'll only leave us with four horses for now." Marta chewed the tip of her thumb. "I don't like it at all, but I suppose we haven't got a choice, have we?"

"Are you actually asking me?" I stepped in front of her. "Because if you'd tell me what the horses were for or where they were going, maybe I could help you work it out."

"It's nothing for you to worry about." Marta gave me a smile just large enough to display her dimples. "We have plenty of supplies here. There's no reason for you to fret."

"I'm not fretting."

"Good." Marta dodged past me and spoke a few whispered words to the woman who minded the horses.

The woman's tan brow furrowed. She pursed her lips, glaring at Marta for a moment before shrugging and going to the tent where the saddles were kept.

"I could help her with the horses, you know," I said as Marta hurried through the trees back up to the main body of the camp.

"She'll have it done in no time," Marta said. "Tirra's quite used to working on her own."

"It's not Tirra I'm fussed about. It's me losing my chivving mind."

"You're not going to lose your mind from a few days' rest." Marta waved a hand in the air as though batting away the foolish notion that the lack of work could be rapidly stripping me of my sanity.

We passed through the clearing where the camp gathered every night—dancing, laughing, talking, perfectly secure in their home far up in the mountains.

I wanted to stand in the middle of the packed dirt and scream. Shout to the entire camp that if they didn't give me something to occupy my time, I might catch fire from the inside out and burn the whole mountain down.

Sleeping brought nightmares. Sitting idle allowed thinking, which brought memories I couldn't bear. I had been reduced to chasing after Marta as she bustled through camp, organizing things in whispers, just so being angry at her would give me something to do.

"If you won't let me help with the horses, food, laundry—"

"There are already people doing all those things," Marta said.

"Then I'll leave camp and gather some plants for healing. You can never have too many supplies if an illness comes."

Marta turned back toward me, chewing on the tip of her chivving thumb again. "I can't let you do that. Liam said you weren't to be allowed out of camp under any circumstances."

A flash of white hot anger burned away the little self-control I'd managed to retain. "Liam says I'm not allowed out of camp? And the chivving slitch didn't see fit to tell me himself?"

"Ena." Marta blushed.

"And why am I not to be allowed out of camp? Am I a prisoner now? Is he afraid there will be soldiers hunting me this high in the mountains?"

"He only wants to keep you safe."

"Don't you even—"

A slow clapping cut me off. I turned to find Cati leaning against a tree in the shadows.

"She's finally cracked." Cati pushed away from the tree, a tiny smile playing on her lips. "I thought it would have happened sooner."

"Cati," Marta warned.

"I bet you were going to explode yesterday." Cati ignored Marta. "Rothford won the bet. I'm out a copper."

"You bet on me losing my mind from sitting still?" I asked.

"That wasn't a very welcoming thing to do," Marta said.

Cati shrugged. "So what's wrong then?"

"I can't just sit around here waiting for precious Emmet to show up," I said. "And I won't be told I'm not allowed to leave camp."

"But Liam—"

"I'm not a child who needs to be kept in the garden." I spoke over Marta. "I'm not useless, and I won't be treated like I am."

"Well, Marta?" Cati crossed her arms, still smiling.

"I suppose," Marta said, looking up to the treetops as though seeking answers from the gods, "there is always a use for more people in the kitchen tent. Neil tells wonderful stories—"

"I don't—"

"Sounds like you don't need Ena's help." Cati stepped between us and looped her arm through mine. "Come with me, Ena. I've got something to keep you busy."

She led me off through the trees, not bothering with a path.

"Wait." Marta chased after us. "Where are you going?"

"To train," Cati said.

"No," Marta said. "Absolutely not. She is not going to train with you. She is to be kept safe until Emmet returns."

"I'm not going to stab her," Cati said.

"She is not a fighter," Marta said.

Cati let go of my arm and rounded on Marta. "I don't care what Liam said. I don't care what Emmet will think. Whatever ends up happening, wherever Ena ends up going, she'll be better off if she knows which end of a knife to shove into someone's eye. Consider her training an investment in her future survival, whether or not she ends up staying with the Black Bloods."

Marta bit her lips together as her face turned bright red.

"Go tally supplies and save Ilbrea." Cati shooed her away.

"If this goes badly, you're taking the blame." Marta gave one final and decisive shake of her head before striding away.

Cati didn't speak again until Marta had disappeared through the trees. "Ready then?"

I wanted to ask what I was supposed to be ready for, but I was too afraid Cati might change her mind and leave me to sit on a stump.

I followed her deep into the trees toward the largest clearing in the camp.

I don't know why they had set the training field so far back from the tents. Maybe it was to keep the clanging swords from making it seem as though the Guilds had come to rip through their canvas homes and kill them all. Maybe it was because there was so little flat space in the mountain refuge, it had to be used where it could be found.

It was a ten minute walk to the open space where the trees had been cut down and the stumps cleared away. The first time I had wandered through the camp, I had wondered at the size of it all. How had so many massive stones been laid to be able to protect a place so large?

But the idea of the mountain shooting talons of stone up around us, as though the rocks themselves held us in their grip, had been frightening enough I'd decided not to worry about how the camp had been formed. If it had that much to do with magic, it was probably best I not know.

The clangs of swords and twangs of bows carried through the trees.

"I meant it, you know," Cati said. "You do need to learn to fight, whatever ends up happening when Emmet gets back. A girl like you needs to know how to protect herself."

"What's that supposed to mean?" I watched as the young man with the flaming red hair hoisted his sword and charged at another man.

"The Guild paun who attacked you—" Cati began.

"Liam told you?"

"Of course, and the sad part is, I wasn't surprised." Cati turned to me, looking at my bodice that showed my curves a bit too well, before staring into my eyes. "You do know you're very beautiful?"

"So men will decide they want to come after me whether I want them to or not?"

"They can try it. But once you know how to fight, you'll be able to slit the throat of the next chivving bastard who tries to touch you." She pulled a knife from her boot and pressed the hilt into my hand. "Sound good?"

I gripped the heavy blade. The weight of it absorbed the hopeless, helpless worry that had been stinging my chest. "All right."

Every muscle in my body hurt. Bruises had formed on my arms and stomach from Cati's blows. We'd both used wooden knives for practice, thank the gods, otherwise I would have been sliced to ribbons.

I'd never seen someone fight the way Cati did. It was as though someone had taught her a fancy dance that just so happened to involve killing people. When the men on the field watched her, their faces filled with a beautiful mix of admiration and fear.

She showed me no pity as she taught me how to block an attack, and I was grateful for it. Even as I sat in the clearing, too sore to join in the evening's dancing, I was grateful for every blow.

She'd let me keep her knife and had given me a sheath so I could tuck the blade into my boot as she had. Having a weapon pressed against me felt like the most powerful secret I could ever hold. I was not helpless, and someday, I would be dangerous.

When the dancers had begun to slow for the evening, Liam walked into the clearing, his pack on his back and dirt covering his boots.

He gave a wave to the ones still frolicking but didn't slow as he crossed through his people and toward his tent. No one stopped him to speak to him.

His footfalls were heavy and his shoulders rounded. He looked exhausted.

We'd climbed through the mountains for days, and even in the worst of it, he'd never looked like that.

I waited until he'd disappeared up the wide row of tents before following him. I gave a nod to Marta, who'd been avoiding me since I'd gone off with Cati, and blushed a bit as the redheaded boy smiled at me.

The music followed me up the lae stone-lined path. Shadows flickered around me as though the night wanted to take over for the tiring dancers.

The flaps on Liam's tent were still swaying when I reached them. I raised my hand to knock, but the canvas wasn't a door. A foolish, nervous fear pressed on the front of my chest. I shook it away and settled for knocking on the tent post.

"What do you need?" There was an unfamiliar, harsh edge to Liam's words.

"Wanted to make sure you were all right," I said. "But if you're bent on being in a sour mood, I won't offer to bring you a mug of ale."

My heart thumped against my ribs as I waited for him to reply.

He didn't.

"Night then." I turned toward my own tent.

Liam pushed the flap of his open.

He stared at me for a long moment, then held out a small waterskin.

I took it, not even needing to get the skin close to my nose to smell the frie. "So you don't want ale then?" I took a sip, letting the fire of the liquor burn away the bit of me that was embarrassed for following him.

"I find the two don't mix well," Liam said.

"Depends on the person, I think." I took another sip from the skin. "A few of the fellows back in Harane took combining the two to a near masterful level. It was rather impressive."

A smile lifted one corner of Liam's mouth.

"So you're all right then?" I asked.

"Fine," Liam said, "nothing you need to worry about."

"So you're worried?"

"That's not what I said."

"As good as. Did it go badly? Whatever it was you disappeared to do?"

He looked at me for a long moment. It felt like he was judging the weight I could bear. Like I was a bridge he wasn't sure was steady enough to be crossed.

"It didn't go as well as I'd hoped," Liam said.

"Want to tell me about it?" I held the frie out to him.

"There are some things it's better for you not to know." He took a long drink.

"Because when my brother decides where I'm to be placed for safekeeping I might go running to the nearest paun soldier and tell them all about your plans to free Ilbrea of the Guilds?" I took the skin and had another drink.

"You wouldn't betray us." Liam leaned against the pole of his tent. "It wouldn't even matter if you felt any loyalty to the Black Bloods—you hate the Guilds too much to offer them help."

"Well then." I ducked under his arm and into his tent.

A bed, a table with two chairs, and a trunk left most of the space in the tent empty.

"Tell me what's wrong." I took a seat at the table before he could argue with me.

Liam stared at me for a long moment, as though warring with himself as to whether or not to toss me out.

I waved the frie at him and nudged the other chair at the table with my toe. "Come on."

My brashness started a steady thrumming in my chest. I don't know if it was the knife tucked in my boot, the frie in my belly, or the simple fact that I didn't care if he got mad at me as long as I got to speak to him.

Liam sighed and let go of the tent flap, shutting out the rest of the camp. "We need more."

"More what?"

"More fighters, more resources." He sat opposite me with a soul-cracking sigh. "We need more everything."

"And you can't get it?"

"I thought I had a chance," Liam said. "I went to speak to one of the other clans—"

"Other clans?" I leaned in.

"There are five clans in the Black Bloods. Unfortunately, none of the others seem to care as much about Ilbrea as we do. I thought telling them what the Guilds had done to Emmet's home would make them see how bad things have gotten. I thought it had worked." He reached into his pocket and pulled out a bird carved of black stone.

He ran his finger along the bird's spine, and its wings shivered as the stone came to life. The bird hopped around the table, its stone-making the only thing giving away that it wasn't a natural creature. Liam held out his palm, and the bird lifted its chin.

A short, tightly wound scroll grew out of the bird's throat. Liam unrolled the paper and read it aloud.

Trueborn Duwead,

Your bravery is the pride of all Black Bloods, but we can see no path forward to a free Ilbrea that will not bring suffering to all the mountain's people. We will continue to protect the magic you bring us and ferry the power safely away from the Guilds' control. If the chance for freedom comes, we will stand with you. Until then, we must protect our own.

Blood Leader Brien

Liam crumpled the paper. "And he didn't even bother to tell me to my face. It sounded like he'd help us. Then I get this when I'm halfway back here."

"Sounds like he's a chivving coward." I held out my hand and the stone bird hopped toward me. "Would you really want someone like that helping you?" The bird leaned into my fingers as I pet its cold head.

"I don't have anyone else." Liam took another drink, watching as the bird nibbled at my fingers. "We do well enough rescuing the ones who want to hide from the Sorcerers Guild. And I'm not saying it isn't important work."

"Freedom for them and one less trained sorcerer ready to kill any common folk who cross the Guilds."

Liam nodded, rubbing his hand across the scruff on his chin. "But it's not enough. How can the other clans not see it? After what the soldiers did to Harane, after what that bastard tried to do to you." He froze, staring at me.

He thinks I'll shatter.

I took a deep breath, testing myself for cracks. "The Guilds torment us. It's how it's always been."

"That doesn't make it right."

"No, it doesn't. Not even a little. But up here"—I let the bird hop up onto my palm as I tried to fit the words into the right order—"I can understand how the other clans ignore it. Up here, the mountains block out the entire world. They swallow everything beyond. All of Ibrea could be on fire, and we wouldn't know. We might not even get a hint of smoke on the wind.

"If I hadn't lived it, if I hadn't watched so many people bleed because of the Guilds, I don't know if I'd be willing to leave the mountains to try and fight the most powerful people in the world either."

Liam passed the skin of frie back to me. The bird hopped up onto my shoulder while I drank.

"There are people dying down there every day," Liam said.

"I know."

"What kind of monsters would we be to ignore that?"

"The kind that stay alive."

"Only until the Sorcerers Guild gets strong enough to conquer the mountains." Liam looked up to the canvas above him. "It'll happen. Maybe not for another generation, but Ilbrea won't leave the mountains free forever. If we just hide and let them slaughter and gain power, then how will we be able to say the Black Bloods deserve aid or freedom when the Guilds come for us?"

"Did you explain it to the Blood Leader like that?"

"I tried. But he's so caught up in this year's rations, he can't think of the people starving outside his control."

"Then find another way to get more people," I said.

"If the Brien won't fight with us, none of the other clans will."

"Who says you have to have Black Bloods? You recruited my brother. Haven't you gotten more out of Ilbrea?"

"Some."

"Then you'll find some more." I nudged his chair with my toe. "You've got magical rocks on your side. You'll find a way."

Liam held out his hand. The bird soared over to him, landed on his palm, and became lifeless. He tucked the bird back into his pocket.

"I—" I began, but Liam met my gaze. Fatigue bordering on defeat filled his dark eyes.

"What happened to Emmet and me when we were young, we're not unique. We're not the only children the Guilds stole everything from. What the soldiers did to Harane, how they killed Lily—she expected it. She knew they'd murder her for helping people eventually."

Liam took my hand in his. His callused palm pressed against mine, the warmth of his touch giving me courage.

"And what that man tried to do to me. No one would be shocked at that either."

"It's not right." Liam squeezed my hand. "People shouldn't have to live like that."

"No, they shouldn't." I leaned closer to him. "And you and I, and the rest of the Black Bloods in this camp, aren't the only ones who see that. There are people who will want to help you. You just have to find them."

"I thought you didn't believe we could overthrow the Guilds."

"I don't. But I don't think you're capable of sitting idly by while the world burns either. And if you're going to fight against the flames, there are a lot of other people incapable of doing nothing who will fight with you. And who knows? Perhaps, if you get enough fools together, you can save us all."

"Maybe." His gaze fixed on my hand clasped in his. He moved his thumb toward my wrist, his skin just barely grazing mine.

The edge of my sleeve shifted, falling up my arm. A flock of bruises darkened my skin. I moved to pull my sleeve down, but he'd already taken my arm in both his hands.

"Who did this to you?" His face turned to stone, even harder than the bird's wings.

"No one."

"Did someone in this camp hurt you?" I could hear death in his voice. He'd already slit one throat to protect me—he wouldn't hesitate to do it again.

I didn't say anything.

"Ena, I brought you here to keep you safe, and if one of my own people—"

"It's not like that." I lifted my arm from his grip.

"It's not hurting you to leave you covered in bruises?"

"She did hurt me, but not like you think."

Liam opened his mouth to speak, but I pressed a hand over his lips.

"It's Cati. She's teaching me to fight. Which does involve hitting me quite a bit, but not in a way for you to get fussed over."

Liam lifted my hand away from his mouth. "Why is she teaching you to fight?" He kept my fingers locked with his.

"Because I can't count on there always being someone around to save me. I have to know how to protect myself."

"You shouldn't have to." He held my hand tighter.

"But I do, and learning something is better than sitting around waiting for Emmet. Besides, since the Brien won't help you, shouldn't you be grateful for anyone who's willing to fight on your side?"

He let go of my hand. "I'm glad Cati is teaching you. She's one of our best."

"She is."

"You should get some rest." Liam stood and opened his tent flap. "I'm sure she'll want to leave more bruises on you in the morning."

"Right." I pushed away from the table and stood, refusing to let the chill night air make me shiver. "Rest well, trueborn Duwead."

I lifted the flap from his hand and let it fall shut behind me.

I closed my eyes, warring with myself as to whether to go into my tent, knowing I wouldn't be able to sleep, or to go back to the clearing, knowing someone might notice I wanted nothing more than to tear a tree up by its roots.

A prickle that had nothing to do with the cold touched the back of my neck. I opened my eyes, searching for whatever had set my senses on edge.

A head of bright blond hair glinted in the moonlight. Marta stood in the trees far off the main path, an over-large mug of ale in one hand, a bowl of stew in the other.

Our eyes met for a moment before she spun on her heel and stalked off into the darkness.

I turned the other way and ducked into my tent. I didn't bother lighting the lae stone. I pulled the knife from my boot and set it under the thin thing I pretended was a pillow. I yanked off my shoes and let the cold bite at my skin as I undressed.

I could hear him through the canvas. He couldn't have been more than fifteen feet away from where I stood. From the soft thumping of his feet, he was pacing in the open space of his tent.

I tried not to picture it. Him pacing and drinking frie. Him plotting to find more people to help save Ilbrea. Him worrying about saving villages and stopping the violence of the Guilds. Him thinking of how to get me away from the mountains and the Black Bloods and him as soon as my brother returned.

I crawled under the heavy layers of my blankets and stared into the darkness at where Liam paced, listening to the sound of his footsteps as I faded to sleep.

When I was a very little girl, my mother swore I would be the death of her. I loved to run and climb and tear down the road on our horse, even though my legs weren't long enough to reach the stirrups.

When I was six, my mother found me sitting on the roof of our house.

She screamed and screamed. My father bolted out of the barn to find my mother wailing like I'd already fallen to my death and me giggling at the spectacle of it all. Soon, the neighbors came to see what the fuss was all about.

The Ryelands' girl had gotten herself into trouble again. No one was shocked, and everyone but my parents seemed to enjoy the afternoon diversion.

While the villagers offered suggestions of how to get me safely down, no one noticed Emmet climbing up the far side of the house to join me. He hated heights, but he thought I was in danger. So he braved falling to come collect me. He took my hand and led me to the side of the house where the boards had cracked wide enough to create handholds for child-sized fingers, and matched me step for step the whole way down.

The adults had been so busy arguing as to whether it would be safe to have me jump and if my father was strong enough to catch me, they didn't notice I'd disappeared from the roof until Emmet led me over to make me apologize to the crowd for causing a fuss and to my mother for making her worry.

"How long did it take you to learn to fight?" I asked, shaking my wrist out, trying to get feeling back into my fingers after Cati's latest blow.

"Does it matter?" Cati tossed her wooden blade from one hand to the other.

"Yes. If you've only been training for a while, then I'm a hopeless slitch who will never get any of this right. If you've been fighting for a long time, then I should resign myself to years of bruises and pain while I try and learn how to not get stabbed."

Cati's laugh rang out over the clanging of the swords next to us.

"And when will I get to use bigger weapons?" I pointed to the blades glinting in the light.

The ginger boy dove under his opponent's sword, leaping back to his feet with a wide grin on his freckled face.

"You won't. I'm teaching you to defend yourself, and keeping a sword tucked under your skirt isn't very practical now is it?" Cati winked at me and mouthed something that looked like *soon*.

She hadn't said anything, but I was fairly certain Liam had

laid out what Cati was allowed to teach me in no uncertain terms.

It really was the most practical course—teaching me how to throw a proper punch, kick someone who grabbed me from behind, and the simplest way to gut someone who tried to hurt me. And, though I was improving day by day, it was still far too easy for Cati to disarm me.

But the idea that Liam had forbidden me from learning the weapons that would be used in a real fight grated against every fiber of my being.

"Let's go again." Cati took her place opposite me, her legs set apart, her wooden blade resting in her hand. She didn't even look like she was trying to hold onto the hilt.

I wiped the sweat off my palms and prepared myself for her inevitable attack.

She waited until I was ready, then began shifting her weight ever so slightly from side to side.

I watched her movements, trying to predict where her attack would come from. Just when I was certain she would lunge at me from the left, she leapt straight for my center and knocked my feet out from under me.

I hit the ground hard, coughing all the air from my lungs, but I managed to hold onto my wooden knife. She planted one foot on my chest. I tapped the back of her knee with my blade before she managed to swipe hers across my throat.

"Well done!" She gripped my hand and hoisted me to my feet.

I sucked air into my lungs as casually as I could while pretending the trees weren't swaying from how hard I'd hit my head on the ground.

"We really should get you a pair of pants to practice in." Cati pursed her lips at my skirt. "Liam might not like it, but that will only make it more fun."

"Right." I blinked at the trees, trying to get them to stop drifting around.

"I'll find you something for tomorrow then."

Cati took her place opposite me again, but I still couldn't look away from the trees. The shadows of them had become familiar in the days I'd spent learning from Cati, but a figure that didn't belong lurked under the branches, staring at me.

I took a step toward the trees and felt the world tilt, as though I'd been knocked to the ground again, as Emmet walked out into the open.

He favored his left leg as though he'd been hurt, but that didn't slow his pace as he stormed toward me.

No, not toward me. Toward Cati.

"What do you think you're playing at?" Emmet pointed to the wooden blade in Cati's hand.

"I thought it was better than using the real thing and risking your sister's life." Cati crossed her arms and glared at Emmet.

"She has no business on the training field," Emmet said.

"Don't even start with me, Ryeland." Cati tapped her blade against his chest.

"Your job is to train warriors," Emmet growled. "She will not become one of your minions. She is not going to fight."

The rest of the people on the field had given up on their own training to watch.

I wanted to say something, but everything inside me had gone viciously cold. I couldn't remember how words were meant to work.

"I am training her to defend herself," Cati spat. "Your sister was nearly murdered. I am trying to make sure that doesn't happen again. She should be able to protect herself."

"It's my job to protect her," Emmet said. "It's my job to keep her safe."

"Grand chivving job you've done of it so far," Cati said.

"She is not yours to train." Emmet stepped in front of me like he was shielding me from Cati. Like of all the things in Ilbrea, Cati was the true danger.

Through the chilling numbness I felt my feet move as I walked around to stand in front of Emmet. I felt the blade fall from my hand and my fingers curl into a fist. My weight shifted as I drew my arm back and punched my brother straight in the jaw.

He stumbled, blinking at me like he couldn't quite make sense of why his face suddenly hurt so badly.

"You do not speak for me." The words scratched like stones in my throat.

"Ena, I—"

"You have no right to say what I'm allowed to do."

"You don't understand—"

"What?" I shouted, letting my voice ring over the field. "What don't I understand, dear brother? That you abandoned me? That you left me with a woman who defied the Guilds every day? Let me grow up in the house the soldiers burned to the ground with Lily swinging out front?"

"I didn't know." Emmet's face paled. "I didn't know Lily was a healer."

"How could you have? You weren't there. You never showed up for long enough for me to tell you the sort of danger that hid beneath the floor in Lily's house. You weren't there when the soldiers murdered her."

"I'm sorry." Emmet reached toward me. "I never wanted anything like this to happen. I only wanted you to be safe."

"Safe." I spat the word. "Safe in a village where the soldiers whip people to death? You're right, that's so much better than being here where my dearest chivving brother has been hiding. The gods would hate you for bringing your sister into this dangerous place where there are no people being hanged from trees."

"Ena, you don't understand. The work I'm doing—"

"Has worse consequences than being executed by the Guilds? Than watching the only thing close to family you have swing?

Than having a chivving stranger save you from being raped in the streets?"

Emmet just stared at me, pain creasing the corners of his eyes.

"Well, you needn't bother yourself with me ever again. You abandoned me a long time ago. As far as I'm concerned, I don't have a brother."

I turned and strode away into the woods.

I forced myself to breathe. To pull air into my lungs like somehow that might make the shattering in my chest stop. I pressed my palms to my stomach, trying to keep my hands from trembling. But all of me had started shaking like I might crack apart at the seams.

The trees began to sway again as my breath stopped filling my lungs and a sob broke free from my chest. I swiped the tears from my cheeks, but more took their place.

My sobs banged against my ribs, threatening to split me in two, but I couldn't make them stop.

I had lost Lily. She was gone, killed, and I hadn't been there to help her. My home had been burned, the life I'd known ripped away, and there was no hope of ever getting it back.

For the second time in my life, I'd been stripped of everything I was and everyone I'd cared for.

I had run from the flames of Harane, but I couldn't escape what had happened. Emmet pretending he cared had fractured the dark place where I'd hidden the reality of what I'd lost.

I wanted the tears to stop. I tried to shove everything back into the void where it couldn't hurt me. But the pain had broken past its boundary, and I didn't know how to shut it away.

A hand touched my shoulder, the weight of it familiar even through the haze of grief.

"Ena," Liam whispered my name.

A deeper crack cut through my chest. Nine years' worth of grief and fear refused to be tucked away any longer.

Liam wrapped his arms around me. I lay my cheek against his chest.

The harder I cried, the tighter he held me. Like somehow he could hold together the shattered pieces of my soul, keep them safe in his grip and make sure no part of me tumbled away and was lost forever.

I don't remember him lifting me, but somehow he was sitting with me cradled in his lap. His cheek pressed to my hair, his body arching around mine.

Sense started to come back as the tears slowed, and part of me wanted to explain. To offer some excuse for why I had shattered into so many pieces. But he had seen the nightmare torment me, and I didn't know if I was strong enough to start the story from its true beginning.

Liam held me without question until the tears finally stopped.

"I'm sorry," were the first words I managed to say without sobbing.

"For what?" He kept his arms tight around me.

I closed my eyes, trying to memorize the way my body nestled into his. "All of it."

"You've nothing to be sorry for."

I coughed out a laugh that made my ribs ache.

"I mean it, Ena. You've nothing to be sorry for."

"I'm not going." I listened to the wind whisper through the branches while I waited for him to speak.

"What do you mean?"

"I don't care what Emmet wants. He is not in control of my life, and I'm not going to let him choose a place to send me."

Liam leaned away and tipped my chin up so he could look into my eyes. "Then where do you want to go? Pick a place, and I'll do everything I can to see you safely there."

"I'm staying here. I want to help you."

"No. Ena, no. You can't stay here. You can't be a part of this."

"Why not?" I wiped the tears from my cheeks, trying not to

think of how swollen my face might be. "You need people, and I can help."

"No, you can't." Liam lifted me off his lap and stood me up.

"I'm useful, and I'm not afraid."

"It doesn't matter." Liam stood.

I didn't back away. "I don't know how to fight, but I can learn. I know enough about healing to be of good use. You should be grateful I want to stay."

"You can't."

"Give me one good reason why not." I laid my hands on his chest. His heartbeat thundered under my palms. "And it better not have anything to do with helping you being too dangerous. Life in Ilbrea is dangerous. If the Guilds are going to kill me, let it be because I was doing something worthwhile. Lily taught me that. It's all I have to hang on to. Do not try to take that from me, Liam."

He looked down at my hands. "This isn't an easy life, Ena."

"I'm not fool enough to think it is."

"If you want to join the Black Bloods, I won't stand in your way."

"Thank you." I took his face in my hands. The rough feel of his stubble beneath my skin sent fire flying up my fingers. "You won't regret this."

He shook his head, and creases wrinkled his brow. "We'll talk to Marta about getting you work to do."

"Good." A tiny shard of something a bit like hope broke through the shattered bits of my chest.

Liam held my gaze for a long moment. "I'll see you back at camp then."

"Right." I watched him walk away, disappearing into the maze of trees.

I sank onto the rock where he'd sat as he cradled me in his arms. One by one, I tucked each of the bits of my life I didn't want to remember back into the shattered void. But the hollow blackness wasn't there to swallow them anymore.

So, I folded the horrors beneath layers of fierce fire. If I was to be a Black Blood, then maybe I didn't need a vast nothing to protect me. Perhaps it was time to use fire to burn the pain away.

"I'm happy to help," I said, careful to keep the smile on my face as Neil squinted at me.

The entire camp seemed to have heard about my punching Emmet in the face. Some seemed offended, others impressed. From the whispers floating on the wind, most of the camp had also heard Emmet shouting at Liam when he was told I would be staying.

I wished I had been there to hear Emmet shout and to hear Liam's defense of my joining the Black Bloods. But the whole thing had been over before I'd trusted my face to look normal enough for people not to know I'd been crying.

As far as I knew, Liam hadn't told anyone what had happened in the woods. I was grateful. If this was to be my new home, I didn't want everyone to know I'd won my place with tears on my cheeks.

Neil pursed his wrinkled lips and leaned closer to me. I don't think his eyesight was that bad. It just seemed to be how he always looked at people.

"Go foraging if you like," Neil said. "I've plenty to keep our people fed, but only a fool says no to extra food in their larder."

"Good." I hurried out of the food tent before Neil could change his mind.

I trusted Liam to tell Marta I needed work, but I didn't want to wait. Crying had left me a kind of tired I hated. But climbing around, foraging for useful things, would leave me the kind of tired that might allow me to sleep.

As much as I longed to run, I kept my pace steady as I walked to my tent to get my bag. I didn't want to risk looking like I was misbehaving as soon as my older brother returned to camp.

I had no reason to think myself unworthy of staying, but knowing how everyone spoke of Emmet made me afraid. Like the Black Bloods might decide they didn't want me, even if Liam himself had said I could stay.

I grabbed my bag and headed east of the camp, to the slopes that cut steeply up the mountain. I searched the ground for berries, or places where some might grow later in the season. If the camp would even still be in the same place when the peak of summer came.

I didn't know where the Black Bloods stayed when they weren't in that camp, or how long they would be there for. I didn't know how they traveled from place to place. I didn't know much of anything. I pressed my forehead to the rough bark of a tree.

The deep scent of the sap calmed me.

Liam was in charge of the camp and of his people, and I trusted him.

I remembered the feel of his arms around me. The warmth of his face beneath my fingers.

I shook my head, flinging aside thoughts of Liam's hand touching mine, and climbed farther up the slope.

I found a patch of mushrooms that were safe to eat, and a bit of sour grass to help season food.

I was so busy searching the ground for edibles, I almost strolled past the boulders that surrounded the camp.

The stones were just like the ones Liam and I had passed between when he brought me into the camp, formed of black rock with the bottoms swallowed by the earth and not a bit of moss daring to mar their surface.

Glancing around to be sure no one had followed, I laid my palms on the boulder. I waited, trying to see if I could feel some pulse or spark of the magic the mountains had granted the stones. I leaned my weight against the boulder as though I were trying to merge my body with the rock.

A laugh at my own foolishness bubbled in my throat before a tingle of something tickled my skin. Not like fire or a bee's sting, because it didn't bring pain. I pressed my hands against the boulder as hard as I could.

A pull.

That was the feeling. Like something inside the stone called to the blood in my veins. My blood answered with a hunger and a wanting that crackled and sparked.

I lifted my hands away, severing the pull of the magic.

A longing tugged at my heart as I turned west and foraged my way back to camp.

I kept looping up and down the slope until my body was tired enough to make sleep a possibility, then headed back to the kitchen tent.

The line for dinner stretched out along the path, so I cut through the back way. I caught a glare from the woman stirring the pot, but I gave her a nod and started unloading my bounty onto the table.

"I know it's the same meal as yesterday," Neil shouted down the line of hungry Black Bloods, "but if the hunters keep bringing back deer, then you'll keep eating deer."

"Couldn't you make something other than stew with it?" a voice called.

I bit my lips together and dumped the mushrooms out of my bag.

"If you don't like the food I'm offering, you can feel free to eat some hardtack," Neil said. "And anyone who takes the hardtack won't be needing any ale to wash it down."

Swallowing my laugh, I snagged a bit of seed bread and a bowl of stew from the table before ducking back out the far side of the tent.

The woman stirring the pot tsked after me, but I didn't stop.

I felt like I'd been wrung out. Every bit of my being was exhausted.

By the time I reached my tent, I'd finished my dinner. I set the empty bowl on the stump that served as my table and lay down on top of my cot, boots and all.

I didn't remember falling asleep or the start of the dream. The pounding of the hooves had been dulled since I'd arrived in the camp, and the terror of the unending darkness unable to consume me. I waited through the nightmare, clinging to the hope that morning would come and wake me, but angry whispers carrying through my tent dragged me from sleep long before dawn.

"We can't." Liam's words drifted through the canvas.

I blinked at the darkness, trying to reassure myself I really was awake.

"It doesn't matter how much it needs to be done," Liam said. "We just can't."

"Why not?" Emmet said in a low, measured tone. Even when we were children, he spoke like that when he was angry. It used to make our mother laugh.

A pain shot through the newly sealed armor of flames in my chest.

"It's too dangerous," Liam said.

"He knew the risks when he agreed to the assignment," Emmet said. "Gabe is willing to sacrifice himself for the cause."

"But it's more than just Gabe we'd be losing."

"You've got to take a chance like this when it comes," Emmet said. "How many people are you prepared to let die?"

There was a thump like a fist pounding a table.

I sat up and ran my hands over my braid, trying to coax the stray strands into submission.

"We aren't going to get many chances like this," Emmet said.

I stepped out of my tent and walked the few feet to the front of Liam's.

"We would be setting ourselves back," Liam said.

Without giving myself time to wonder what the consequences might be, I knocked on the pole of Liam's tent.

Liam and Emmet fell silent.

I had time to look up at the stars in the moonless sky before Liam opened the flap of his tent.

"Ena, are you all right?"

I ducked under his arm and into the tent. "Oh, I'm just fine." I smiled at Emmet, taking a tiny bit of pleasure at the new bruise on his cheek. "I was actually sleeping fairly well until you two started worrying about Gabe's fate. I hope the poor fellow is all right. From the way you talk, he might as well be a sheep lined up for slaughter."

"This has nothing to do with you," Emmet said.

"Then maybe you should be careful talking about poor Gabe ten feet away from my bed." I sat in one of the chairs.

"I'm sorry, Ena," Liam said, not lowering the tent flap, "we should have been quieter."

"It's fine," I said. "What's a little lost sleep compared to the sacrifices Gabe is willing to make?"

Emmet looked from Liam to me as though waiting for Liam to kick me out. When Liam said nothing, Emmet leaned across the table toward me. "Ena, we're discussing important things here. Matters of life and death."

"Sounds like it." I crossed my arms and leaned back in my chair. "Of course, when you're dealing with the Guilds, sneezing at the wrong moment can be a matter of life and death. So, what makes Gabe's impending doom so important to the Black Bloods?"

"It's not your concern," Emmet said.

"Ena"—Liam let go of the tent flap—"I know you want to stay here."

"And you agreed that I can." I swallowed my glee as the veins on the sides of Emmet's neck bulged through his skin.

"But there are some things it's best if fewer people know," Liam said. "The work we're trying to do is dangerous. We may not have the forces to fight on a grand scale, but if we keep the small things we do hidden, the people we have are safer."

"Sound reasoning," I said. "But, as I already know about Gabe's death wish, since you failed to take into account that fabric is easy to hear through, is there anything I can do to help?"

"Yes," Emmet said. "Go back to bed."

"Because you think I'm a useless child or because you just don't like me?" I asked.

"Because you don't belong here," Emmet said. "You're not a Black Blood. You're not a fighter or an assassin. You've no experience killing people. You can't help."

"How many lives have you ended?" I looked to Emmet's hands, foolishly expecting the blood of the people he'd killed to be staining his fingers.

"Enough," Emmet said.

"And what about Gabe?" I hid my shudder at Emmet's cold glare. "Is he an accomplished killer? Does Cati need to go and make the kill for him?"

Emmet glanced to Liam.

"We couldn't risk losing Cati either." Liam pressed his knuckles to his temples.

"Sounds like whoever you want dead isn't worth very much trouble," I said.

"He is." Liam paced the open space in the tent. "That's the problem. We have a chance to rid Ilbrea of a monster."

"But you don't want to sacrifice one of your own?" I asked.

"Ena, you should go," Emmet said.

Liam stopped. He looked at Emmet and me both staring at him.

"I would be losing more than just one good man," Liam said.

Emmet gripped the edge of the table.

"We would be losing a spy we spent a long time putting in place," Liam said.

"Because if the spy kills the monster, he'll have outed himself and most likely be hanged?" I said.

"It has to be done," Emmet said.

"But how many lives will be lost if we don't know what's happening in their ranks?" Liam began pacing again.

I watched him tramp back and forth across the tent, treading the dirt path his boots had worn.

"Gabe can't slay the monster without anyone knowing?" I asked.

"I don't want to shock you, but it's usually pretty easy to tell when someone's been killed," Emmet said.

"I'm aware," I said. "I've seen more than my share of killing and corpses."

Emmet looked up at me.

I turned my back on him, focusing my gaze on Liam. "But does he have to stab the monster in front of a crowd?"

"No," Liam said, "but trying to make a death look like an accident would take more resources and men than we have."

"It doesn't need to look like an accident," I said. "Just poison the monster, and people will think he died of an illness."

"What?" Emmet said.

"It wouldn't even be that hard. A few years ago, Han decided she hated her husband, baked him a pie filled with shadow berry pulp. He died, and no one thought anything of it until Han went mad from the guilt and tore about town half-naked, confessing her crimes. If Lily didn't know Han had poisoned her rat of a husband, no one else would have guessed at it either. Lily had to treat shadow sickness all the time."

"Shadow sickness?" Liam asked.

"In children, mostly." I nodded. "Shadow berries smell sweet, and they grow in the shade of other berry bushes. The little ones eat them without knowing they've done anything wrong. By the time their parents notice they're sick, they're most of the way to dead.

"You can save them if they haven't started coughing blood yet, but that's the first symptom most people show. Got so bad last summer, parents started rushing their children to Lily if they found a trace of berry stains on the little ones' faces."

Liam sat down on his bed.

"You can't be considering this," Emmet said.

"Does it look like a normal illness?" Liam asked.

"Close enough to a fever fit, you can't tell unless you know what they've been eating," I said.

"It could work." Liam looked to Emmet. "Gabe could poison the chivving bastard, and no one would need to know it was him."

"We are freedom fighters," Emmet said, "not murdering mad women."

"If you're trying to kill a monster, does it really matter how you do it?" I asked. "Have the Guilds ever once stopped to think about what the good way to murder us would be?"

Emmet shook his head, but didn't look at me.

"Could you make the poison?" Liam asked.

"No," Emmet said.

"I'm not asking her to deliver it," Liam said, "only to make it. Could you do it, Ena?"

I bit my lips together, trying to sort through the realities of making a tonic not to save, but to kill. "Theoretically, yes, but I've never tried making a poison before. My work with Lily was always on the lifesaving end of herbs."

"Then we'll come up with another plan." Emmet stood.

"If I can get my hands on some shadow berries, it shouldn't too hard to mix them down into something subtler than a deadly pie." I stood up as well, looping around the table to stand closer to Liam. "I'd have to test it to be sure it was strong enough, and we'd have to choose the right way to mask it to be sure poor Gabe isn't caught serving something that tastes like poison."

"Who are you going to try the poison on?" Emmet asked.

"You could volunteer," I said.

"Where can you find shadow berries?" Liam asked.

"They grow all over around Harane, anywhere people haven't found them to rip them up," I said. "I've heard tell of children dying of shadow berries in other places, too, so they've got to be spread out along the mountain road."

"You haven't seen any in the mountains?" Liam looked up to the peak of the tent.

"No." I followed his gaze, though I didn't see anything but plain canvas above us. "The soil isn't right, I suppose."

"She can't go near the mountain road," Emmet whispered. "Liam, please."

Liam met my gaze, a battle warring behind his eyes.

I couldn't tell which side I should be fighting for.

"She'll only have to go far enough out of the mountains to find the berries," Liam said. "After that, you can stay with her in the woods while I take the poison on to Gabe."

"Congratulations, Ena. You've just agreed to kill a man." Emmet stormed out of the tent.

29

"I should be going with you." Cati shoved stockings into my bag. "I should be going instead of you. What does Liam think he's playing at?"

"I'm happy to help." I passed her the few fresh rolls I'd been granted, along with the packet of hardtack and dried meat Marta had given me for the journey.

Marta hadn't said a word to me as she passed off the food, turned on her heel, and hurried away.

"If he needs a woman, it should be one who hasn't just arrived here," Cati said. "I don't want to hurt your feelings, Ena, but it's not as though you're ready for a fight."

"I know that," I said.

Liam had warned me not to tell anyone of our plans to mix poison. I didn't know why it mattered if Cati knew or not, but I'd only just been allowed to join the Black Bloods and had actually wheedled my way into being given something important to do, so I only shrugged under Cati's glare. "Maybe he thinks they'll need a healer. I don't want to brag, but I've a fine hand for stitching flesh together."

"That is a valuable skill." Cati tied the top of my pack closed. "Just try not to forget everything I've taught you while you travel. And if anyone tries to hurt you—"

"Gut them?" I laughed.

"Be careful." Cati squeezed my hand. "That's all I ask."

I let her lead me out into the bright morning. She gave my hand one final squeeze and headed off toward the training field to torment some other student.

It seemed strange to be leaving camp. I'd never packed to leave a place with the intention of returning.

A few people gave me curious looks as I walked toward the paddock. I held my head high and my shoulders back, ignoring the weight of my pack. I'd salvaged a few small things from the kitchen tent when Neil hadn't been looking. I didn't know if the weight of the items felt heavier because they'd been pilfered or because of what they were meant to help me do.

Marta waited by the side of the paddock, watching as Tirra checked the saddles on four horses.

"Who's the fourth?" I looked to Marta. "Are you coming with us?"

"Me?" Marta gave a low laugh. "Not me. I, unlike some people, remember the promises I've made and intend to keep them."

"What?" I dodged around Marta. Dark circles stained the pale skin under her eyes. "Are you all right?"

"Why wouldn't I be?" She gave a smile that didn't show her dimples.

The tromping of boots came up the path to the paddock.

"Safe journey." Marta turned on her heel and strode away, barely bothering to give a nod to Liam, Emmet, and the red-haired boy.

A stone weighed heavy in my stomach. I wanted to chase after her and ask what I'd done to make her mad. But Liam had reached the rail around the paddock, Emmet was glaring at me, and I was too afraid I might already know why Marta no longer liked me. So I watched Tirra minister to the horses instead.

"Are you a comfortable rider?" Liam asked.

"She loves to ride," Emmet said.

"I can answer for myself," I said. "And if I was a slitch who couldn't ride a horse, wouldn't now be a bit late to be worrying about it?"

The red-haired boy chuckled.

I waited patiently while Tirra glared at each of us before passing over the reins of a horse. I was given a beautiful brown mare who didn't fuss as I strapped my pack of pilfered goods to her back. She wasn't the sort of horse one would dream of riding through fields, but she didn't look like she was going to drop down dead either.

No one spoke as we rode out past the edge of the camp. Liam led, then the ginger boy, then me, with Emmet riding in back as though making sure I didn't run away.

As we passed beyond the boulders that protected the Black Bloods, the pull of the magic within the stones sparked in my veins. I took a breath, letting the scent of the forest dissolve the heat in my blood.

The branches on the trees left patches of shadow scattered across the ground. I kept myself busy, scanning every plant in view, trying to find the treasure we sought. Trying to ignore the growing whispers of Lily's voice creeping into the back of my mind.

You fool of a girl. Leaping right out of the only safety you've ever known.

The day slipped past as Liam led us on a winding trail down the mountains. The slopes on this side were far kinder than the ones we'd climbed farther east. The horses didn't seem to mind them at all. Though, I suppose the paths through the mountains were what they were used to traveling.

We rode until dusk neared.

Liam stopped beside a stream and hopped off his horse. "We should rest here. There won't be another chance for a while."

"You know the path that well?" I climbed down from my horse, gritting my teeth to hide how sore my legs already were from riding.

"He's a trueborn," the ginger said. "Even the Guilds' fancy map makers couldn't know the mountains as well as Liam."

"There are some places in the mountains I'm sure I'll never know," Liam said. "But I have learned this is the best path for the horses to reach the mountain road."

"And the fancy map makers of the Guilds are too coward to do much exploring in the mountains anyway." The ginger began tending to the horses, removing their saddles and tying them close to the stream.

"What's your name?" I knelt by the edge of the bank and splashed chill water on my face.

"Finn," ginger Finn said. "Nice to meet you, Ena."

"You as well." I took a long drink of the water, feeling its cold trickle all the way down past my lungs. "How soon do you think we'll reach the base of the mountains?"

"Tomorrow," Liam said.

"We really did take the long way then," I said.

Liam caught my eye and held my gaze for a moment. "The paths in and out of the mountains aren't the same."

"And there are only a few men can survive?" I dried my hands on my skirt. "I'm thankful I've had such a fine guide."

Liam chose a spot and laid out the black stones around it. Emmet gathered wood for a fire while I pulled the few bits of almost fresh food from our packs.

The dread didn't trickle into my stomach until the sun began to fade from the sky. I had been so excited to be doing something that might hold a bit of meaning, I hadn't really thought through the actual journey.

Finn said cheerful things every few minutes when the silence seemed to become too dull for him, but the rest of us didn't speak much. Once Finn had finished eating, he untied his bedroll from his pack and laid it on the ground.

My heart raced as though the nightmare had already begun. I had to warn Finn that terror would come for me while I slept, but I couldn't warn Finn without Emmet hearing.

No one in the camp had mentioned me screaming in my sleep, but the four of us were packed in together. There was no god I could think of to silently beg for mercy, and whatever thin veil of safety had comforted me in my tent had vanished.

Emmet would know about the nightmare soon enough. As soon as I started screaming, he would know something was wrong. But Emmet hadn't been there on the night the terrible dream had been born. Even he wouldn't understand the darkness that trapped me.

Liam unrolled his blankets, leaving a space between him and Finn large enough to fit my bedding. "You should get some sleep."

"I'm not tired." I met Liam's dark eyes, trusting the fading firelight to hide my fear.

"We'll need you rested when we reach the valley." Liam unrolled my bedding and laid it out beside his. "Don't worry, Ena, I promise to keep you safe."

"We've got magic stones," I said. "Why would I be worried?"

Finn laughed from his bed.

I took a long time untying my boots and retying my pack. The others had all lain down by the time I crawled under my thick blankets.

I lay, staring up the branches crisscrossing in front of the sky, wondering if I should find a sharp rock to put under my back to make sure I didn't fall asleep.

I was a chivving coward. I would have to sleep eventually, but the idea of Emmet knowing the monsters that still stalked me...

Liam's fingers grazed the back of my wrist. The panic in my

chest ebbed. He laced his fingers through mine and squeezed my hand. He didn't let go.

When I woke in the morning, our hands were still locked together.

30

"It's not that I mind berry picking. It's just not what I pictured when we left camp." Finn popped a handful of blackberries into his mouth. "Definitely worse ways to spend an afternoon."

"Thanks, Finn." I weaved between the trees, searching for a briar patch that might hide our quarry. "Just be careful not to eat anything you shouldn't."

Finn's eyes widened.

"Don't worry. You can eat blackberries. I'll tell you when we find the poison kind," I laughed, trying to shake off my fear.

We were searching for berries to murder a monster. As much as I hated the Guilds, as often as vengeance for the horrible things they'd done had flitted through my mind, I'd never actually thought through the process of killing a person.

"They are much sweeter than hardtack," Finn said. "I really doubt hardtack should be eaten."

"Better than starving, I suppose." I moved on to the next patch of trees. A few low plants grew in the shadows, but nothing like what I was searching for.

"Maybe." Finn sounded unconvinced.

Liam and Emmet walked close behind, leading the horses and keeping an eye out for anyone who might want us dead. At least, that's what it felt like with Emmet keeping one hand resting on the hilt of his sword and Liam holding a fistful of rocks.

We'd reached the edge of the forest before midday, and Liam had turned our path north, keeping us within the safety of the trees and out of view of the mountain road.

"Supposing we don't find the death berries," Finn said.

"We will," I said with as much determination as I could after hours of fruitless searching.

"But if we don't," Finn said, "you could find something else that would work, couldn't you?"

I pinched my nose between my hands. "I don't know. There are plenty of plants that could kill a man, but I don't know how we'd drop flower petals into a paun's stew."

"We'll keep looking then," Finn said.

The low rumble of Emmet muttering carried from behind, but I couldn't make out the words.

"What?" I rounded on him.

He stared stone faced at me.

"What were you saying?" I asked.

"We might be too far north," Emmet said. "We're more than fifty miles above Harane. Shadow berries might not grow here."

"We've got horses," Finn said. "We can ride south."

"They should grow up here," I said. "We just have to find them."

"Or maybe we should accept this as a sign from the sky and go back," Emmet said.

I tipped my face to the sky and laughed. "You would rather let a monster torment people than let me help. Well, I am not a coward, and I am not helpless, Emmet Ryeland. I'm not going back up that chivving mountain until we've found the chivving berries."

I turned and stalked toward the edge of the forest.

"Ena," Liam called after me. "Ena, where are you going?"

"I've always seen shadow berries in the open, so I'm going out into the open," I said.

There was a muttering of curses before boots pounded after me.

"Ena, you can't." Liam took my elbow.

The sun peered through the trees just ahead of us, unobstructed by the shade of branches.

"Soldiers could be hunting for you," Liam said. "We're fifty miles north of Harane, but we're only fifty miles. If you had stuck to the mountain road, you could have easily walked this far."

"So you want to give up?" I yanked my arm from his grip.

"I want to keep searching the forest," Liam said.

"Just keep walking north in the trees and hope we get lucky?"

"We need to keep heading north anyway. And this is already the easiest path for us to safely travel. We're only looking along our way."

"Way to where? Is Gabe in the north?" I waited for a moment, but he didn't answer. "Because if he's not, we're wasting our time. I'll dodge out of the trees and do a quick search around. It's not as though soldiers are quiet when they travel. If I hear any trace of a great host of murderers coming my way, I'll run straight back into the forest."

"We need to head north," Liam said. "We have a friend there. We'll need to see her before I can go to Gabe."

I seized that one tiny seed of information he'd been willing to give since we'd left the camp, setting it aside to think about later.

"Will we need the poison for when we meet her?" I asked.

"Yes," Liam said. "There would be no point otherwise."

"Then I suppose when we get to her, you'll finally have to let me out of the woods to search."

"Do these look poisonous to you?" Finn held a bright red berry in the air.

I peered at the low weeds Finn had been digging into. "They won't kill you, but they'll make you wish you were dead."

Finn let his handful of berries tumble to the ground. "Good to know."

"Don't they have bird bushes in the mountains where the Black Bloods live?" I asked.

"Not really." Liam bowed me north. "We've got plants in the mountains near Lygan Hall, but none like this."

"What's Lygan Hall?" I marched north, carefully searching for any sign of shadow berries, though I knew full well I wouldn't find a chivving thing.

"It's our home," Liam said.

"The camp's called Lygan Hall?" I asked. "It's a nice name, but a bit fancy for the tents, don't you think?"

"Can you imagine those tents being Lygan Hall?" Finn tossed a tiny green thing to me. "Can you imagine living in those tents year round?"

I looked at the thing he'd tossed me before scowling and tossing it back. "Can you imagine mistaking a tree tip for a berry?"

"At least I'm trying to help." Finn winked.

"You can eat that if you want," I said. "Might not taste the best unless you're brewing ale."

"Hmm." Finn popped the bright green bud in his mouth and chewed. "I've definitely tasted worse when Neil's in charge of the kitchen."

"Is he not in charge of the kitchen in Lygan Hall?" I asked.

"Things don't work the same way there," Liam said. "People have homes. Most cook for themselves."

A wide patch of fallen trees blocked the path in front of us. The ground beneath them had collapsed, leaving a dark crater under the tangle of trunks.

"If people have homes at Lygan Hall," I said, climbing up onto the trunk of one of the wider downed trees, "why are you living in tents?"

"Camp is closer to the mountain road," Liam said. "It makes it easier to do our work. We can't stay year round—we'd freeze to death come winter—but for the warmer months, it helps to get more done."

"And helps us protect the people we care about at home in the Hall." There was an edge to Emmet's voice.

I walked across the trunk, heading toward the center of the sunken-in earth.

"Careful, Ena," Liam said.

"How does it keep them safe?" I took a long leap onto another tree, picturing Emmet's terrified face as I jumped.

"The mountains protect us," Liam said, "but going back and forth as much as we do, we'd risk someone managing to follow us home."

"There's not a Black Blood in the camp who wouldn't die before giving up the path to Lygan Hall," Emmet said.

"Not that the Guilds would be able to follow the path," Finn said.

I climbed down close to the cracked earth.

"Ena, what are you doing?" Emmet said.

"Looking for berries. Didn't you know?"

There was nothing in the darkness beneath the tangled branches but a dug out lair where some great beast had made its home. From the scratches in the dirt, the animal would have had no trouble tearing out Emmet's intestines.

Or mine, for that matter.

My heart battered against my ribs as I scrambled onto the highest of the downed trees' trunks and ran to safety on the other side. I leapt down onto solid ground, not sure if I should be grateful the animal hadn't been home or terrified it was out in the woods.

"Is Lygan Hall beautiful?" I resisted the urge to glance behind to make sure the others hadn't been eaten alive.

"I think so," Liam said. "Not like the grand halls the Guilds have built with gold and blood. But the Hall is beautiful in its own way."

"I'd like to see it someday," I said.

"You're one of us now, Ena." Liam gave a small smile that actually reached his eyes. "I don't know where else you'd go come winter."

We spent the next ten miles walking and searching. Finn ate everything I knew wouldn't kill him, while I got more eager to go search out in the open as the sun drifted down. Emmet stayed silent and angry through it all.

The forest we trekked through was the same as the one that bordered Harane. The mountains that blocked us to the east were the same range I'd seen my whole life, but somehow it felt as though no one had bothered to tell the trees.

The air in the woods had a different taste than it did near Harane. The ground had a spring to it, too, like there was something alive hidden right beneath our feet. I tried not to wonder what magic might lurk in the forest floor. If the legends of the stones in the mountains holding magic were true, what other wonders had been hiding from the Guilds?

Liam switched with Finn, taking his place at the front of the group. Between searching for berries, I watched Liam's shoulders growing tighter and higher.

We're almost there.

I thought the words a dozen times, but didn't dare say them.

When the light had begun to slant through the trees, Liam stopped, rolling around the stones in his hand before turning to look over my shoulder.

I glanced behind to find Emmet staring back at Liam.

"No." Emmet gripped the hilt of his sword. "Absolutely not."

"Absolutely not what?" I looked back to Liam.

"We can't," Emmet said.

"Can't what?" I asked Emmet.

"I'll go out," Emmet said. "I know what the berries look like. You make camp in the forest, and I'll meet you here tomorrow. I'll bring the shadow berries with me."

"You want to go tromping out of the woods and leave us here?" I asked.

No one bothered to respond.

"It's better this way, and you know it," Emmet said after a long moment.

"No." I rounded on Emmet. "I don't know it, because you're a chivving slitch who doesn't say anything when he speaks. I need to find the shadow berries, not you. I have to make the poison, not you. Because I'm the only one among us who has even the faintest notion of how poisoning a person should work. So once again, me, not you."

Finn let out a low whistle.

"I am going out of these trees to find what I need to make this whole chivving trip worthwhile," I said. "Now, either you can come with me, or you can hide in here and wait for me to come back. But if any of you so much as mentions it being too dangerous for me to be out where the soldiers might spot me, so please the gods I'll poison the lot of you."

"You're a fool," Emmet said.

"Don't." Liam stepped forward. "We'll head into the city and search along the way. If we can't find anything, we can come back out and look again tomorrow."

"You think she'll be pleased to have four of us knocking on her door?" Emmet asked. "And that's if we can get through the city without trouble."

"Why would there be trouble?" I said.

Emmet scowled at me with one eyebrow raised.

"Fine." I stomped over to the horses and pulled my bedroll free. I draped my blanket around my shoulders and shook my hair from its braid, letting it hang limp over my face. I gave a cough that would have made Lily cringe.

"Ena?" Finn said.

"No one is going to get close enough to a sickly girl to see if she might have been around when a soldier got his throat slit." I glared at Emmet. "Besides, of the four of us, aren't I the one who's done the least to anger the Guilds?"

"Shockingly, I think she might be right." Finn shrugged.

"But we've all been careful to keep our faces away from soldiers," Liam said.

"I'm a girl. I'm certain the last thing those soldiers were staring at was my face."

Emmet gripped the hilt of his sword so hard, if it had been wood, I'm sure it would have broken.

"Unless you want to tie me to a tree, I'm walking out of these woods." I looked to Liam. "Would you like to travel together, or should I just be on my way alone?"

Liam stared at me for a long moment before speaking. "We stay together. We'll go straight to Mave's and wait there until tomorrow."

"She won't like it," Emmet said.

"I don't like it." Liam headed to the edge of the woods, still clutching his fistful of stones.

I kept close on his heels, not letting myself look back at Emmet for fear he might come up with some better argument for keeping me hidden.

It only took a few minutes for us to reach the tree line. The sunset glimmered over the valley beyond.

A city built of stone and spires sat nestled in the bend of a roaring river. I'd never before seen a river so wide, with a current so fast, I'd have no hope of swimming across it.

On the far side, a second river flowed between two rocky cliffs, racing toward the city and down behind the silhouettes of the buildings. The mountain road stretched from north to south in front of us, but a smaller road by the big river was where dozens of wagons had gathered.

There were more buildings than I'd ever seen in one place, and no trace of the hint of Harane my heart had been longing for.

As Liam led us toward the city, the weight of how little I knew of the world sank in my gut.

31

The stench of sweaty men and horse dung tainted the scent of the river and the tang of spices coming from the carts.

Young boys lifted crates larger than themselves off the boats bobbing in the river, hauling them up the dock and into the waiting wagons. The wagon men leaned against the sides of their carts, chatting while the children did the work.

"Are those men Guilded?" I asked, keeping a close eye on the river dock as my horse followed Liam toward the city.

Liam's neck tensed before he looked at the wagons. He studied the people there for a moment before speaking. "No, just laxe."

"What?" I guided my horse to ride beside Liam.

"I thought you were supposed to be ill," Emmet said.

I gave a great cough in his direction. "Better?"

"Do you not call your merchants *laxe* in Harane?" Finn asked. "Or are they not filthy enough to have earned that title?"

"There isn't a merchant class in Harane," Emmet said. "The village isn't big enough."

Finn gave a low whistle.

"Everyone in Harane works to survive," Emmet said.

Doesn't everyone everywhere work to survive?

The question crept toward my lips, but I swallowed it, too afraid they might decide I was ill-prepared to meet the frightening world of a proper city and send me back to hide in the woods with whatever clawed beasts lurked there.

"So the laxe make the children work for them?" I asked.

"They pay whoever needs coin," Liam said. "Sometimes children, sometimes adults, whatever tilk they can find."

"And the Guilds allow it?" I watched as the sun reached the tops of the low mountains to the west, casting the great city into golden shadows.

"The Guilds encourage it," Liam said. "They have to get their fancy robes, wine—"

"Jewels, shoes, houses," Finn added in.

"The Guilds only do their own work," Emmet said, "and they aren't going to go bargaining with the tanner to have a saddle made. The merchants sell to the Guilds. Profit off the Guilds abusing the common folk in Ilbrea. The lot of them are nothing but filthy collaborators."

"Ink for the scribes, blood for the healers, steel for the soldiers, wind for the sailors—land for the makers of maps to behold, and for sorcerers, magic, to defend royals' gold." Finn spoke in a sing song voice. His cheerful verse sent a shiver down my spine. "No bankers, traders, or builders in the Guilds. Those low positions are filled by merchants."

"Traitors," Emmet said.

"I think you've made your opinion clear," I said. "Though I can't say I remember anyone asking you to speak."

Finn chuckled.

"It takes all types to keep Ilbrea running." Liam looked back at Emmet. "We have to remember who the real enemy is."

Emmet's face hardened, but he nodded.

"If we make good time to Mave's, we might even be able to get a decent meal," Liam said. "The streets shouldn't be too crowded tonight."

I tried to picture streets crowded with people. Enough people in my path that it would change my time going from one place to another. I couldn't imagine it.

The walls surrounding the city rose up thirty feet, with turrets sticking up at steady intervals. Tall, thin windows had been built into the stone. I peered into the shadows of each, trying to spot a person staring back at me.

High gates stood open at the end of the road, and a line of wagons, horses, and people waited to be let into the city.

"Twelve soldiers," Emmet said, his fingers twitching as he reached toward the sword he'd tied under his pack.

Men in black uniforms flanked the gates.

My heart leapt into my throat, and I pulled the blanket higher around my head.

"We'll be fine," Liam said, either to Emmet or me—I don't really know.

The scent on the wind changed as we reached the back of the line of people waiting to enter the city. Hints of baking bread, strong frie, and too many people packed together wafted through the gates.

"It shouldn't be taking this long to get through." A woman perched on a fine horse spoke to the young girl tending the horse's reins.

"I'm sorry, ma'am," the young girl said.

The woman glared down as though expecting the girl to have something more than an apology to offer.

I gave a rattling cough that grated my throat.

The woman shifted her glare toward me, horror filling her face as she lifted her sleeve to her nose and turned back to the gates.

My horse fidgeted beneath me as we made our way closer to the soldiers. I watched as a farmer was let in with his giant containers of milk, and a merchant with wooden crates slipped a few coins into a soldier's hand before being allowed through. A young man entered the city, his arms wrapped tightly around the waist of a giggling girl.

We never would have survived in Harane if the Guilds had guarded who went in and out of the village. If they had been able to see who had snuck off with a giggling girl and had the chance of checking any goods that came down the road to us, half the town would have been whipped on a weekly basis.

But we hadn't survived anyway. They hadn't lurked over us every day, only come to kill us when the fancy struck them.

"What is your business here?" A soldier glared between the four of us when our turn came. He wasn't as soft as I would have expected from someone told to guard a gate. His chiseled jaw, narrowed eyes, and firm grip on the sword at his hip made it seem as though he expected an attack rather than a pair of young fools back from rolling around in the forest.

"We're traveling north on the mountain road and seek a warm place to stay for the night," Finn said.

I glanced over to Liam, but he was looking daftly up at the wall as though he'd never seen something so big in his life.

"What's your business in the north?" the soldier asked.

"I've got a friend in Marten who might be willing to marry my sister," Finn said.

The soldier glared at me.

I gave another rattling cough.

"We want to get her rested and well before we get there." Finn gave a hopeful smile. "We've money to pay for a good room."

"Is she catching?" the soldier asked.

"No," Finn said, "her lungs have always been a chivving wreck. But if we get her rested, she'll look well enough he might take her."

Anger rolled in my stomach, and I gripped my reins to keep from punching Finn in the back of his chivving head.

The soldier eyed me for another moment before giving a low laugh. "May the gods help you in getting that one married." He stepped out of our way.

"Thank you, sir." Finn gave a little bow and led us in through the gates.

The wall was thicker than I'd imagined it to be when we were looking at it from the outside. We traveled under twelve feet of stone, which loomed over our heads as though waiting to drop and murder us, before riding out onto the cobblestone streets of the city.

The people didn't spare a glance for the soldiers waiting by the inside gate. Women in fancy silk dresses strode past on the arms of men in finely made coats. Children ran by, giggling as though the soldiers weren't even a threat to be feared.

"This way," Liam said when I'd fallen too far behind our party. "We have to get the horses settled."

Finn stopped in front of a wide stable with a giant white horse painted across the front.

"What is this place?" I stared at the entrance of a pub that had a sparkling silver sign above the door, which read *River of Frie*.

"Frason's Glenn." Liam took my hand, helping me down from my horse. "It's a trading port. Ships stop on the northern coast by Ilara. Some of the goods stay there. Some get loaded onto smaller river boats and brought down here. Then the laxe load them onto wagons and haul them south to be sold."

"So"—I pulled my pack free from my horse, dodging out of the way of a cart selling sweet bread and honey—"this whole town only exists because people earn coins off the goods from the river."

"The whole of Ilbrea only exists because someone is making coin. The only thing that changes from place to place is whose pockets get heavy and whose back gets whipped." Finn took the reins of my horse and tried to hand them to a gangly boy who stared open mouthed at me. "Take the chivving horses." Finn flapped the reins at the boy. "I promise you haven't a chance with the girl."

Finn waited until the blushing boy had gotten all four horses inside before leading us down the street.

I stayed close to Liam, taking his arm as we passed a towering building made of white stone. People in red, blue, white, and purple robes lingered by the glittering metal doors.

I had heard of Guilded folk beyond the normal soldiers, scribes, and healers we dealt with in Harane. I'd seen the black, white, and red robes marking each of their Guilds. I'd even seen a sorcerer in purple robes once. But to see a pack of Guilded paun, chatting on the stone steps that some poor fool had carved swirls and leaves into, sent a cold sweat on the back of my neck.

A lady healer tipped her head back and laughed to the twilit sky. Joy filled her face like there was no duty that called for her time besides standing with her fellow paun enjoying the late spring evening. Like there were no common folk in need of her aid.

Good folk who went hungry to pay their taxes to the Guilds so they could have the right to a Guilded healer's aid. Good people who would die because the lady in the red robes was standing on the steps instead of saving lives.

My stomach twisted so hard I thought I might be sick on the stone street.

Liam took my hand, holding it tight as we passed shops with sparkling glass windows. Dresses, lace, boots, sugar cakes, books—everything I could imagine anyone wanting to spend coin on was displayed in the shops. Lamps burned brightly, inviting customers in, even though the sun had faded from view.

Emmet took the lead, veering off the main street and onto a narrow road lit by lamps that hung from the sides of the stone buildings.

There were fewer people on this street, and most of the businesses had already closed for the day, though the colorful signs describing their trades still hung in the shadows.

There was beauty in the details of the signs, almost as though someone had made up a competition for the most intricate plaque. I didn't know which would win—the cut out of a platter of sweets that had been carved so deep in places, it looked like I might actually be able to pry a slice of cake free, or the woman with long hair, where each strand seemed to have been painted on individually.

My shoulders relaxed as houses took the place of shops, and lamps only hung on the corners of the cross streets. The darkness and quiet might have been frightening if I were alone, but with the others, the isolation seemed safer. Fewer prying eyes and less of a chance someone might spot the girl from Harane who had run from a dead soldier.

Just as I began to wonder how big the city was and how much longer it would take to reach Mave, laughter floated up the dark street. A quick melody of a cheerful tune came a moment later.

Emmet picked up his pace, leading us around the corner and closer to the music.

"Where is that coming from?" I asked.

"Mave's," Liam said.

We reached a set of tall stone buildings that blocked the street we had been traveling down. There were no windows on the first floor of the buildings, but on the second, third, and fourth stories, bright light shone out of the windows. Swirls and flowers of twisted iron surrounded the small balconies that dotted the buildings.

A few of the balconies had been taken by couples enjoying the darkness. Others sat vacant, as though inviting people to come and fill them.

The song ended, and a cheer rose from beyond the buildings.

Emmet shook his head and cut through an alley toward the music.

The dazzling light of a hundred lanterns bathed the square beyond. Five buildings surrounded the open space, all facing each other like old men gathering to gossip. A fiddler, a drummer, and a woman with a tin whistle stood on a high platform at the center of it all.

Around the sides of the stage, young men in matching orange shirts minded great barrels of drink. People stood in line, waiting for their chance at the barrels.

The players began another song, and the crowd hollered their joy.

A man darted out of the barrel line, sweeping a girl into his arms and leading her into a dance. In a few moments, the whole square had filled with couples dancing.

I smiled under the cover of my blanket. I didn't recognize the song, but it was nice to see that even people who lived with soldiers at their gate could find a moment of joy in music.

Emmet led us around the edge of the dancers to one of the buildings on the far side. On the front of the building, the windows started on the ground floor, peering out over a wide porch packed with tables. Men and women filled the seats, some sitting on each other's laps when there were no extra chairs to be had. Plates of food and glasses of chamb had been set out on every surface. Smoke drifted from pipes, laying a haze over the whole scene.

"Fresh ones!" a girl called to no one in particular as she peeled herself off a man's lap and sauntered toward us.

Her blond hair had been pinned up, leaving only a few curls to drip around her long neck. The laces of her bodice had been pulled so tight, she was one quick move away from her breasts falling out and making her having worn anything on top utterly pointless. Her painted red lips curled into a smile as her gaze drifted from Finn to Liam then finally landed on Emmet. "This is turning out to be a lovely night."

"We're here for Mave." Emmet stepped in front of our group.

"Why?" The girl narrowed her kohl-lined eyes.

"Mave and I are old friends," Emmet said.

"Pity." The girl shrugged and headed toward the pale blue painted door. She didn't bother shutting it behind her.

I peered through the doorway to find more tables. Girls dressed to please the men around them, and handsome young men with their shirts unbuttoned prowled through the crowd.

"What is this place?" I whispered to Liam.

"Mave's brothel," Liam said.

"Why are we standing on the steps of a brothel?" I asked.

A pair of red-haired girls led a man inside. One of them had already begun unlacing her bodice.

"Mave's a good friend," Liam said.

A woman stepped into the doorway, blocking out the room beyond. I don't know if it was the mass of dark curls surrounding her face, her perfect features and dark complexion, or the way she held herself that made me forget to breathe. She tipped her head to the side, and a slow smile spread across her face.

"I didn't think I would see you here again," the woman said.

"Hello, Mave," Emmet said. "It's good to see you, too."

"Should I be returning the compliment or kicking you out of my square?" Mave stepped forward. The lantern light caught her dress, glistening off the tiny beads that had been sewn into the maroon fabric.

"You should be pulling down your best bottle of chamb and bringing us in." Emmet stepped forward, reaching for Mave's hand. "Have I ever brought anything you haven't wanted to your door?"

Mave crooked an eyebrow. "More than once. And I don't like having filthy girls dragged to my home. You know my thoughts on men who do such things."

"She's my sister," Emmet said. "The blanket's just to make her feel safe on her first trip into Frason's Glenn."

Mave looked to Liam for a long moment before nodding. "Then welcome, weary travelers. May you find rest and the best of life's comforts within my walls."

The music from the square carried up to the second floor window, drifting into the parlor where Mave had left us.

A painting of the seven-pointed star of Ilbrea hung over the mantle, though no fire burned in the stone hearth beneath. Blue fabric woven into a flower pattern covered the walls and the furniture that took up the center of the space. Three chairs and one, long fainting couch surrounded a table made of rich, cherry-stained wood.

I sat on the very edge of the seat I'd been given, too afraid of tainting the fabric with my forest filth to get comfortable.

"Not like Harane then?" Finn winked at me.

"Careful." Liam nodded to the open window.

Finn shrugged and leaned back in his chair.

"You can take the blanket off," Liam said.

"Right." I lifted the blanket over my head, folding it up before laying it at my feet. I ran my fingers through my hair, weighing how awful it must look against how much the others would laugh at me for digging in my pack to find my wooden comb. For all the world, it felt like I'd been brought in front of the Queen herself.

"Not everywhere outside Harane is like this," Emmet said. "Most places are closer to the village. But Frason's Glenn has a lot of money—"

"And coin buys fancy things," I cut across him. "I am smart enough to have figured that out for myself."

"Just be kind to Mave and she'll like you," Emmet said.

"Of the two of us, which usually has trouble with being kind?" I asked.

"Enough," Liam said. "We made it into the city without any fuss. Let's not go feeding the shadows ourselves."

A knock on the door kept me from answering.

A man in a bright orange, silk vest stepped into the room without waiting for us to answer. He carried a tray of food with a bottle of chamb sitting right in the middle.

"Compliments of Mave." The man set the feast on the table, took a moment to look at each of the men, and went back out into the hall.

"By the gods, I'm hungry." Finn dove toward the table, grabbing a roll and a slice of meat before the rest of us even stood.

"Are you always hungry?" I examined the bowl of berries, plate of cheese, pile of fresh baked rolls, slices of meat, and bottle of chamb.

"I was born starving, and it hasn't stopped since." Finn spoke as soon as he'd swallowed. "Honestly, when my mother found out I'd chosen to travel outside the Hall, she openly wept. The neighbors all said it was because she loved me so much, but I'm smart enough to know they were tears of joy that she wouldn't have to worry about feeding me any longer."

"Smart woman." Liam smiled. A bright, comfortable smile without any trace of the hardened Black Blood I had followed through the mountains.

The door swung back open.

"Now that I've fed you"—Mave sauntered into the room, closing the door behind her with a sharp click—"tell me why I should let you stay here. Unless, of course, you've come to enjoy an evening of the flesh, in which case eat up and go choose a partner before all the good ones have been claimed. Don't worry"—Mave looked to me—"I can find someone for you as well."

Heat flooded my face.

Liam walked to the window and pulled it closed. The glass dampened the music but didn't block it out. He looked toward the door.

"We're safe." Mave sat on the fainting couch, fluffing the folds of her skirt around her.

"We need a favor, Mave," Liam said.

"I thought as much," Mave said. "Why else would I find a true-born Black Blood in my home?"

I glanced toward the door, waiting for everyone from the square to come storming in to murder us.

"Do you have any prisoners?" Liam asked.

Mave smiled. "As far as you're concerned, no."

"We need one, Mave," Emmet said.

"Why?" Mave asked. "Who of yours was foolish enough to be caught and important enough to be traded for?"

"No one," Emmet said. "We're not looking for a trade."

"We're looking for a victim," Liam said.

Mave stood, poured herself a glass of chamb, and sat back on the couch. She watched the bubbles rising in her fluted glass for a moment before speaking. "Victim for what?"

"Poison," Emmet said.

Sour rose in my mouth.

"We're planning something," Liam said. "I've got to know everything will work as needed."

"So you want someone to poison?" Mave said. "Should I just haul a victim in here? I'm sure there's plenty of filth in the square who deserve a bit of death."

"We aren't murderers," Emmet said. "But your prisoners are

already going to be executed for crimes against the people of Frason's Glenn. They might as well do a bit of good on their way out."

Mave sipped her chamb.

I looked to Liam who gave the slightest shake of his head. I nodded and stayed silent.

"I like you Emmet Ryeland," Mave said. "I'd go nearly so far as to consider you a friend."

"Thank you, Mave." Emmet knelt in front of her and kissed her outstretched hand.

"But there are some risks I can't take, even for friends," Mave said. "I won't put my family in that kind of danger."

"There is no danger," Emmet said.

"Having Black Bloods in my home is a danger," Mave said. "Bringing you to my dungeon is too much to ask."

"We wouldn't need to go." I waited for Emmet to glare at me for speaking, but he kept his gaze fixed on Mave. "I could give you the poison, and you could just…" I swallowed, wishing I had my own glass of chamb. "Tell me how it worked. How long it took for the symptoms to show, and how quickly your prisoner died."

"We're trying to make a difference," Liam said. "This is how we save lives."

Mave studied my face for a long moment. "Fine. I'll let your brew be the end of one of my prisoners. It's not how things are usually done, but I can make an exception. Though, a debt like this will need to be repaid."

I gripped the edge of my seat, no longer caring about the dirt on my fingers contaminating the fancy fabric.

Emmet looked to Liam.

"Our aim is worth owing a friend a debt," Liam said. "I will see you repaid for the prisoner and for sheltering us while we are in Frason's Glenn."

"The shelter I give freely out of friendship," Mave said. "The prisoner is what comes with a price."

"Thank you, Mave." Emmet kissed her hand again.

"Do you have the poison?" Mave asked. "I have a paun fit for the task."

"Not yet," I said. "But I will soon. Tomorrow night, after I've had time to search outside the city walls."

"I'll search," Emmet said. "We can't risk you being seen."

"Why would that be?" Mave sipped her chamb.

I stood and poured myself a glass. "I was a bit too near a soldier who ended up dead."

I heard the rustle of her skirt before she took my chin in her hand. "You're pretty."

"I know." I met her dark eyes, willing myself not to flinch.

Her gaze swept down to my breasts and back up to my face. She took a bit of my hair and rubbed it between her fingers before tracing the line of my jaw.

"Mave," Emmet said.

"Do you want to hide in a filthy blanket?" Mave asked.

"No," I said.

"Would you like to roam free, not worry about who spots you?"

"Yes."

The right corner of Mave's mouth twisted into a smile. She leaned in and kissed my cheek. "Good girl."

The scent coming off her skin sent my head swimming, like she had somehow bottled sunshine, firelight, and longing and had found a way to bathe in their perfume.

"You boys get washed up before the stink of you taints my parlor forever. You, girl—"

"Her name is Ena," Liam said.

"Ena, come with me," Mave said. "By morning, I'll have you fit to catch the eye of every soldier at the gates."

"We don't want her to be seen." Finn froze with a slice of cheese halfway to his mouth. "Unless I've missed something."

"No one questions the feathers of a beautiful bird. They only marvel at her beauty and let her fly away. Come." Mave reached for my hand.

I downed the rest of my chamb, letting the bubbles tickle my throat as I took Mave's hand and followed her out of the parlor.

The sound of voices carried up the stairs from the floor below. A man gave a booming laugh. A chorus of female titters answered.

"Mave." The man in the orange vest bowed as we passed.

"You're free to go." Mave gave him a nod.

The man slipped back down the stairs to the first floor.

"This way." She led me down a long hall with doors on either side.

I bit my lips together, trying to focus on the sounds of Mave's rustling skirt instead of the noises coming from the rooms around us.

We stopped at a narrow door at the end of the hall. Mave pulled a key from the folds of her skirt and slipped it into the lock. "Don't go wandering while you're here. I like your brother, but that doesn't mean I'm willing to trust you with a key."

"Yes, ma'am."

A staircase waited for us through the door. There were no fancy fabrics covering the walls here, only bright, unstained paint. Voice drifted down the stairs, but they weren't the same as the raucous crowd below.

"Charge her double and make her buy you a bottle of frie next time," a girl said.

"Double wouldn't cover it," another girl laughed. "She's as sweet as a lamb, but there's only so much a girl can take."

We stepped up into a brightly lit room, and everyone around us froze.

"Mave." A girl in a pink robe was the first to spring to her feet.

The other four were up a moment later, nodding to Mave while keeping their eyes locked on me.

Mave looked at each of the girls in turn, though what she was searching for I had no idea.

"Is everything all right, Mave?" a girl with bright blond hair asked after a long moment.

"I have a project for you, Nora." Mave put a hand on my back, guiding me toward the blond. "This little bird angered the wolves. Give her a new pair of wings."

"Of course, Mave." Nora bowed her head, then narrowed her eyes as she studied me. "She'll be beautiful."

"Good girl." Mave swept back toward the stairs. "Now I've got to manage her brother."

I watched Mave disappear down the steps, feeling the stares of the five women prickling the back of my neck.

"Who's your brother?" the girl in the pink robe asked.

"I..." I felt as though I were withering under their gazes. "I'm not sure you'd know him."

The girl in pink raised an eyebrow.

"Emmet Ryeland," I said.

"Emmet's here?" A girl with chestnut curls started toward the stairs. "*The* Emmet?"

"Leave it, Lolli." Nora caught her arm. "I don't think Mave would like you storming in."

"How do you know my brother?" I asked.

A chorus of laughter rang from the girls.

Nora fluttered a hand for the others to stop. "The poor thing is covered in mud. At least show an ounce of compassion." She bit her red painted lips to stop her own giggle. "Now come with me, little bird. Stories of Emmet Ryeland are best told in the daylight."

"What's that supposed to mean?"

Nora didn't answer my question, but I followed her anyway.

This floor hadn't been built on the same pattern as the one beneath. The stairs had brought Mave and me up into the large room where the girls had been sitting. There was space in the room for twenty more to have seats at the table, near the fireplace, or by the bookshelf. I blushed as I tried not to think of where the others who normally sat in the room might be.

Nora led me down a brightly painted, narrow corridor. The rooms lining either side were quiet. Some of the doors had been left open. I slowed my steps enough to peek into one of the rooms. A plain, wooden-framed bed stood next to a rack of beautiful gowns.

"We never leave this floor without our paint on," Nora said. "It's safer that way."

"Safer?" I ran a few steps to catch up.

"Soldiers wear armor to protect themselves. We wear paints, powders, and silk. We step into battle every time we leave the safety of the haven Mave has built for us. I, for one, would never be foolish enough to go into battle unarmed." She stopped in front of an open door.

A set of four brass tubs took up the center of the room, with shelves and mirrors lining the walls. Two of the tubs had women in them.

"Fresh blood?" One of the girls sat up out of her tub.

I averted my gaze from her naked breasts.

"Oh, she won't make it long," the girl said.

"Ha!" the other bathing girl laughed. "When you first came here, you couldn't look at a naked man without vomiting."

"Oy." The first girl splashed the second, sending a wave of water onto the floor.

"Hush, both of you." Nora held up a hand, and the two fell silent. "Either mind your baths or get out."

The first girl ducked sheepishly under the water, while the second picked up a sponge and dabbed at her arms while staring at me.

Nora sighed. "I will never understand these girls. Ah well. Get your clothes off. We've got to get you clean before we start on the real work."

"Right." I reached for the laces on my bodice but couldn't manage to make my fingers work. "A proper bath would be nice."

"By the Guilds." Nora swatted my hands away and untied the knot herself. "We sell pleasure to people at an exorbitant rate. We aren't perverted, and we won't eat you alive."

"Unless you've got the coin to pay for that sort of thing," the sponge girl said.

"I don't think we could convince Mave to agree to host such a horror." Nora wriggled my dirt-covered bodice over my head. "I've seen some strange things in Mave's halls, but there are limits to everything." She unbuttoned my skirt, and it fell to the floor. "Get your shoes off, and I'll find a comb."

I untied my boots, tucking my knife into the bottom where the hilt wouldn't show, and tried to ignore the dark smears of dirt I'd left on the tile floor.

"What sort of new feathers are you hoping for?" Nora pulled a basket down from the shelf.

"I don't know," I said. "I mean, I haven't thought about it."

"You should cut her hair short," the sponge girl said. "A bunch of the Guilded have been asking about short-haired girls. I think it might be a fashion in Ilara."

My stomach rolled at the idea of a Guilded paun touching me. Pain ached in my throat where the soldier had tried to squeeze the air out of me.

"Hush now." Nora petted my cheek. "Breathe, little bird. Just breathe."

"Who hurt you so badly?" the sponge girl said. Or maybe it was the other one. The room had started to go blurry around the edges.

"Out, both of you," Nora ordered. She didn't look away from me or take her hand from my cheek. "No one here is going to hurt you. No one in Mave's home will make you do anything you don't want to do."

The baths sloshed as the girls got up and scampered out of the room.

"We'll get you in a warm bath and give you a fresh set of armor." She took my hand, leading me to the tub on the far right side of the room. "You share Emmet's blood. Whatever wrong the world has done to you, you're strong enough to survive."

"I am." I pulled off my shift, let it fall to the floor, and stepped into the hot bath.

"It's really not frightening here." Nora pressed a brick of soap into my hand and knelt behind me, lifting my hair away from the water. "We're lucky. You're lucky Mave let you up here. Outsiders aren't permitted above the second floor. I don't think she would have allowed it if you weren't Emmet's sister."

"The most amazing luck." I scrubbed at my hands with the sweet-smelling soap. I'd only been away from the camp for two days, but it had already begun to feel as though I might never be properly clean again.

"Are you staying with us?" Nora ran a thick-bristled brush through my hair.

"I'm only here for a day, maybe two, I suppose. Not that there would be anything wrong with staying." The last part tumbled out.

Nora laughed softly. It was the gentlest laugh I'd ever heard. If the wind could laugh as it swept through a summer field, I think it would have made the same sound.

"Our way of life isn't for everyone," Nora said. "There are times I wish I hadn't chosen it."

"Why did you?" I scrubbed at my arms. "If you don't mind my asking."

"My father drank away any money that would have seen me into a decent marriage. Duck down."

I dunked my head below the water, reveling in the silence for a moment before coming back up into the world.

"I had a few men who wanted me anyway." Nora ran her fingers along the teeth of a carved comb. "But I didn't want any of them. To marry a man I didn't love, to spend the rest of my life rolling on my back for him, and then popping out his screaming children, I couldn't stomach it.

"I could have found work as a domestic for a Guilded or a merchant, but then I would have spent the rest of my life toiling in someone else's home only to die old and lonely, owning nothing of my own. With all those years of drab misery laid out in front of me, I couldn't turn down what being a part of Mave's family provides."

"What do you mean?"

Nora started working through the ends of my hair with her comb. "By the time I'm not fit to work the downstairs anymore, I'll have enough coin for ship passage south to the kingless territories with plenty left over to live comfortably for the rest of my life. I'll be done working before I'm thirty."

I tried to imagine that sort of riches, but I couldn't. Cal's family had more income than anyone I'd ever met, but even they couldn't survive if they stopped working.

"It can't be said for the poor souls who whore on the streets." Nora stood and went to the shelves on the right hand wall. "If they aren't beaten to death and manage to stay healthy, they still barely make enough to eat and have a solid roof. The Guilds forget our profession existed long before they took control of Ilbrea, but Mave never forgets. She's built a family, and strength. I wouldn't be surprised if she's the richest woman in Ilbrea outside the Guilds."

"And when you're done, you'll sail away from the Guilds forever?"

"Exactly." Nora held out a thick, black cloth.

I stood and let her wrap me in the soft fabric.

"I'll gladly pay the price for my freedom," Nora said. "I won't ask what brought you to Mave's door, but is what you came here for worth the cost the stars will demand?"

I touched my neck, where the remembered pain had pounded. "Yes."

"Good." Nora kissed my cheek. "In case Mave didn't warn you, beauty is not a pleasant process."

34

I ignored the pain in my neck and shoulders that having my head tugged at strange angles all night had brought, but I couldn't get my fists to unclench as Nora flitted around me, dabbing pink on my cheeks.

"I'll leave your hair down," Nora said. "The color brings a nice contrast to your fair complexion."

I didn't bother trying to answer. After protesting her using the kohl pencil on my eyelids, I learned Nora didn't actually care what I thought of the manner in which she preened me. It had been two hours since she'd finished with my hair and dragged me into her room. She dressed me and painted me like I was nothing more than her doll. A doll she preferred to remain mute at that.

Nora dabbed a bit of tingling cream on my lips. "It really is a pity." She looked at me as though waiting for me to speak.

"What's a pity?" I asked, careful not to let any of the cream get into my mouth.

"That you were born so pretty," Nora said. "It's a waste. Do you know how many girls come crawling to Mave's door who would give their left tit to be half so beautiful as you?"

"No."

"Well, it's a lot." Nora pulled the blanket from around my shoulders. "I'll have to make you a box of treasures when you leave us. It would be wrong to dress you in armor and leave you helpless when it washes off."

"Thank you."

"Come take a look." Nora waved me toward a floor to ceiling mirror in the corner of her room.

Let there be something left of me.

I stepped in front of the glass, examining myself from my toes up.

The boots were the same pair Cati had found for me back at the camp. The long, deep green skirt had more material to it than I was used to. The fabric was finely woven, soft with a hint of texture that pleased my fingers as I trailed them into my pockets.

The black bodice cut low in front and left no need for imagining the curves of my body. Nora had pulled the neck of my shift down to meet the bodice, displaying enough of my chest to send heat to my cheeks.

"Don't blush, you'll ruin the look." Nora squeezed my hand.

The deep brown of my hair had been swallowed by black dye.

Like a raven's feathers.

I took a deep breath, straining against the laces of my bodice, and looked up to my face.

I still looked like me, but the girl in the mirror was different. Fierce and powerful in her beauty. A more romantic version of me, one meant for moonlight and love. The Ena Ryeland that would exist if I had been created in a daring story.

Is this how Cal saw me?

"No one will suspect you've ever even passed through Harane. You are a true girl of the city now." Nora furrowed her brow. "Do you hate it? I could go a bit further with your face, but you've said you aren't staying here—and that much paint would be suspicious on the road."

"You've done wonderfully." I managed to make my voice cheerful. "It's just very different. I'm not used to it."

"That's the point." Nora leaned her head on my shoulder. "If you don't feel like you, what chance does the rest of the world have of picking you out in a crowd?"

"None." A blissful sense of freedom tamped down my trepidation.

If the soldiers who had been in Harane saw me on the streets of Frason's Glenn, they'd never guess I was the girl they'd attacked a few short weeks ago. I shifted my weight, letting the sheath of the knife hidden in my boot press into my skin. If the soldiers came after me again, I would not be helpless. I wouldn't allow myself to be.

"We should get you down to your brother." Nora took my hand, drawing me away from the mirror. "I'm excited to see what the great Emmet Ryeland thinks of my work."

"Why do people here know Emmet?" I followed Nora out into the corridor that ran between the sleeping quarters of Mave's girls.

Nora laughed, then whispered, "I'm not sure I'm the best one to tell that tale."

"You said it was best told in daylight, and the sun has risen." I slowed my steps as we reached the big room that led to the stairs.

A girl in a deep blue dress slept in a chair next to the bookshelves. Another girl sat at a table, sipping out of a steaming mug.

"By the Guilds, last night flew," Nora said.

The girl with the mug looked up. "Maybe for you."

"Oh hush." Nora wrinkled her nose at the girl and dragged me toward the stairs.

"Just tell me," I said.

"I wasn't even there," Nora said, "so I couldn't do a proper job."

"But—"

"Ask one of the kitchen folk about the time a naked boy

caught the square on fire." Nora pulled a key from her pocket and unlocked the door at the bottom of the stairs. "You'll get a far more accurate and thrilling rendition than I can provide."

We stepped out into the hall, and Nora locked the door behind us.

Women in plain dresses bustled between the rooms on the second floor, hauling buckets, baskets, and rags. They nodded to Nora and me but kept buzzing about their work, moving in a manner that seemed to imply they'd performed these very same tasks a hundred times before.

There was no music pouring in from the square and no laughter drifting up from below. The sound of the floorboards creaking beneath my feet felt like an intrusion on the quiet of the women's morning work.

"Do you know where the others I arrived with are?" I whispered to Nora as we passed a room where the bed had been turned on end. "Liam and Finn?"

"They might be on the fourth floor, sleeping in the men's rooms," Nora said, her voice barely above mine. "If not, they'll be in the kitchens."

"Are the men not fed where they sleep?"

"They are, but Mave eats in the kitchen. If your friends came to see her, that's where they'll be." Nora let her hand glide along the banister as we climbed down to the ground floor.

The great room that had been packed with people the night before sat empty—all the chairs carefully tucked around the tables with not a rogue chamb glass lying around to ruin the perfection. The faint sounds of voices and pots clunking together carried from the far back of the dining room.

The temptation to sit down at one of the tables and revel in the shining solitude grew in my stomach, but a low rumbling voice kept me at Nora's heels.

"I'm not sure it's worth the risk," Mave said as Nora swung

open the door to the kitchen, "but if anyone has a manifest, it's him."

I opened my mouth to ask what sort of manifest was worth any sort of risk but lost my question in marveling at the sheer size of the kitchen. The space was bigger than any of the houses in Harane. Larger even than the tavern. Five iron stoves sat along one wall, with a fireplace large enough to burn a bed at one end, and a sink the size of a bath at the other.

"There she is." Mave's words drew my gaze to a long table in the center of the room. She'd changed out of her maroon gown and into a finely made day dress of the same color.

Liam and Emmet sat opposite her.

Liam turned toward me, freezing with his mug halfway to his mouth, while Emmet stood, glowering at me.

"Emmet"—Nora stepped forward, extending her hand—"how lovely to see you with your pants on."

"What have you done to her?" Emmet looked from Nora to me.

"Exactly what I was told to do." Nora planted her hands on her hips. "I created a new and glorious creature and spent the whole night working on it. Some gratitude would be in order."

"Say thank you to Nora, Emmet," Mave said.

Emmet clenched his jaw for a moment before speaking. "Thank you, Nora. No one would suspect this girl is my sister."

"I would." Liam lowered his mug.

Nora turned to me, tapping her lips with one, well-manicured finger. "I could take her back up and change the color of her hair."

"No." I stepped away. "Getting my hair to black was bad enough."

"I don't think the soldiers will know it's her." Liam stood, his chair scraping against the stone floor. "But she looks the same to me."

My heart flipped in my chest so hard I was certain everyone

could see its movement through the fabric of my bodice. "Then I'll be going out of the city today?"

"I still don't think—"

"I wasn't speaking to you," I cut across Emmet.

Liam studied me, the line of his jaw set like stone. "We can ride out together. Hopefully, we won't have to go too far."

"I should fetch Finn, then." Emmet started toward the door. "If we're going to go, the sooner the better."

"You and Finn have other things to attend to," Liam said.

"They can wait." Emmet stood in the doorway, glaring at Liam as though he could change his mind through sheer force of loathing me.

Liam didn't flinch. "I'll keep my word, Emmet. I hope I can trust you to keep yours."

Emmet looked at me, his eyes resembling our father's more than I remembered.

"We won't go far," I said.

Emmet looked back to Liam and nodded.

The entire kitchen stayed frozen as Emmet's footsteps thumped away.

"Must be an exciting outing you have planned," Nora said when the only sound left was the girl in the corner scrubbing out a stove.

"Get yourself to bed, Nora," Mave said. "You need your rest."

"Yes, ma'am." Nora bowed her head and floated out of the kitchen.

"Feed the girl." Mave seemed to speak to no one in particular, but a man in an orange coat appeared before I could think to look for him, bearing a tray of pastries the likes of which even Cal's mother could never have dreamt of.

The man bowed and extended the tray toward me. My fingers hovered over the confections as I tried to choose between the shiny one with the chopped nuts on top, the thing filled with jam, and a roll that looked so fluffy I wasn't sure it counted as food.

"We should go," Liam said.

"Let the girl pick something to eat," Mave said. "Beauty is a tiring process, and she's had a hard night."

I picked the nut-covered thing.

The man winked and kept his tray toward me. I grabbed a fluffy roll as Liam waited by the door.

"Thank you," I said. "Thank you, Mave."

"Get out before Liam has a fit." Mave shook her head, her curls bobbling around like a living crown.

I slipped out the kitchen door behind Liam, barely able to believe I'd not only gained two cakes for breakfast, but was also going to be riding out of the city without Emmet.

Bright morning sun bathed the square outside Mave's house. The men sweeping away the debris of the revelry paused as Liam and I passed, holding their brooms steady as though wanting to be sure they didn't kick a stray bit of dirt onto my skirt.

I waited until we were out of view of the workers to bite into my breakfast. The sticky sweetness of the nut-covered pastry made me feel like a little girl who had stolen a bit of pie.

"Are you all right?" Liam glanced sideways at me.

"Fine." I held the roll up to him. "Want some?"

He shook his head. "Mave's already stuffed me full."

Liam weaved a different path through the streets than the one we'd followed Emmet on the night before. He turned down an alley so narrow it looked like people shouldn't be allowed to cross through. Before I could ask where he was taking me, we'd stepped out into a square packed with market stalls.

"How often do you come here?" I asked over a vendor's shout of, "Morning remedies! Take a swig and clear your head."

"It depends." Liam took my arm, guiding me past a man selling vegetables and eggs and a woman offering slabs of meat. "I only make my way to Frason's Glenn when I've no other choice."

A pack of children ran by. The girls had ribbons in their hair. The boys had bright rosy cheeks. This wasn't the Frason's Glenn

I'd seen the night before when only the laxe and the night workers had been out. In the fresh morning air, normal people filled the city.

Buying milk, trading gossip, looking for a new packet of needles. Doing normal things like Black Bloods and monsters were no more than myths. I studied the people as I passed, wanting to memorize the beautiful blandness of it all.

The more I watched the people, the more I realized they were watching me as well. I ate the fluffy roll as quickly as I could, just waiting for someone to come charging after us.

We passed out of the square and onto a wide road. No one chased us, but the man with the candle cart and the little girl selling flowers both stared at me.

"Liam," I whispered, "I think people might recognize me."

I felt his arm tense beneath my touch, but he didn't change his pace. "Who?"

I swallowed hard, trying to rid myself of the urge to be sick on the cobblestones. "All of them. They keep looking at me."

Liam scanned the street. I stepped closer to him, holding his arm tight.

He didn't speak until the gate came into view. A line of people had already gathered to exit the city. "They don't recognize you. They just want to look at you."

A prickle sprang up on the back of my neck. The feeling of being watched by a horde drained the warmth of the sunlight from my shoulders.

Liam's tone held no trace of fear as he chatted with the gangly stable boy, asking for our horses.

I steeled my courage and looked at the people around me, searching for the eyes of a monster that sought to destroy me.

Instead, I found a tiny boy with his fist in his mouth as he stared up at me, and an older woman who smiled gently as she looked at me like she was remembering someone else. A boy my age blushed scarlet when I met his gaze.

They all watched me like I was a curiosity. A beautiful bird who had landed in a garden and would soon fly away and be forgotten.

I am wearing my armor, and they don't even see it.

The stable boy brought me my brown mare, and Liam and I rode through the gate, past the soldiers and the river docks, and to the open fields beyond.

35

I know my memory of that day isn't right.

I remember the sun kissing my face and the wind lifting my hair as I rode through the fields beyond the reaches of Frason's Glenn.

I remember laughing with abandon.

And Liam laughing with me, the deep tambour of his joy burning in my soul with a fire I didn't understand.

I remember the sun glinting off my darkened hair in a new way, and somehow not being frightened by the change.

If the perfection in my mind were somehow true, the first blooms of spring had begun to appear, and white flower petals clung to the green fabric of my skirt as I wandered, searching for treasure. The sweet perfume of the blooms tickled my nose, and I tucked a pink flower in my hair.

We rode for miles, searching and knowing the city waited for us, but somehow still wanting to ride a bit farther. To find another meadow to wander through, Liam by my side, a solid pillar of a man that somehow made the sun burn brighter.

The way his eyes burned brighter when we found the shadow berries and piled them into a black pouch. The way he kissed the back of my hand and thanked me for helping him while in the same breath telling me he would find a way to see the rest of our work through without me. I didn't have to do anymore.

But I did.

Walking away from him, from what had begun the moment I'd decided to follow a Black Blood into the mountains, was impossible. So I touched his cheek, the warmth of his skin calling to every bit of my being, and told him I would do the work that needed to be done.

I remember the ride back to Frason's Glenn being too short.

I remember desperately wishing my time by his side would never end.

I remember the smoke hovering over the western edge of the city and drifting out over the river, like morning mist gone mad. Trying not to breathe in the smoke because I didn't want to lose the scent of sunshine and spring the day had left etched in my soul.

But I know not all of the perfect sunshine can be true. Such wonderful days do not exist in a world ruled by the Guilds. Their torment taints even the brightest joy.

I will never know how much of that day was truly how I remember it. I rode out of the city an innocent girl who had never done anything a decent man would judge as wrong.

I returned to the gates a Black Blood with the power to murder hidden in her pocket.

The Guilds had stolen so much from me. My innocence I gave willingly to destroy them.

There were more people trying to exit the gates than enter when Liam and I joined the end of the line. The sun had begun to sink, and the smoke left an ominous haze over the city.

I wished I had a cloth or something to hold over my face, but the clothes Nora had dressed me in left lifting my skirt to my nose as my only choice. I might have been tempted to try it, but the black pouch of berries burned in my pocket, and I was too afraid of calling attention to myself to do anything more than wrinkle my nose at the stench and wait patiently in line.

Liam kept his horse next to mine as we moved slowly forward.

I glanced around before leaning toward him. "Are they searching people?"

The thought brought me no fear. I doubted the soldiers were smart enough to know the berries in my pocket were deadly. And, even if they did, it would be easy enough to pretend I was a fool bringing bounty home to be made into a tart.

Liam didn't answer right away. He sat up straight, staring at the gate, looking angry at being kept from his supper. "They're searching the people leaving, not entering."

"Leaving?" My brown mare shifted as I stood in my stirrups, trying to see past the gate.

One by one, the people entering crept past a pack of soldiers searching every person exiting the city. The soldiers had pulled down all the crates from a man's cart, leaving the merchant with bolts of fabric lying in the dirt.

Another man had been stripped of his pack and stood pale-faced as a young soldier dug through his possessions.

Why? Why should they care what leaves their protected city?

I opened my mouth to ask, but a different question came out. "Will you promise me they're safe?"

Liam kept his gaze fixed on the gate.

"Liam?" I gripped my horse's reins.

"We should be able to make good time once we get through the gate." Liam gave me a smile that didn't reach his eyes.

All the joy from the day's sunshine drained from my chest.

"Keep moving in." A soldier climbed up onto a stack of crates so he towered over the crowd. "If you don't want us to shut the gates and keep you all out for the night, keep moving in."

"We're trying," an older man in a fine coat shouted up at the soldier. "Don't blame us for your soldiers blocking our path."

I flinched, hunching my shoulders out of instinct. There were people in line behind us, but not so many I couldn't turn my horse and ride away.

A scuffling came from the front of the crowd, inside the gate where I couldn't quite see.

"Stay, Ena," Liam said.

"I am a soldier of the Guilds," the man on the crates spoke above the growing voices by the gate. "Any citizen of Ilbrea who questions my authority will be taken to the prison and dealt the Guilds' justice."

Prison.

I rolled the word around in my head, trying to reason through the Guilds locking up the man who had spoken rudely to the soldier instead of just whipping him on the street.

"I'm sorry," a woman wailed from the front of the crowd. She was inside the gates, hidden from view by five soldiers. "I've done nothing wrong. Please!"

"Stay, Ena," Liam said again, as though he could scent my desire to run.

But as the woman wordlessly screeched, I wasn't sure which way I wanted to run. To the forest, or toward her? I had a knife in my boot and berries in my pocket, but neither would have done much good against so many paun.

The soldiers parted as two of them grabbed the woman. She screamed as they dragged her down the street.

"Help her," I whispered.

Liam looked to me, pain filling his eyes. "I can't."

I reached across the distance between us, needing to feel his skin against mine to assure myself I hadn't fallen into some new nightmare.

The line started moving forward more quickly. The people exiting the city plastered themselves to their side of the road, keeping their heads bowed and staying silent as the soldiers searched them.

Liam moved to ride behind me as we passed under the stone wall and into the city. Ruined skeins of yarn, trampled food, scattered papers, and a shattered doll lay on the ground. Parts of people's lives the soldiers had cast into the dirt without care.

The stable boy stood in front of the white painted horse, his hands behind his back and chin tucked as he watched the soldiers search a fresh batch of tilk.

"Do you still have space?" Liam hopped down from his horse and reached up to help me.

I didn't argue that I could chivving well climb down from a horse without his help. The soldier outside the gate had started shouting again, and Liam's hands on my hips soothed my desire to flee.

"I do." The boy didn't look away from the gate.

"What happened?" I asked.

Liam wrapped an arm around my waist, keeping me close to his side.

"Not sure," the boy said. "Bells rang across the city. There was a bit of a panic about a fire spreading and burning all of Frason's Glenn. Then people said we wouldn't burn, but there were bandits out to steal all our gold. Then the soldiers came.

"Truth be told, I doubt any of what I heard is even true. I can't think of a sane reason any bandit would break into the sailors' offices. There are plenty of places with more gold in them. And if they wanted to break in, why do it during the day?"

"I can't see any sane purpose for it," I said.

The stable boy smiled at me. "I'm glad I've not lost my reason." He stepped forward, taking charge of our horses. He glanced to the gate before leaning in close to Liam and me. "If you want to know what I really think, some Guilded slitch got drunk off their knob and set their office on fire. Now the whole city's stuck paying for the fool's mistake."

Liam gave a laugh that might have sounded real if I hadn't known him. "You just be careful not to down too much frie and light the stable on fire."

"I care for these horses as if they were my own." The boy gave a nod. "Most of them are good as babes, and even the chivving bastards among them deserve a safe stall and fine hay."

"Thank you for taking care of them," I said.

The boy bowed. "I am at your service." He blushed and led our horses away.

Liam gave a laugh that came closer to real. "We should have you fetch the horses when we leave. He might not charge you for their keep."

I aimed an elbow at Liam's stomach. He dodged away, but

kept his hand on my back as he guided me through the city. He walked just behind me, as though terrified someone might sneak up and try to steal me away.

We cut back through the square where the common folk had been doing their morning shopping. The vendors were still out finding buyers for their wares, but the cheerful note the scene had held earlier had vanished. Shoppers moved quickly from one stall to the next, taking the goods they wanted and handing over coins with barely a word exchanged. The children had disappeared altogether.

"What did you send them to do?" I asked.

Liam led me into the tight alley without answering.

"What did you ask them to do that's affected a whole city? Liam"—I stepped away from his hand and turned to face him—"what have they done?"

Liam ran his hands over his face. "Nothing that should have caused this. If everything went as I'd asked, there shouldn't be any fuss or fire. Maybe it's not them at all."

"Do you really have any hope of that?"

"I'm not one to give up hope." Liam laid his hand on my shoulder, his fingers touching my bare skin. "But I'd like to get to Mave's and find out what's happened."

"If Emmet's gone and mucked everything up with Mave—"

"Come on." Liam skirted around me and took my hand, leading me out onto the street.

We heard the music coming from Mave's long before the backs of the buildings that surrounded her square came into view.

While the market had gone quiet, Mave's folk seemed to have taken the smoke in the air as a sign from the stars that the revelry needed to be bolder than before. Seven musicians stood on the platform, playing for a packed crowd who whooped and hollered along with the tune.

The girls on Mave's porch swept from man to man, flirting and teasing as easily as butterflies flitting from bloom to bloom.

Nora perched on the edge of a table filled with men who gazed at her like she was a goddess fallen from the sky.

She wore her armor well.

I recognized her face, her hair, the way she smiled in a pitying way at the men who fawned over her. But there was a façade covering the Nora who had spoken gently to me as she dyed my hair and painted my face.

She'd become a knight, going into battle against all mankind.

She is a beautiful warrior.

A man leaned back in his chair to look at me as we crossed the porch. Liam tucked me close to his side, wrapping his arm around me. The man raised an eyebrow and turned back to his drink.

The dining room had filled with patrons as well. The scent of roasted meat and fresh baked cakes wafted from the kitchen. Men in green, chest-baring vests roamed the room as the girls had on the porch. Men in orange carried silver trays heavy with glasses of chamb.

"Can I help you, love?" A girl stepped in front of the stairs, blocking our path, and eyeing Liam.

"I'm Emmet's sister." I tipped my chin up, meeting her gaze.

Her face paled, and she fumbled for the pocket in her skirt. "You should come with me."

"Why?" I followed her up the stairs. "Is he all right? What happened to him?"

The girl spun on the steps and glared at me. "Don't ask such questions in front of the guests."

"Sorry." I stayed close on her heels as we cut through the long corridor of rooms.

Some of the doors were still open. The beds had been made and the lamps lit.

If something were horribly wrong upstairs, life below

wouldn't be continuing uninterrupted. But Mave kept her business going while holding prisoners and planning executions. If she could do a thing like that, there was no way to know she wouldn't have my brother's corpse upstairs while her family plied their trade in the long line of rooms.

The girl unlocked the door and stepped aside. "They're on the top floor."

"Thank you." I ran up the steps to the girls' floor.

The big room was empty. I climbed the stairs to the floor above. Another large room, built like the one below but painted a calmer hue, waited at the top of the steps.

Two men stood from their seats at the table.

"Where are they?" Liam asked.

"In the back." One of the men eyed me. "It might be best if she waits out here. It's not a pretty thing."

I ran down the hall without bothering to reply.

"Ena." Liam chased after me. "Ena." He grabbed my arm. "Let me go in. Let me see what's happened."

"Don't be a chivving slitch." I didn't have to ask what door I was looking for. Both Finn's voice and the smear of fresh blood on the handle gave it away.

Gritting my teeth against the feel of blood-covered metal, I opened the door.

The room was small, like Nora's. But instead of beautiful gowns, this room had been taken over by the spilled contents of Finn's pack, a pile of bloody clothes and bandages, and a bowl of red-stained water.

"What under the stars have you done?" I glanced between my brother sitting in a chair, looking pale as a corpse, and Finn kneeling beside him, trying to tie on something they seemed to think was a proper bandage.

"Evening, Ena." Finn gave me a fleeting smile. "Your new hair looks lovely."

"Thank you, Finn." I lifted my skirt over the blood-stained shirt on the floor. "Emmet, what have you done to yourself?"

Emmet glared at me, wincing as Finn tugged on his bandage. "I didn't do anything to myself. Things didn't go as planned, and I had a bit of a run in with a sword."

"If I didn't know better, I'd think you were trying to be funny." I shooed Finn away.

"We got the papers." Finn leaned against the wall.

"What chivving papers?" I knelt beside Emmet.

Liam shut the door and leaned against the frame. "Cargo orders for the river boats."

"That's what you're bleeding for?" I untied Emmet's bandage. "Did you start the fire in the city, too?"

"We didn't have much of a choice." Emmet hissed through his teeth as I began unwrapping the thin cloth they'd used to bind his arm. "We got into the sailor's office saying we had a shipment coming in and needed to know where they'd want it."

"Paun bought it, too," Finn said. "Went searching through the records for where we should deliver our grain. Got him out of the room, got everything we wanted from his desk. Then a soldier walked in from the street, shouting about needing supplies before we could fade into the distance."

"And the soldier carved you up on your way out the door?" I asked.

"More or less," Emmet said.

"How long ago?" I peered at the cut. It was longer than my hand and deep enough to need stitches, though the edges were clean and not too swollen.

"A couple of hours," Emmet said.

"It should have stopped bleeding by now," I said. "Could Mave not find a healer?"

"I won't have trouble brought on Mave's head over my bloody arm," Emmet said.

"You're a fool, Emmet Ryeland." I sat back on my heels. "Your arm needs to be cleaned and stitched if you don't want a nasty infection."

"I'll be fine." Emmet pulled his arm away from me, sending a fresh trickle of blood sliding down his skin.

"How many men have said that only to end up armless or dead?" I looked toward my pack, hoping against hope Lily's basket would appear. "Liam, I need a sturdy needle, thread, strong liquor, clean water, soap, and a bandage these fools haven't made a mess of."

"No," Emmet said, "absolutely not."

"Don't fuss like a baby. It won't take long."

"You're going to stitch him up?" Finn said.

"Of course I am."

"She's not," Emmet said.

"Liam, go fetch the supplies to stitch up this fool." I glared at Emmet as I spoke.

The door clicked closed behind Liam.

"We don't have time for this," Emmet said. "Mave is going to her dungeon tonight. You have to make her the poison."

"Did you even find the mythical berries?" Finn asked.

I pulled the pouch from my pocket and tossed it to him.

"Work on the berries, Ena," Emmet said. "I'll be fine."

"Stop arguing with me and be grateful I'm here." I dug in my pack, pulling out the things I'd pilfered from Neil. A tiny pot and a tight-knit sieve were all I'd brought with me. It didn't seem like enough now that it was actually time to brew something to kill a man.

"Finn, empty the berries into the sieve," I said.

"All right." Finn took the pot and sieve from me.

Footsteps thumped toward the door.

"I've got everything but the soap and water." Liam came back, a bottle of frie in one hand and a needle, thread, and bandages in the other.

"I'm coming," a voice called from down the hall. A boy my age stepped into the room, carrying a bowl of steaming water and a brick of soap. He wore only a thin green wrap around his waist that hid absolutely nothing.

"Get out of here dressed like that," Emmet said.

"You"—I nodded toward the boy—"get me a spoon and two empty vials."

"Yes, ma'am." The boy ran out of the room.

"Press the berries through the sieve." I looked to Finn while I washed my hands in the near burning water.

"With my fingers?" Finn asked.

"Sure," I said. "Just don't lick them afterward."

I took the bottle of frie from Liam, pulling out the stopper with a pop.

"Ena, you're being ridiculous," Emmet said.

I lifted his arm, twisting the gash toward the ceiling. "This is going to hurt." I poured frie into his wound.

Emmet gave another satisfying hiss through his teeth.

"I've got the berries pressed through." Finn held up his deep-violet stained fingers.

"Find a bit of thin cloth." I took the needle and thread from Liam's outstretched hand.

"Can we send the naked boy to get that, too?" Finn asked.

"Just use a bit of the bandage you ruined." I held the needle in the lantern's flame.

"But it's all been bled on," Finn said.

"You only need a bit, and there are some clean patches." I threaded the needle and knelt back down beside Emmet. "Besides, I think the man we're making it for will have bigger things to be fussed over than how cleanly we strained the juice."

Emmet laughed.

I looked up to find a faint glimmer of true mirth playing in the corners of his eyes.

"This is going to hurt, but I honestly don't feel too badly about it." I stuck the needle into my brother's flesh.

37

I'd washed the blood and berries off my hands before I'd even left the men's floor. Mave had come to take a vial of the dark liquid. I'd tucked the other vial into my pocket as she led me downstairs to a room at the very end of the row on the third floor.

The bed was made and the lantern lit. I'm sure Mave told someone to make the room up for me, but it didn't seem like it at the time.

With the music still playing and laughter rumbling up from below, it felt as though the house itself were a living creature. And the animal made of stone and wood had created a room for me. A little cave where I could rest huddled in its embrace.

I hadn't slept in more than a day. I should have been able to topple down onto the clean bed and drift instantly away. But I couldn't. I scrubbed my face and hands in the washbasin, and stared out the window at the dark street instead.

Had I been facing the square, I could have watched the dancers and musicians. But my window gave me a view of the sleeping city away from the revelry.

A boy passed beneath my window, moving like he was

hurrying somewhere. I wondered if maybe Mave had given him the poison.

No one had told me who would be feeding the man the berries I'd mixed. All I'd been offered was a promise of a full report as to how it had worked once the thing was finished.

If I'd done my job well, a man would be dead by morning. A man whose face I would never see, whose name I would never know. If it was even a man at all.

The air in my room pressed against me, too heavy for me to breathe properly. I unlatched my window, swung the tall panes inside, and stepped onto the small balcony beyond. The chill night air kissed my bare neck, easing my nerves.

"Don't be a fool, Ena," I whispered to the darkness. "You begged to be here. The choice has already been made."

"That doesn't mean you have to be happy about it," Liam said.

I looked up, half-expecting him to be floating in the air, hovering on his stones.

Instead, he leaned over his railing, watching me from the balcony above mine.

"What we're doing is right," Liam said. "It's for the good of all tilk. That doesn't make it any easier."

"No. It doesn't."

Liam looked up toward the sky. The sliver of moon cast shadows on his face.

I wanted to be closer, to gaze into his eyes and see what had truly kept him awake to this horrible hour of the morning. I wiped my palms on my skirt and stepped up onto the metal railing that bordered my balcony.

"What are you doing?" Liam looked down as the rail clanged beneath my boots.

"Climbing." I stood perched on the metal rail for a moment, testing my balance and reveling in the wind blowing around my ankles.

"Ena, get down from—"

I jumped, catching a spiral loop on his balcony in each of my hands. My arms burned as I pulled myself up. I enjoyed the pain of it, the way my muscles remembered how I wanted them to work. I got myself high enough to sneak my toe onto his balcony, and pushed the rest of the way up with my legs. Keeping my back to the open air and my hands on the iron, I looked down at the ground far below.

There was nothing between me and falling but my own strength and calm head. Such a simple path to death with no tricks, plotting, or malice to be found.

"Can you climb over to this side now?" Liam said. "Before the wind gusts and you fall?"

"Wind wouldn't knock me over." I kicked a leg up and over the railing, careful to keep my skirts low enough to not give the sort of show the people downstairs sought. "Maybe if there were a horrible storm, but not a normal wind."

"I'd still rather you stay on this side of falling." Liam leaned against the rail opposite me.

We stood together in silence for a moment. The crowd on the other side of the building cheered as a new song began.

"I suppose it's good thing I didn't have my heart set on sleeping," I laughed.

"You should try anyway," Liam said. "We've a long ride ahead of us tomorrow."

"Even if the berries don't work?" I gripped the rail behind me. The edges of a metal flower cut into my palms.

"They will."

"I hope." I sat on the ground, bending my knees to fit in the small space that was no wider than the window. "It's an awful thing to hope for."

"Maybe." Liam sank down, scooting toward the edge so both of us could fit. "But Ilbrea will be a better place without him."

"Are you sure?" A knot I hadn't noticed before squeezed my stomach tighter.

"I asked Mave who the prisoner was. I thought you might want to know eventually, even if not for a long time. Questions about things like this tend to linger."

I looked up to the stars fighting to shine against the lamps on the streets below.

"Who is he?" The question caught in my throat.

"A Guilded scribe."

I let out a long breath.

"He embezzled tilk taxes," Liam said. "Made it look like some of the farmers north of here hadn't paid."

"Were the farmers killed?" My hands shook.

Liam reached forward, taking my hands in his. "One. Two others were whipped and stripped of their land."

"That scribe is a murderer."

"And the Guilds would never have given him true justice. They'd have kicked him out of the Scribes Guild at worst—sent him to a lesser post more likely."

"Where he could destroy more people's lives for his own selfish greed."

"He'll never harm anyone again." Liam held my hands tighter. "The people he hurt may never know justice was given, but at least they're safe from the monster who placed his desires above common folks' lives."

"Then I'm glad I had a hand in his end. Does that make me awful?"

"Not to me." Liam gave a tired smile. "Not to any of the Black Bloods in the camp. This is the only scale we can fight the Guilds on right now. We do the best we can to stop one monster at a time."

"And tomorrow we ride to Gabe? Help him slay a beast?"

Liam leaned forward, looking straight into my eyes. "We ride to rid Ilbrea of a man who has harmed hundreds of innocents."

"Good."

He let go of my hands and leaned back against the railing. "You should get some sleep. It'll be a long day tomorrow."

"Sleep isn't something I'm very good at." I nudged his leg with my foot. "You've seen it. Better not to disturb the people below my room."

"You shouldn't have to carry such a burden."

I shrugged. I hated myself for not having anything brave to say.

"The nightmare"—Liam pulled something from his pocket and held it up to the sky—"what happens?"

"Does it matter?" I leaned in, examining the thing he held between his fingers. A small black stone, like the ones he'd protected us with in the forest, glinted in the hint of moonlight.

"Perhaps." Liam rolled the stone between his fingers. "Maybe it's only the way the Black Bloods live, but I was always taught you can't fight a monster you can't name."

"There is no monster in the dream." I looked up at the moon, holding on to its faint light so the darkness of the nightmare couldn't surround me. "I honestly don't know if it would make sense."

"Just try."

"Has Emmet told you," I began, fighting to keep my voice steady with every word, "has he told you how our parents died?"

"Fever took them both."

I looked to Liam, searching his face for a lie. But I could see it in his eyes. He honestly believed that was what had happened to them both.

"Emmet's a liar." I laced my fingers together, tucking them under my chin. "Or maybe he doesn't remember. He was so sick when it happened, maybe no one told him."

I waited for Liam to ask a question, or to defend Emmet, but he just sat watching me.

"I was the first to catch the fever. It wasn't that bad for me. I felt chivving awful, but I got better in a few days. Then Emmet and our mother took ill. They didn't get better."

The long-forgotten scent of sweat and sick brought bile to my throat. "Emmet could barely breathe. Mother got so bad she started having seizures. Lily came. She did everything she could, but they were beyond her help. We needed a proper healer. But there's never been a Guilded healer assigned to Harane. The nearest is in Nantic, thirty miles north of the village."

"That's too big a territory." Liam clasped the stone between his hands.

"The villagers in Harane have been asking for a healer since before I was born. But the answer is always *just ride to Nantic*. Father had started to get the fever by the time Lily said she couldn't help us any further. I was well enough, and I loved to ride, so he told me to race for Nantic. Set me up on the horse and told me not to stop for anyone. My mother and brother would die if I didn't find the healer before sunrise."

Tears pooled in the corners of my eyes, but I couldn't reach up to brush them away. My body had frozen, trapped in the memory of that terrible ride.

"The sun had set, but I knew the way. There's only one road between Harane and Nantic. All I had to do was follow it. I rode and rode, crying, begging the horse to go faster, but the night stretched on, and there was nothing but darkness and the pounding of the horse's hooves.

"The poor creature collapsed before we'd even reached the city. So I ran. I ran and ran, until there were finally buildings along the road. I didn't know where to find the healer, so I just kept screaming for help. An old woman came out of her house. She was kind. She led me to the healer's door. But there was a note pinned up. A soldier had broken his leg on the crossroad, and he'd gone to tend to the wound.

"The woman begged me to come into her house. Promised me food and a bed, but I had to find the healer. If I didn't, Mother and Emmet would die. I found the crossroad and ran west. There was blood in my shoes, and the road swam in waves as I tried to keep going. I found the camp just after sunrise. I begged the soldiers to help me, to take me to the healer. I told them my family would die.

"They just laughed. Their own healer had gotten too drunk to help anyone, so they had called for the one from Nantic. I told them I'd raced all the way from Harane for help, I sobbed and pleaded. They spit on me, and hit me, and tossed me out of their camp. By the time I could stand again, the sun was already high."

"Ena." Liam took my hands, guiding them away from my chin. "I'm so sorry."

"It took me two days to walk home." The heat of my tears tortured my face. "By the time I got there, Mother was dead. Those soldiers arrived a few hours after me. They'd come to collect spring taxes. Father didn't have the money. He'd sent it to the scribe in Nantic to get the papers so mother could be buried. The soldiers threatened to take our fields. Father argued.

"He stood there, screaming at a silver-haired soldier holding a shining sword. When the soldier got tired of it, he ran father through. My father bled to death in the cold mud. The soldiers left me weeping next to his corpse. They rode away like nothing had happened."

Liam pressed my hands to his lips. "You survived, Ena. I'm sorry for what those bastards did to your father, but the horrors of the nightmare, you survived those soldiers in the real world. You're strong enough to survive them in the dream, too."

A horrible laugh cut through my throat. "The nightmare never gets that far. I'm trapped on the ride to Nantic, knowing I won't make it. Knowing my parents will die because I failed."

"That's not true." Liam touched my cheek, brushing away my tears. "Your mother died because she was ill, because the Guilds didn't see fit to make sure there was a healer to help her. Your father died—"

"Because the greed of the Guilds murdered him? I know. Lily told me that for years. I can repeat her whole speech if you want me to. None of it changes the nightmare."

Liam leaned away from me and took his hand from my cheek. I thought he'd given up, realized there was nothing to be done to help a girl who'd let her parents die because she couldn't ride fast enough.

But a deep blue light glimmered in his hand, emanating from the stone. He breathed onto his palm and the light grew brighter.

"I wish I could take away what happened to you." He pressed his finger onto the stone, bending the light. "I wish I could change the past so your father never placed that responsibility on your shoulders. I wish I could make the healer be in his home and force a shred of compassion into the soldiers' hearts." He pinched the stone between his fingers. "None of those things are within my power, but at least the nightmare can stop."

The stone faded to a shining black oval with a hole pinched through near the center. He pulled his purse of coins from his pocket, untied the leather cord that held the bag shut, and tucked the loose coins away.

"I wish I could protect you from more, but at least I can let you sleep." He strung the leather through the stone. "May I?"

I leaned forward, holding my breath as he lifted my hair to tie the cord.

"It won't protect you from monsters, but it will keep you safe from your own mind."

His face was so near, only a breath between his lips and mine.

A pull began at the center of my chest where the stone touched my skin. A burning that reached deep into my veins as though my blood itself had discovered longing.

He brushed the rest of my tears from my cheeks with his thumb.

"Liam…"

He pressed his lips to my forehead. "You should rest now."

Our gaze met, and the whole world froze. There was no sound from the square, no wind chasing in the coming storm—nothing had ever existed but Liam and me.

His fingers touched my lips, and I leaned into his warmth.

His lips grazed mine, and I forgot to breathe. A hunger like I'd never known ached inside me.

Before I could memorize his taste, he stood, letting the cold night air reclaim me.

"Mave will be looking for us at sunrise." He pushed his window open. "You should get some sleep."

A wave of laughter carried up from the dining room below.

"Right." I stood, sliding my fingers over the smooth pendant at my neck.

"You can cut through here and take the stairs down."

"I'd rather climb."

"Be careful." Liam stepped inside.

"Emmet and Finn," I said before the window closed, "they were seen by the soldier at the sailor's office. They can't be given new feathers like me. They won't be able to travel with us."

"They didn't leave any witnesses behind." He closed the window, and I was alone in the night.

I climbed down to my bed and lay on top of the covers, waiting for the world to come crashing down on me, or for the Guilds to come burn me alive. But the flames that singed me didn't come from the torches of evil men.

I stared at the ceiling above, wishing I could close the short distance between us. Wanting to taste his lips again if only for a moment, just long enough to be sure I would remember the feel of his hand on my cheek.

But sleep came instead, and there was peace in the darkness.

38

Tap, tap, tap.

I opened my eyes, blinking at the early morning light spilling in through my window.

Tap, tap, tap.

It took me a moment to remember how I had ended up on a soft bed in a fancy, painted room.

"Yes," I called.

"It's Nora. I've been sent to collect you."

"Come in." I sat up, running my hands over my face. My fingers grazed my lips and heat burned in my chest.

Nora stepped into my room carrying a small leather box. "By the Guilds, your hair."

"What?" I leapt to my feet. "What's happened to it?" I ran to the mirror, afraid it had somehow become orange or purple or some other outlandish color.

The black had stayed in place while I'd slept, but the mass of my hair had tangled in an almost impressive way.

"You can give a mouse peacock feathers, but it takes them more than a day to learn to fly." Nora set the leather box on the windowsill and pulled out a brush. "You're going back through the gate today, and you can't do it looking like a gutter snipe."

"Are the others up?" I wondered if Liam had slept, if he'd had even a moment to remember kissing me.

"They're all locked in Mave's parlor."

"Without me?" I started for the door.

"Come back here."

"There are things they could be talking about that I need to know."

Nora dodged around me and planted herself in front of the door. "The man died. He was a fat, old slitch, and it took an hour for him to go. It wasn't pretty either. Whoever you have in mind for that potion, I hope they deserve a painful death."

"They do."

Nora hugged me tight. "Then I'm glad the Black Bloods have found someone like you." She gave a shaking sigh and stepped away. "Now, let's get you ready to go."

"I didn't know you knew." I let her lead me to the mirror without a fight.

"I've been helping Mave for years." Nora combed roughly through the knots in my hair. "I have private clients around the city. It makes my coming and going at odd hours an easy thing to explain."

"What else is Mave talking to them about?"

"One thing at a time, little bird. You haven't earned Mave's secrets, only Liam's."

Heat rushed to my cheeks at the sound of his name.

Nora looked at me in the mirror, one eyebrow raised. "Guard your heart with that one."

"I don't know what you—"

"Liam loves his cause. I don't how much affection he has left for anything else." She pulled a tin of powder from the leather box. "I hope this will all fit in your pack. I cut it down to the bare minimum of what a girl really needs to survive."

I glanced into the kit of weapons Nora had chosen for me. She'd packed more powders and pigments than Karin could have thought up in her wildest daydreams.

"I've already tucked a few clean clothes into your pack. Eyes shut."

I closed my eyes, careful to keep still as she drew the kohl across my lids.

"Thank you, for all of this," I said, "but you really don't have to."

She bopped me on the nose. "Of course I do. Eyes open. The world may be cold and cruel, but that doesn't mean we shouldn't help where we can."

"Thank you." I hugged Nora again.

"Promise to take care of yourself in your travels, and that will be thanks enough for me." She dug back into the box and pulled out the cream. "Lips."

It only took her a few minutes to primp me back into a well-groomed bird. We walked arm-in-arm down through the empty dining room and into the kitchen. The boys stood around the table with Mave, their coats on and all our packs ready.

"She's fit to travel." Nora presented me to the group.

Emmet tossed a warm roll to me and turned to dig in his pack. Liam didn't look my way at all.

"Thank you, Nora," Mave said.

"It's been my pleasure." Nora tucked the box into my pack.

"Can you even ride in a top that tight?" Finn asked.

I swatted him on the arm. "Faster than you can."

"We should be on our way." Liam hoisted his pack onto his back. "We've a long road ahead, and the sooner we're out of your hair, the better."

"Are you sure you wouldn't rather take my path out of the city?" Mave asked.

"We need our horses." Emmet kissed Mave's hand. "Thank you, Mave, for all you've done."

Mave took Emmet's face in her hands. "Be safe, and come back again someday."

Emmet nodded and headed for the door.

I tucked my roll into my pocket. My stomach had started to squirm too much to consider eating.

"Pleasure meeting you both." Finn gave a nod and followed Emmet.

"Trueborn," Mave said, "don't forget what we're fighting for."

"Never." Liam picked up my pack, balancing it on his shoulder.

"I can take that." I reached for my bag.

"A girl dressed like you wouldn't be carrying a pack in the city." Liam held the door open for me.

"Take this and be well." Mave lifted a bundle of black fabric from the table and pressed it into my arms.

"May we meet again in a land of freedom." Nora kissed my cheek.

"Thank you." I gave them both a brief smile and walked out into the dining room.

Finn and Emmet stood on the porch out front, watching the men cleaning the square.

"Do you think the soldiers will be searching people at the gate?" My voice echoed strangely in the empty room.

"Probably." Liam didn't say anything else as he ushered me out of Mave's house.

I clutched the black fabric tight and touched the pendant at my neck. The smooth stone held the warmth of my body, it had no imperfection in its making, and it was very much real.

What have I done to anger you?

I wanted to ask Liam, but as we weaved through the streets, more pressing questions had to come first.

"Do we have anything we can't let them find?" I asked.

"Not that you need to worry about," Emmet said.

"We're traveling together," I said. "We'll be searched together."

"You and Finn will go through first," Liam said. "He knows which way to ride. We'll catch up to you."

"We should stay together." I clutched the fabric closer as panic crept into my chest.

"You don't trust me, Ena?" Finn clapped a hand to his heart. "You have wounded me beyond healing."

"It's not that."

We entered the market square. The children were back out, running and laughing as though the soldiers weren't a thing to fear.

The noise of the shoppers made speaking softly impossible. The man selling milk joked merrily, and a drunk woman laughed above the rest of the chatter.

We reached the far side and stepped out onto the main road. I slowed my pace to walk beside Liam.

"What if something goes wrong at the gate?" I asked. "How will we know? What if you can't find us? It makes more sense to stay together."

"Ride with Finn, we'll catch up," Liam said. "Emmet."

Emmet stopped, waiting for Liam and me to reach him.

"Let them get their horses before we do," Liam said. "I don't want the soldiers guarding the gate to see us at the stable together."

Finn took my pack from Liam's shoulder. The bulk seemed absurd on his smaller frame. "See you on the road."

I looked at Emmet and Liam but couldn't come up with a thing to say that would let us all stay together.

I tried to think of an argument to make as the stable boy blushed and passed me the reins of my horse. But the poison lay tucked in my pocket, and the papers Liam had wanted badly enough to warrant theft were with him.

Liam's decision made sense.

I mounted my horse and draped the black fabric over the saddle in front of me. A carved wooden clasp caught my eye. A little bird to fasten the neck of a thick black cloak. I smiled, sending a silent thank you to Mave and Nora.

The soldiers gave a quick search through our packs and sent us on our way.

"All we've got to do is ride," Finn said. "They'll find us."

He headed north to the glenn that bordered the city. I followed him, hoping to soon hear hooves pounding behind me.

39

For the first hour, it was easy to make excuses for why Liam and Emmet hadn't caught up to us. I made Finn stop in the trees by the glenn so I could scavenge for a few more supplies. They hadn't come by the time I ran out of reasons to linger.

I looked behind as we took the road that headed west, but they still weren't there.

When the storm came and lightning split the sky, I took comfort in the downpour. With the rain whipping across us, blurring the road and the towering trees surrounding us, they could have been riding just behind and we wouldn't have seen them.

It wasn't until the lights of the town came into view that I gave in to the dread that had threatened for hours.

I was soaked through. Mave's cloak had protected me from the storm for a while, but the protection wasn't meant to last forever.

The rain finally slowed to a manageable pace as Finn led me into the town of Marten.

I clutched my reins with half-frozen hands, studying the stone buildings around me.

The place looked more like Harane than Frason's Glenn. No great wall surrounded the houses that had been built close together like those at the center of Harane. But, if whatever fool had placed the businesses in Harane had also been charged with the planning of Marten, here their gamble paid off.

Shops, a tanner, two taverns, and a proper inn had all been packed together on the main road with more businesses on the two streets that cut through it like a cross. The buildings were taller than the ones in Harane, built three and four stories high to make up for not being able to expand from side to side.

The houses were all made of sturdy stone, and most had their shutters closed tight. I couldn't remember which houses in Harane had even bothered with shutters.

Finn turned down a smaller road and stopped at a tavern that looked a bit sadder than the others we'd passed.

There was no music pouring through the windows. The front door had been solidly shut against the storm, and the paint on the sign out front, which read *The Downy Loft,* had been worn away in places so I had to squint to make out the words.

"They've a stable back here," Finn said. "You stay with the horses, and I'll run in and get us a room. I think..." He scrunched up his face. "I think it would be better if we shared, told them we were together. I don't fancy the idea of leaving you alone in a room here."

I gripped the stone pendant. "Whatever you think is best."

He passed me his horse's reins and dashed inside.

I held my breath, playing out a beautiful scene in my head.

Liam and Emmet would appear behind me. Liam would be cross that Finn had left me alone in the dark. Emmet would say something rude about my needing to be more careful.

We would all go inside and have a hot meal and cup of frie to warm us up. Emmet and Finn would fall dead asleep, and Liam and I would be alone.

I would tell him I'd been worried about him. That I was sorry if I'd somehow tricked him into kissing me, but if he wanted to, I would be happy to kiss him until all the stars fell from the sky.

"They've had a hard ride." Finn came back out of the tavern, leading a sour-looking girl behind him. "If you could give them a bit of extra attention, I'd be very grateful."

"I love gratitude," the girl said. "It does so well when buying food at the market."

"Too right you are." Finn untied my pack from the back of my saddle. "Just see that you care for them as you'd like me to care for you."

I slid off of my saddle, not bothering to hide my wince as my legs protested being asked to straighten.

"I've gotten us a nice room, my love." Finn took my hand, awkwardly shouldering open the door as he balanced both our packs. "I'm told there's already a fire burning in the grate, and the kind lady who owns the place has promised to send up frie and soup."

The murmurs in the dining room, not that a place like that deserved such a fancy name, stopped as everyone turned to look at me.

I resisted the urge to wipe my face in case any of Nora's paint had dripped all the way down my nose. Keeping my chin high, I followed Finn through the crowd of men. Two older women sat in the booths tucked up along the walls. I tried to give them the same sort of smile I'd have given Nora, but both just stared at me.

The wooden stairs had filth lodged in the corners and creaked as we climbed them.

"Second floor, third room down, my love." Finn let go of my hand to fish a key out of his pocket. "We'll get you dry and settled in no time."

"I doubt I'll ever be dry again."

Finn stopped at the third room down and fitted the key in the lock, which gave a heavy thunk as it turned.

The woman who'd rented us the room hadn't lied about the

fire in the hearth. The flames crackled mercifully in the grate, the bed had been laid with thick blankets, and before we could close the door, a little boy thumped up behind us with a tray of soup and frie.

"Thank you, sir." Finn set our bags aside and took the tray from the child. "Would you be a fine gentleman and fetch us a pitcher of hot water to wash up with?"

The boy grinned and ran down the hall.

I closed the door behind him.

"It could be worse." Finn set the tray down on the shaky table beside the bed. "It could definitely be better, but it could be worse."

"They'll know to find us here?" I unfastened my cloak and hung the soaked fabric on a nail beside the fireplace.

"It's the choice Liam would make." Finn kicked off his boots. "Can't say I agree with him, but such is life."

I sat in one of the two spindly chairs in front of the fire, letting the flames warm my fingers before I even bothered trying to untie my boots.

"Here." Finn pressed a cup of frie into my hands. "Drink up before you lose a finger."

"I'm not in much danger of that." I sipped the frie, wrinkling my nose as the liquor burned its way down my throat.

"Can't be too careful with those types of things. We can always have the boy bring more up."

"Will Liam and Emmet find us tonight?" I took another sip of frie. "Will they ask what room we're in?"

"Not unless there's a reason for us to run." Finn sniffed his soup before daring to sip from the bowl.

"What if they've already arrived and decided to stay somewhere else?"

"They haven't."

"What if they got lost along the road?"

"They didn't."

"What if they were stopped at the gate and are trapped in Frason's Glenn?"

"Eat your soup." Finn nodded toward the bowl on the table.

"When are we supposed to meet Gabe?" The bowl nearly burned my fingers, but I drank anyway, grateful for the distraction as panic welled in my stomach.

"It's not so much a set time," Finn said. "His regiment is stationed just north of Marten. As far as I know, they aren't set to move anytime soon."

"So we just sit here and wait?"

"No. We wait for the lad to come back with some water to wash up, order some more frie and something other than week old soup to eat, then go to sleep and dream of better food for breakfast."

"You really do think only of food, don't you?" I downed the rest of my soup.

"Food, freedom, and love, sweet Ena. Those three things occupy all the space my mind has to offer."

I slept on the bed while Finn curled up near the fire. Lying under the heavy blankets, I clutched the stone pendent, trying to promise myself I was brave enough to sleep. As the storm's wrath began again, I finally drifted off.

When I woke in the morning, the storm hadn't changed. So little sun peered through the thickness of the rain, it was nearly impossible to tell day had come at all. The floor creaking as Finn paced was the only thing that dragged me from my dreamless slumber.

"What's happened?" I asked as soon as I managed to remember where I was and what we'd come for.

"Nothing." Finn stopped midstride. "Just lots of rain and a bit of thunder, but now that you're awake, we might as well go and eat."

I rubbed my hand over my face. "Why don't you go down and order us some food while I try and make myself presentable."

"If that's what you want." Finn flipped the lock on the door. "I just didn't want to have you wake up alone." He stepped out into the hall. "See you down there then."

"Squeaked the floor to wake me up and ran for food," I said after the door had closed behind him.

I took my time brushing my hair and painting on my armor, checking the vial I'd hidden in my bag to be sure it was safe, making sure the other plants I'd gathered in the glenn hadn't been ruined by the rain. I dawdled for as long as I could.

There were only two possibilities I could think of. Either Liam and Emmet were downstairs, in which case they would still be there watching Finn eat an extraordinary amount of food even if I lingered in my room.

Or they weren't downstairs. The soldiers had caught them with the papers they'd taken from the sailors. They'd been trapped somewhere awful and needed Finn and me to rescue them. They could already be dead.

I didn't know if I was brave enough to face that possibility.

I tore the brush through my hair one last time and headed downstairs.

The scent coming from the kitchen promised a better meal than the soup we'd had the night before. Voices carried from below, though I didn't recognize any of them.

Holding my breath, I stepped down into the dining room.

The same two women sat in the booths along the wall. Another woman stood behind the bar, polishing metal mugs with a rag browner than my boots. A pack of men waiting for drinks from the woman leaned against the bar, and a few others sat at the tables dotted around the room.

The young boy shuffled from the kitchen, carrying a tray laden with food, heading toward a table near the door where Finn sat, his red hair as bright as a beacon against the dull brown surrounding him.

There was no one else sitting at his table.

My nails bit into my palms as I walked toward him, keeping my face calm so no one would see my panic.

"There you are, my love." Finn stood and pulled out a chair for me. "I'm afraid I've already eaten my breakfast, but I didn't want you to eat alone, so I ordered another round."

I stared down at the roast pig, vegetables, and porridge on the little boy's tray, wanting nothing more than to throw the food against the wall.

"I'm not very hungry." I sank down into the seat opposite Finn.

"Well, eat what you like and I'll finish the rest." Finn set a plate in front of me.

I stared at him.

"Perhaps some tea for my love, young sir." Finn smiled at the boy. "It seems she needs a bit of perking up."

The boy bowed deeply and backed into the kitchen as though Finn and I were the King and Queen of Ilbrea.

"We don't have time to eat." I spoke through clenched teeth as Finn skewered a roasted potato.

"Of course we do."

"They aren't here."

"I figured that out for myself, shockingly enough." Finn popped the potato into his mouth, closing his eyes at the ecstasy of food.

"Finn," I said, gripping the edge of the table to keep myself from tossing the tray aside, "they could have been captured, they could be dead. We have to ride back to Frason's Glenn and find them."

"That's the part where you're wrong." Finn ate another chivving potato. "What we have to do is wait right here and make sure no one notices us lingering. So we eat."

"We can't just—"

"Hush now, my love." Finn held his potato laden fork to my mouth. "You've got to eat, darling. I know you're exhausted from the trip, but I promise we can rest here for a few days."

I bit the potato from his fork as the little boy shoved a tea tray onto our table.

"Thank you, young sir," Finn said.

The boy backed away again, giving an even larger bow, his face split in a wide grin.

"They might not have stuck to the road," Finn said in a much softer voice. "If something went wrong at the gate, then they're probably keeping to the wilds. Which would mean, if we headed toward Frason's Glenn on the road, we'd miss them. They'd arrive here. We'd be nowhere to be found. Liam and your brother would think we'd gotten ourselves killed, and that is a type of wrath I don't care to see."

"We can't just sit here forever." I shoved another chunk of potato into my mouth to keep from screaming.

"Not forever." Finn took my hand. "We wait a few days. Get our gift to our friend on our own if we have to. If they still haven't come, we head home."

"Without them?"

"To find them there." Finn looked up to the spiderweb-strung ceiling. "That's why Liam split us the way he did."

"What do you mean?" I leaned across the table.

"There are paths through the mountains that are open to Liam and me that you and Emmet wouldn't be able to travel alone."

"You're a trueborn?" I whispered.

"No." Finn laughed. "Thank the gods I'm not. I'd never want to carry that sort of responsibility. But the mountain runs through my veins. As loyal as you and Emmet may be, the mountain cares for those born of her child."

I buried my face in my hands, picturing the mountain swallowing Liam and Emmet whole.

"I've seen Liam get out of scrapes that would have killed the best paun," Finn said. "And, to be honest, I've seen Emmet get out of a lot worse. They are fine. We have to focus on getting our own work done, or there will have been no point in leaving camp. Except escaping Neil's cooking for a while. That is quite the welcome change."

I poured myself a cup of tea, letting the steadiness of my own hands give me courage. "So, where do we find our friend?"

"We can look for him tonight." Finn held his cup up for me to pour for him. "If you want no part in it—"

"Tonight will be fine. I have a few more things to do before we meet him anyway."

I spent the day in our room, working on things that would have horrified Lily.

Or maybe she would have been proud. Maybe she would have smiled, glad the skills she had taught me would have a hand in saving lives, even if one man had to die to do it.

I looked up every time a floorboard squeaked in the corridor, hoping it would be Liam and Emmet, terrified it would be a soldier come to hang me. The day passed without either happening.

When night came, I hid three packages in my pocket and polished my armor.

The rain had turned to a fine mist by the time I walked out of The Downy Loft, arm-in-arm with Finn. He hadn't said exactly where we were going, only that I should look my best. He had put on a clean shirt and run my brush through his hair.

We wandered up the side street where we'd been staying. I studied each building we passed, better able to see them now than when we'd come into town in the rain. The buildings were a bit sadder than I'd thought, with the mortar between the stones crumbling. The paint on the doors peeled away in places, and the shutters all had heavy hooks on the inside, as though ready to be locked against a terrible storm at a moment's notice.

"Are most towns this sad?" I leaned in close to whisper in Finn's ear.

"Only the ones who have an army camped on their doorstep," Finn said. "If a demon were lurking in the garden waiting to steal your child the moment they showed a lick of magic, you'd stop caring about everything but keeping your doors locked tight, too."

"What?" I tugged on Finn's arm, stopping him midstride.

"Didn't Liam tell you why we were coming to kill Drason?"

"No." A heavy weight pressed down on my chest. "I never even asked for his name."

"The Sorcerers Guild noticed a strange number of sorci children being born in Marten." Finn drew me into his arms and spoke close to my ear. "They sent Drason and his men to investigate. He's been stalking the city for more than a year, trapping the children born with magic, then taking their mothers, too. The children are shipped to the Sorcerers Tower in Ilara. We haven't been able to figure out where the women are taken."

A heavy weight sagged in my stomach as I looked at the hooks on the windows. Locks could keep out a storm but not the Guilds.

"This is why we slay the beast." Finn squeezed my hand and led me onto the main road.

Light and music poured through the taverns' windows. Soldiers in uniforms roamed the streets, but not as though they were patrolling. A fair handful of them seemed to be very drunk for the sun having just gone down, and the rest seemed intent on joining the stumblers soon enough. They strode through the town without a hint of guilt for the pain they'd caused.

Finn stopped in front of a common man carrying a sack on his back. "Sorry, sir." Finn gave a little bow. "I'm looking for a recommendation for a lively tavern."

The man wrinkled his brow. "They're all right behind me."

"Yes, I can see them." Finn gave a smile that would have looked foolish on anyone else. "But I wanted to know which you'd say was best."

"Fiddler's Mark." The man nodded. "Good barkeep, good ale, good music, and I've seen them wash the glasses once or twice before. There are soldiers in there, but..." The man shrugged and shook his head.

"Thank you very much, sir." Finn bowed and stepped around the man as though to lead me to the tavern.

But when the man had turned a corner and was out of sight,

Finn veered away from Fiddler's Mark and back out to the center of the street to step in front of a young man with a lady on each arm.

"Excuse me, folks," Finn asked. "Which tavern would you recommend?"

"Fiddler's Mark," the girl to the left of the boy said. "We're going. You can come if you like." She gave Finn a wink as the boy led her away.

"What are you doing?" I asked as Finn stopped to stare into the window of a bookshop before looping back out to walk down the street.

"Whenever the soldiers camp close to a town, they always flock to find a drink away from their commanders," Finn said. "Gabe will be at the most popular tavern, not recommended by the soldiers, but the locals. That's how we find him."

Finn asked three more people which tavern would be best. Only one answered anything but Fiddler's Mark.

"I think it's time for a drink." Finn smiled as the elderly woman he'd spoken to toddled away.

"No food?" I asked.

"Of course food," Finn said. "But I was thinking we'd start with a drink and have food to celebrate a job well done after I've finished our work."

"No."

"Fine," Finn sighed. "Food first if you insist."

"I'll be doing the work. Not you."

Finn stopped ten feet in front of the door to Fiddler's Mark. He dragged me away from the cheerful music and into the narrow alley beside the tavern.

"What are you talking about?" Finn whispered.

"I'm giving it to him, not you."

"Don't be a chivving fool, Ena." Finn held out his hand. "Give me the vial and let's be done with it."

"There's more than just the one vial. Liam wanted to be sure Gabe wouldn't be found out."

"Which is why you've brewed the berries," Finn whispered.

"A single death from an illness, taking a commander no less, would still be suspicious."

"So we should just kill the whole regiment? I'm not opposed to it, but I think we should have spoken to Liam about this new idea."

"I'm not talking about killing." I leaned in as though moving to kiss Finn's cheek. "If a group of people take ill and one doesn't recover, they'll blame the food or the gods and not spare a thought for anyone plotting."

"By the stars, Ena."

"I have everything I need in my pocket. I just have to give it to him and be sure he knows how to use it."

Finn leaned against the tavern wall.

"I can do this, Finn. Trust me. I'm sure I'm right."

"Chivving cact of a god's head. Do you not understand, Ena? Liam and Emmet will both kill me if they ever catch wind of me letting you do this."

"They don't need to know." I took Finn's face in my hands. "But I do need to be sure Gabe understands what he's got to do, or the wrong person could die."

"You've literally cornered me." Finn kissed my cheek. "If you get yourself captured or killed, I will never forgive you. I may seem cheerful enough, but I've stone in my blood and fury in my heart."

"I'm terrified of you." I took his hand, leading him back out of the alley.

A chorus of whistles and laughter sprang up as a pack of soldiers spotted us stepping out onto the main street.

"Didn't know they had such beauty available in Marten." One of the soldiers gave a mocking bow.

Heat rushed to my cheeks.

"Oh, Emmet is going to murder me." Finn looped an arm around my waist and ushered me into Fiddler's Mark.

The place was packed with as many men in black uniforms as there were in common clothes. Women dotted the crowd, some huddled together at tables of their own, others mixed in with the men.

I wanted to tell the women to run away, to hide from the soldiers.

But Lily had told me to hide, and my world had been burned in my absence.

A long bar took up one side of the room. Three women poured for the customers, and a panicked-looking man ran food from the kitchen. A woman sang on a stage tucked into the far corner, surrounded by four men playing stringed instruments.

"I hate to say it, but the locals have decent taste." Finn weaved through the tavern, searching for an empty table. "If I could smell anything from the kitchen over the liquor in the air, I might even be excited about dinner."

"How do they do it?" I watched a pair of tilk men laughing as though the soldiers at the table beside them weren't their enemies.

"Allowing your hate for the Guilds to show only gives them reason to suspect you and your family." Finn pressed his lips to my forehead. "Better to drink with a demon than to have him look too closely at your children."

A sick feeling rolled through my stomach.

Finn tipped my chin up and spoke loudly enough for the people around us to hear. "Give me a laugh, girl. If I'm going to pay for our drinks, that's the least you can do."

I hovered on the edge of telling him I owed no man my smile before coming to my senses and giggling as the woman onstage pulled out a pipe to play.

"There we are." Finn darted to the back of the room where a table had yet to be claimed.

We were far from the front door, nestled against the wall, with a flock of drunken soldiers between us and the way out.

"Are you sure we want this table?" I asked. "We could wait for another."

"This is perfect." Finn pulled out a seat for me. "You wait here, and I'll grab us a round of drinks."

He walked away before I could tell him the nerves in my stomach might make drinking anything a disaster.

I unbuttoned the carved bird fastening at the neck of my cloak and let my fingers graze my stone pendant to be sure it was still there. Even after wandering in the chill mist, the stone still held a blissful warmth to it. I draped my cloak over the back of my chair, sat, and began watching the people around me.

Gabe had been placed as a spy among the soldiers, so he would be wearing a black uniform. But beyond that, I couldn't guess what he might look like. Of the Black Bloods I'd met, there didn't seem to be one trait that ran amongst all of them. Between Finn's red hair and Liam's dark eyes, any man in the room could say they had been born a Black Blood and I'd have no way of knowing if they were lying.

"Here we are." Finn set a mug down in front of me. "The woman who owns this place swears by her ale. It may be awful, but honestly I was too afraid to order anything else."

I laughed and took a sip of the bitter brew that tasted like dried flowers.

Finn leaned in to whisper in my ear. "He's here."

"Where?" I started searching the crowd for Liam and Emmet before realizing who Finn was talking about.

"Table on the far side of the bar, facing the door to the street."

"Are you sure?"

"Of course I'm sure, I've met the fellow before." Finn tucked my hair behind my ear. "He's got two others at the table with him. Gabe will stay late. We'll wait and hope his friends leave."

"Do they call him Gabe?" I trailed my finger along Finn's cheek.

"Gabe Louers is his name registered with the Guilds."

A big man in a soldier's uniform came in from outside, giving a booming laugh as though making sure everyone in the room would notice his entrance.

"This"—the man raised his arms toward the sky—"this is an evening to celebrate."

A roar of approval shot up from all the soldiers.

"This, this could be a long night." Finn sighed as the big man lumbered his way to the bar.

Other soldiers followed him, buying drinks for everyone in sight.

I shuddered even thinking of reasons a paun soldier would want to celebrate.

"Maybe we should try again tomorrow night." Finn took a long drink of his ale.

I sipped from my own cup. "No. We should get it done tonight."

"We'll be here till morning."

"What does Gabe look like?" I ran my fingers through my hair, making sure it hadn't been matted by the mist.

"It doesn't matter until the place clears out." Finn took my wrist.

"It does if I want to do a little flirting." I glared at him. "Just tell me what he looks like, and I'll go see if I can spot a way to talk to him."

"You do realize if anything happens to you, I'll be killed. By the Guilds' hand or Emmet's, I will die."

"I'm well aware. Now tell me before I start shouting *Gabe* to see who answers."

Finn froze for a moment as though thinking through his chances of getting me out of the tavern quietly.

"Blond, curly hair, devilishly green eyes, and a scar on his lip that makes him look like a rogue."

"Sounds fascinating." I yanked my arm from Finn's grip and stood. "Try not to panic while I'm gone."

"Thanks."

Pressing my shoulders back, I started through the tables. I didn't know if it was taking off my cloak or not being held close by Finn, but more men eyed me as I worked my way toward the front of the room.

I can be Nora. I have the armor she's given me. I can have her strength as well.

I scanned the tables I passed, offering little smiles to the handsomer men.

"A fine evening." A man in common clothes nodded to me as I passed.

"I don't fancy the mist." I turned away from him.

His friends' laughter followed me as I made my way toward Gabe's table.

I spotted him without trouble. While Finn's description of Gabe's eyes and scar had been accurate, he had understated the color of Gabe's hair. Flaxen ringlets topped the head of the soldier who sat laughing with his friends.

My gut told me to hate him. Laughing with a pack of soldiers, probably telling stories of the tilk lives they had destroyed.

He is one of us.

I fixed a coy smile on my lips and walked up to his table.

The men stopped laughing as they spotted me.

"Good evening." One of the soldiers nodded, his gaze drifting none too subtly to my breasts.

"Not really," I said.

You are brave. You are a warrior.

"The man I came in with is a horrible bore. You"—I pointed to Gabe—"come buy me a drink. I've asked all the locals and they promised this is the best place to find decent ale."

I ignored the simmering disappointment on the other men's faces.

Gabe stood, downing the rest of his frie. "If a man was fool enough to bore you, then please allow me to be the one to regain the dignity of my sex."

"What a kind man." I held out my hand for him, taking his elbow as he stepped away from his table. "Is Fiddler's Mark ale really wonderful?"

"It's not to be missed."

I kept my gaze fixed on Gabe's face as we waited at the bar, carefully ignoring the stares of the other men.

"Two ales please," Gabe called when he caught a barkeep's eye. "It's not usually this hard to get a drink around here. I suppose everyone's come out now that the storm's passed."

"Pity it's so crowded." I leaned closer to him. "I was hoping we might be able to get a table to ourselves."

Gabe unhooked his arm from mine and laid his hand on the back of my waist. "I don't care the size of the crowd. I'm sure I can find us a private table."

"Here you are, Gabe." The barkeep shoved two mugs our way with a smile for Gabe and a glare at me.

"This way." He wrapped his arm around my waist and led me closer to the musicians.

The woman had begun singing.

"As the stars gleam above, so our love shall survive,
As the moon falls from the sky, our children will thrive."

"Fellows," Gabe said, stopping at a table filled with boys who didn't seem old enough to be wearing soldiers black, "do us a favor and find other seats."

Two of the boys leapt to their feet. The third stared at me wide-eyed until his friends hauled him away.

"That wasn't too hard." Gabe pulled out a chair for me.

I sat and he moved to sit across from me.

"Sit here." I patted the chair beside me. "No point in putting a whole table between us."

Gabe smiled and sat.

I took a deep breath, trying to think of how to say who I was.

The players started a new, faster song.

"So where is he?" Gabe asked.

"Who?" I twisted in my chair, leaning close to him.

Gabe trailed a finger from the top of my bodice, up my chest, and to the pendant at my throat. "The one who made this. Where's Liam?"

42

"I don't know." I leaned closer, pressing my lips to his ear. "But I have a gift he's sent for you."

"A gift?" Gabe tipped my chin so my lips brushed against his. He tasted of ale. "What sort of gift would I be sent?"

"Poison to slay a monster."

"That doesn't sound like Liam." He traced his nose across my cheek and nibbled the bottom of my ear.

"It was my idea. A way to keep you in place while getting rid of the beast."

"I've no experience in poison." He kissed the side of my neck.

I tipped my head to the side, offering more skin for him to explore. "That's why I'm here. All you have to do is exactly as I say." I shifted to sit on his lap, draping one arm around his neck.

Gabe's eyes widened.

I whispered in his ear. "There are three things in my pocket." I took his hand, guiding it down my hip to where my treasures hid in the folds of my skirt.

The song ended, and everyone in the tavern cheered.

I tipped my head back, laughing at the racket of the drunken men.

Gabe pulled me closer to him, slipping his hand deep into my pocket.

"Gabe's having a good night," a burly man hollered through the crowd.

I winked at the man as Gabe kissed the skin just below my pendant as though there were no one watching us.

The musicians struck up a fresh tune. Men began stomping in time with the song. The sound of their thumping rattled into my chest, shaking my lungs.

I tipped Gabe's chin up, kissing him, then guiding his lips to the side of my neck.

"The little vial is for the beast. It'll have a taste of berries. Slip it into his drink."

Gabe ran one hand up the side of my ribs, while the other stayed in my pocket.

"Dump the powder into a small food pot, there's enough to make ten men ill. Make sure it's not too diluted, or it won't work."

"What will it do?" He lifted me, shifting my weight so my torso pressed against his.

"Nothing they won't survive." I twined my fingers through his ringlets. "The pouch of berries is for you. Eat them as soon as the others show signs of illness."

"Why?" The ridges of his muscles tensed.

"To be sure you look like one of the fallen." I kissed him as fear flitted through his eyes.

"What will it do to me?" His lips teased mine as he spoke.

"You'll wish the gods would take you for a few hours and be fine by the next day." I rested my forehead against his. "Compared to being hanged, whipped, or burned alive by the paun, your suffering won't be much."

"When should it be done?"

I hadn't thought about the when, hadn't thought about setting a time to end a man's life.

I looked toward the ceiling, wishing the room were quiet and I could have one moment to think through the best time for murder.

Gabe kissed the top of my breasts, his tongue grazing the skin just above my bodice.

I gripped his ringlets, tipped his head back, and kissed him, trying to tell him I was sorry for giving him such a terrible task and for the pain my plan would cause.

Forgive me. May we meet again in a land of freedom.

I whispered in his ear, "The first chance you get. Let it be done."

I kissed him on the cheek and stood. His hands trailed along my waist until he couldn't reach me anymore.

I walked toward Finn, to our table in the back of the room.

A man took my hand as I passed him. "Did he not have enough to please you? I can promise I do."

I didn't look down to see the man's face. I couldn't see anyone in the tavern but Liam, standing at the back of the room. His jaw set and eyes dark.

43

"That's not what I brought you here for." A hand pinched my arm, dragging me away from Liam.

"What?" I blinked, trying to get my eyes to focus on anything besides Liam's face.

Someone shook my arm. "I pay to bring you here, pay for our drinks, and this is how you thank me?"

My gaze found a head of red hair and a livid face.

Men sniggered as Finn dragged me through the tables toward the front door.

"I have never met such an ungrateful, wretched whore in all my days." A light shone in Finn's eyes, a glint of something between triumph and warning.

I pulled my free hand back and slapped him hard across the face. "If you'd like me to pay attention to you, perhaps you should try being more interested in me than ale."

Finn pulled me to him and kissed me. I wrapped my arms around his neck, and leaned my weight against his body.

He scooped me up and carried me to the door. "This night is for me, and I'll not be sharing you." He kicked the door open and strode out into the misty night, still cradling me in his arms.

A round of hoots and cheers to lift the roof of the tavern followed us toward The Downy Loft.

"Tell me you got him everything he needed," Finn whispered as he turned onto the side street.

"He has everything, and I gave him as clear instructions as I could."

"May the gods bless you, Ena." He kissed my temple. "That was a damn fine performance."

"Did Liam see?"

"Liam and Emmet came in about when I thought Gabe was going to tear your bodice off with his teeth." Finn set me down in front of The Downy Loft. "I'm not sure what your brother thought of Gabe nigh on rolling his sister in the middle of a bar, but I don't think anyone could suspect anything but sex came of that meeting."

He opened the door, and the scent of stale soup greeted us.

Finn wrinkled his nose. "I wish we could've eaten elsewhere, but it seemed best to make a dramatic exit before more fiends came looking for a taste of you."

The little boy ran out of the kitchen, his face bright as he beamed up at Finn.

"Young sir"—Finn bowed—"I'd like any breakfast leftovers you have brought straight up to my room, along with a bit of frie."

The boy bowed so low it looked like he might tip over.

"And a pitcher of hot water for washing up," I said.

I could still taste Gabe and Finn. My neck burned where Gabe had kissed my skin. I wished I was back at Mave's where I could soak in a bath and wash Gabe's scent from my skin.

"Come on, my love." Finn took my hand, dragging me toward the stairs. "The night is young, and we mustn't waste it."

The two women hunched in the booths furrowed their brows at me as we passed.

"A bit of food and a nice night's sleep," Finn whispered as he closed the door to our room behind me. "Liam and Emmet are here, we've done our work, and tomorrow we can turn our attention toward getting home."

"Right." I untied my boots.

"Unless Liam wants to linger until the thing is done." Finn paused halfway through unbuttoning his jacket. "I'd rather be well away, but Liam is the one in charge."

"We'll see what he says."

Tap, tap, bang.

Finn opened the door and ushered in the little boy. I took the pitcher from the tray and went straight to the wash stand in the corner.

"That will be all for the evening, young sir."

I poured water on the cloth and scrubbed at my neck. Liam had seen. Had been standing there watching as Gabe...

I moved the cloth to wipe the kohl lining from my eyes, but I wasn't ready to remove my armor.

"Eat." Finn held out a plate of food. "It's cold but still better than the gray soup."

"Thanks." I sat by the fire and ate cold potatoes, listening for boots in the hall. "Do you think he'll be caught?"

"Gabe's smart. He'll find a way to do as you instructed."

"I hope so."

Boots thumped up the stairs.

I held my breath.

Knock, knock, knock.

Finn was on his feet before I could decide if I thought it was soldiers or Liam and Emmet, and which possibility was more terrifying.

Finn opened the door, and Liam and Emmet stepped through. Neither spoke as Emmet closed the door behind them.

"I'm glad you've made it here safely," Finn said. "Was it trouble at the gate?"

"What under the chivving sky were you thinking?" Emmet

tossed my black cloak down at my feet. "What sort of madness has taken your mind?"

"It worked," Finn said. "We've done what we set out to do."

"You put my sister into a pack of men." Emmet stepped toward Finn, seeming to tower over him as anger pulsed from his skin.

"It was my idea." I set my plate down. "And truth be told, I didn't give him much of a choice."

"What?" Emmet rounded on me.

"I needed to speak to Gabe myself, to be sure he understood how to use everything I gave him." I brushed my skirt off and stood. "I made Finn tell me who Gabe was and went after him myself."

Emmet's jaw tightened.

"And if you're looking for an apology, you won't get one from me." I tipped my chin up. "Frankly, I think I did a wonderful job. No one will think anything of Gabe having a bit of fun with a girl, so if you're searching for any words to say to me, you'd best start with *thank you.*"

"Thank you for playing the whore to aid our cause," Emmet said. "I'm glad you take such pride in placing yourself in danger."

"Would you say such a thing to your beloved Mave's girls?" I growled.

"I don't like them putting themselves in danger either, but they aren't my chivving sister." Emmet stormed out of the room, slamming the door behind him.

"That went about how I expected." Finn dug his fingers into his hair. "Shall I make sure he doesn't tear apart the town stone by stone, or would someone else like to claim that pleasure?"

I stared at the door. There were things I wanted to scream at Emmet but had nothing to say that would make him any less angry.

"I'll do it then." Finn grabbed the bread from his plate and his coat from by the fire and slipped out the door.

I couldn't bring myself to look at Liam. I didn't want to see the same anger in his face I'd gotten from Emmet.

"What did you give Gabe?" Liam said.

I picked my cloak up off the ground and hung it on the nail by the fire.

"You said *everything*," Liam said. "What did you give him besides the shadow berries?"

"A powered root to cause a fever for some of the other soldiers, bird berries for Gabe to eat to get a bit sick as well."

"You asked him to poison himself?"

"He'll be fine. He may wish he'd never heard of food, but it'll keep him out of the way while people are worrying about the beast's death."

Liam paced the room.

"Tell me I wasn't right," I said. "Tell me I didn't protect Gabe."

Liam kept pacing.

"It's done." I spread my arms wide. "I got the work done. And if you don't like—"

"You could have been killed." Liam's boots thumped against the floor in a maddening rhythm. "If you had been caught carrying poison, you'd have been hanged."

"Any of us would have been. I knew this was dangerous going into it. Didn't you?"

"You walked into a room packed with foul paun men, teasing them, luring them—"

"That's what Mave's primping made me fit to do."

"I saved you from that soldier in Harane. I didn't do it so you could throw yourself straight back into a den of beasts. Letting Gabe paw you like that, do you have any idea what sort of ideas that puts in evil men's—"

"Stop chivving pacing."

Liam stopped, still staring at the wall in front of him.

"Look at me."

He didn't move.

"I said look at me." I took his face in my hands.

He met my gaze, his eyes dark and unreadable.

"I had Finn," I said. "I was safe enough."

"You think Finn could protect you from a whole tavern of paun soldiers?"

"You sent me away with him. If you trust him with my safety, shouldn't I?"

He hadn't shaved since the balcony. The stubble on his cheeks had lost its coarseness.

"If Finn had been caught, we both would have hanged anyway. The ending was the same if either of us failed."

Liam stepped away from me, rubbing his hands over the place where my fingers had touched his cheeks only a moment before.

"I said that I wanted to be a Black Blood, that I wanted to help."

"By letting Gabe kiss you with a room full of men leering at you?"

"It had to be done."

"Not by you!"

I stepped forward, close enough that I had to tip my chin up to look into Liam's eyes. "What are you mad about? That I got it done, that I let Gabe touch me, or that you ever kissed me in the first place?"

Liam's gaze drifted down to my mouth. I remembered the feel of his lips against mine, and the burning of wanting flared in my chest. I leaned closer, begging the stars for him to take me in his arms and kiss me.

"Ena." He brushed his thumb over my lips and trailed his fingers down the side of my neck.

"Do you want me or not?"

Our eyes met, and then he was kissing me.

He wrapped his arms around my waist, drawing me toward him. He tasted of fire and honey and sweet winds and freedom. I parted my lips, wanting to savor more of him.

He held me closer. His heartbeat thundered in his chest, keeping time with mine.

I laced my fingers through his hair as my hunger for him burned as bright as a star destined to consume worlds. Every bit of my being knew nothing but wanting Liam.

His hand moved up my ribs, his thumb grazing the side of my breast.

I gasped as heat seared through me. I pressed myself to him, feeling every ridge of his body against mine.

"No." He stepped back.

My head spun at the absence of his touch.

"No." He stared past me, through the window to the night beyond.

"Liam." I reached for his hand.

He shook his head, turned, and walked out the door, leaving me frozen in place.

I have never believed in true love or happy endings. They are not things that have ever existed in my world.

I have always believed in pain. In agony that cuts so deep, you fear your very soul will pour out of the wound and be lost to you forever.

That torment I know well. It is as familiar to me as the scent of the air after a storm.

But my soul has never poured out of me. Somehow, I have always woken up the next morning.

Mine is not a happy love story. But there is a monster to be slain, a multitude of demons that torment our land. As long they steal innocent souls, at least I have a beast to battle.

That fight must be enough to keep me breathing.

Finn had slept on top of the covers next to me. He'd tried to sleep on the floor beside the fire, but given the bruise growing on his cheek, I'd insisted he rest somewhere soft.

I woke before he did in the morning and lay in bed, fingers wrapped around the pendant on my neck.

Part of me cherished it, a bit of Liam that was mine even if I couldn't have him. Part of me wanted to throw it out the window as a first step in shedding all thoughts of how badly I wished he were lying in bed beside me.

But I'd slept through the night, and that was a gift even the horrible mixture of shame, hurt, and longing that buried me couldn't convince me to toss aside.

The sounds of movement on the street below began just after dawn. The rattle of cart wheels fighting through mud and mumble of sleepy voices made the morning seem so peaceful for a town that had a regiment of soldiers camped nearby.

The scent of burned food drifted up the stairs. I forced myself to grin as I imagined the little boy telling Finn there was nothing for breakfast as every edible scrap in the place had been turned to ash.

Finn woke, sniffing the air. "It that breakfast?"

"You are a mockery of yourself." I tossed my pillow at his back.

"That implies a consistency of character that is difficult to find." Finn sat up. "So, I will take it as a compliment."

He gave me a lopsided grin, wincing as his swollen cheek moved. The bruise on his face took up most of the left side of his jaw. The right side, where I'd slapped him, had only been left a bit pink.

"Emmet should be walloped for hitting you." I crawled over him and out of bed. "What was the slitch thinking?"

"He didn't hit me." Finn gingerly touched his cheek.

"Did you fall and smack your face on something fist-shaped?" I tore my brush through my hair a bit harder than was wise.

"No." Finn grabbed his boots and tugged them on. "He got into a fight with some local boys, and I got punched trying to get the poor slitches out of Emmet's way before he pummeled them into the dirt."

"Why would he do that?"

"I imagine he pictured each of them as the men from the tavern who were quite openly fantasizing about shoving themselves inside his sister."

"Finn!" I tossed my hairbrush at him.

He caught it and began brushing his own hair. "I did manage to ensure no one sustained life-threatening injuries in your brother's rampage. I should be given quite a bit of credit for that feat."

"Credit to you and an earful for Emmet. How has such a chivving fool managed to keep himself alive?" I picked up the box Nora had given me.

"You've never seen him fight, have you?"

My fingers hovered over the tins of powder. Part of me wanted to throw it all away, like somehow I could blame the paint for luring Liam close enough that I thought I could have him. But there were soldiers all around, and I couldn't go back to being the girl from Harane, even if that was what a very large part of me wanted.

"Do you think we'll ride out today?" I brushed pink onto my cheeks.

"I doubt it. Liam and Emmet don't have horses."

"What?" I froze with a brush of pigment halfway to my eye.

"I haven't heard the full story, what with the neck kissing and fighting, but they made their way here on foot."

"No wonder it took them so long." I tamped down the tiny bit of sympathy that rose in my chest at the idea of the two of them traveling through that storm on foot.

"I'm sure it will be a delightful story." Finn inched closer to the door. "Once we get some food in them, and make sure Emmet's gotten past his rage at having a beauty for a sister, we can ask them to tell us the whole thrilling tale."

He stopped with his hand on the doorknob.

"You can go." I trailed the kohl along my eyelid.

"I'll wait." Finn shrugged. "Wouldn't want to leave you alone."

He gazed longingly at the crack in the door as though the scent of burned food were somehow appealing.

"Are you afraid of facing them without me?" I laughed. The feel of it grated against the wound in my chest.

"Not afraid, just wise enough to better my chances with your presence."

I finished drawing on the face of someone who cherished their beauty and let Finn lead me from our room.

"Well, my love," Finn said as we stepped down into the dining room, "a bit of breakfast, and I'm sure we'll both feel better about last night."

A hint of smoke drifted out of the kitchen and lingered on the dining room ceiling, swirling through the spiderwebs. The woman behind the bar had red in her cheeks. I couldn't tell if the hue had been born of anger or tears.

Emmet sat alone at a table, facing the front door.

"We could ask the boy to bring food to our room," I whispered to Finn.

"I hear the kingless territories are beautiful this time of year," Finn said. "We could hop a boat and leave Ilbrea behind forever."

I nudged him in the ribs. "Do not tempt me, Finn, or you'll find yourself on a ship sailing south."

"We all must have dreams." Finn laughed.

Emmet turned toward the sound, glowering as though his glare could burn the world.

"You woke up cheery." I set my face in a pleasant grin, delighting as Emmet balled his hands into fists on the table. Cuts and bruises marked his knuckles. "A good night's sleep can fix the worst of woes. Though those"—I pointed to the fresh wounds—"could use a bit of care. Have you even bothered to wash them properly?"

"I'll order some food." Finn darted toward the bar.

"Of course, in a place like this, who knows how clean the water is?" I said. "We could find some strong liquor to pour on them. I'll have to check your stitches, too. I'm sure not all of them are still in place after you ran around like a chivving fool last night."

I waited for Emmet to say something. I wanted so badly for him to scream and rage so fresh anger could drown out the hurt in my chest.

"Do you want to die of infection?" I sat opposite Emmet, blocking his view of the door. "It's a terrible way to go, but I suppose it's your choice to make."

He inched his chair to the side to see around me.

I stood, leaning in toward him. "Answer me, Emmet."

"I've lived through far worse than this with no one to tend my wounds. I'm not concerned about scrapes and pulled stitches. A few more scars won't damage me. Now sit down and pretend to be a proper girl."

"A proper girl?" I perched on the edge of the table. "What makes a proper girl? Should I find myself a nice man to marry, stay out of the way while the men do the work?"

"I'm not fool enough to expect such a thing of my sister." Emmet laid his hands flat on the table. "But as you played whore and assassin last night and we still need to get back to the mountains alive, a smart girl would sit nicely and eat her chivving breakfast. The best we can hope for is no one taking notice of us."

I slid into the chair to Emmet's right, clearing his view of the door. "Is that what you were doing when you went out to pick a fight last night? Was that you not being noticed?"

"At least I kept my clothes in place."

Finn froze beside our table.

"I wish you hadn't waited so long to tell me shifting my skirts upsets you," I said. "From now on, I'll have to make a point of being naked as often as possible."

"Perhaps I will eat in the room." Finn backed away.

"Of course not." I pushed the chair opposite me out with my toe. "*Proper* people eat breakfast in the dining room, and we must appear *proper*."

"Right." Finn sank down into his chair, his ears turning pink as he glanced between Emmet and me. "I asked about breakfast. It might be a minute as there was an incident, which we can all smell, of course, but I've been promised there will be edible food available soon."

"Good," I said, "we can't have you going hungry after you so bravely helped Emmet last night. As a matter of fact, I think Emmet should thank you for saving him from himself."

"That's not necessary." Finn widened his eyes at me.

"Of course it is," I said. "You got hit in the face for him."

"You're the one who slapped him," Emmet growled.

"Oh, Finn didn't mind that," I laughed. "Matter of fact, I think he liked it. The kissing wasn't bad either."

"Ena!" Finn said at the same moment Emmet leapt to his feet and a bell rang outside.

Everyone in the tavern froze.

The ringing came closer, like whoever held the bell was running along the street.

"What does the bell mean?" I whispered.

Emmet glared at the front door, and Finn shook his head.

I crept toward the bar as the ringing came closer still. "What does the bell mean?" I whispered to the barkeep.

"Someone is searching town for the healer," the woman said. "They ring the bell to call her if she's not at home."

A sense of dread trickled into my stomach. If the healer were being called, then the time had come for the beast to die.

But soldiers traveled with their own healers.

That didn't make a difference nine years ago.

I dug my nails into my palms to keep my hands from shaking as the ringing moved past us.

Nantic's healer had been helping the soldiers when my mother died because their own healer had been drunk. Maybe this healer was drunk as well. Maybe the soldiers' healer had been confounded by the poison and wanted help. Maybe it wasn't a soldier who needed help but a woman gone into labor.

Movement in the dining room resumed as the ringing faded away.

I walked silently back to the table and took my seat. "Where's Liam?"

"Finding new horses," Emmet said.

"Probably best you didn't go with him. Who knows if you punched the stable boy last night?" My joy in needling Emmet had vanished.

We sat at the table, waiting for food, as the bell rang again, traveling back in the opposite direction.

I buried my hands in my pockets to hide their shaking. If the healer had been called to the camp and a tilk was looking for the healer as well, then it would be my fault their call for aid was going unanswered.

I could help. If someone was ill or bleeding, I should help. But offering my skills to strangers could too easily end in my being hanged.

The bell had long since faded away by the time the little boy brought us a tray of food.

"Thank you, kind sir." Finn's bow lacked it usual playful joy.

The boy didn't seem to notice.

We ate half-cooked potatoes and some sort of meat. The three of us kept glancing toward the door, searching for Liam.

"Does he have enough money for two horses?" I asked after a long while.

Emmet nodded.

A sound began in the distance, not the ringing, but a different noise. A steady booming like the beating of a massive drum.

I stood and crept toward the bar again. "What does that mean?"

"I've no idea." The woman furrowed her brow.

There was something in the booming that made me afraid, though I wasn't sure why.

"I'm going to look for Liam." Finn stood as I returned to the table.

"No, you're not," Emmet said.

"We need to leave," Finn said.

"And if he shows up a minute after you walk out?" I took Finn's arm. "You're the one who said we couldn't risk missing each other in the wild."

"Fine." Finn pinched his nose between his hands. "You get our packs, I'll make sure the horses are ready."

I shoved one more cold, crunchy potato into my mouth and headed for the stairs. Emmet's boots thumped against the wooden floor as he followed me.

"You don't think I can get my pack without a man toying with my breasts?" I asked as I hurried up the stairs.

"I have my own bags to gather."

We split ways as he ran two stairs at a time to the floor above. I shoved the few things Finn and I had used back into our packs, hoisted them onto my shoulders, and draped my cloak over my arm. The tightness of my bodice made it hard to breathe while bearing the extra weight.

The door to my room flung open before I could reach it.

"Ena." Liam stood in the doorway, sweat slicking his brow, worry marring his eyes.

"What's wrong?"

He lifted Finn's pack from my shoulder. "We have to go."

"Why?" I followed him down the stairs, lifting my skirt so I could run. "Liam, why?"

A dozen horrible possibilities raced through my mind.

Emmet ran down into the dining room the moment after we'd arrived.

The booming had grown louder in the few minutes we'd been gone.

Boom. Boom.

The women who had been in the booths were gone. The barkeep had disappeared as well.

"Where's Finn?" Liam asked.

"Getting our horses," I said as Liam shoved me out the door.

Two new horses waited for us, tied up outside The Downy Loft.

The booming carried from the main street, and voices sounded over its resonance.

"Emmet, take Ena. Ride to the edge of the woods." Liam

yanked my pack from my shoulder, tying it onto the back of his horse.

"You take her," Emmet said. "I'll go with Finn."

"He's in the stable. He's right behind us," I said as Liam grabbed me around the waist, lifting me toward the horse. "We should—"

A familiar clink of metal carried from the north, a sound I had only heard a few times before and would grow to know too well by the end of my life.

I broke free from Liam's grip.

"It's not too late." Emmet met Liam's eyes.

Finn tore around the corner, the reins of our horses in his hands.

The main street fell silent.

"We are not mud!" a voice shouted. "We are not filth to be abused. Our women do not give birth for the pleasure of the Guilds. Our children are not born to be hoarded by the Sorcerers. Our lives are worth more than waiting to die at the hands of the golden demons."

I walked toward the shouted words. I had never heard such things spoken of in the open, let alone shouted for an entire town to hear.

The clinking came faster, surrounding us from the south and the west as well.

"We have spent years convincing ourselves we deserve to be punished, to have our children stolen by the Guilds. If we have suffered for so long, then the stars must have ordained our punishment."

A hand took mine, but didn't try to hold me back as I continued toward the voice.

"But the gods have seen fit to teach us how wrong we have been. Drason is dead. The monster who tormented us has been killed by the gods. They have brought illness among his men. The gods themselves have smiled upon us. They have set us free."

I reached the corner and looked down the main street.

A hundred people surrounded a wagon.

A man stood on top of the wagon, a club in one hand, a wide-stretched drum in the other. He tipped his face up to the sky. "What will you do with that freedom?"

The world seemed to slow as the man on the wagon looked back toward the crowd. The clinking stopped, and an arm wrapped around my waist, pulling me toward the side of a building.

"You have not been granted permission to gather," a voice shouted.

A sea of black had closed off both ends of the main street and come up behind us to block our path back to The Downy Loft.

"Disperse at once." A soldier stepped in front of his fellows. The golden star stitched onto the chest of his uniform glinted in the light.

"The gods have granted us freedom from you." The man on the wagon raised his arms toward the sky. "The beast Drason is dead. Leave our home."

"This town, all land in Ilbrea, is the property of the Guilds," the soldier said. "You dwell here at their pleasure."

"My family's been on our land for five generations," a woman shouted. "How can that not give us a claim to it?"

"There is no claim but the Guilds'." The soldier took another step forward.

The men behind him matched his movement.

"They claim our land, our blood, our children." The man on the wagon struck his drum with a boom that shook my ears. "The gods have freed us from the monster, and we will not lose that freedom."

"The Guilds will send a new commander," the soldier began. "Commander Drason's death—"

"Is a miracle," a young man shouted. "Chivving bastard got what he deserved."

A roar of approval rose from the tilk.

"Get out of our town!" a woman shouted.

"He deserved to die twenty times for what he stole from us." A girl reached down and picked up a clump of mud.

I watched her gather the dirt in her hand. Watched her throw the filth at the soldiers. I strained against the arm that held me, as though I could somehow outpace the flying mud and catch it before it struck its mark.

The scraping of swords clearing sheaths cut through the shouts of the mob.

"We will not allow you to steal the freedom the gods have granted us!" The man banged his drum. An arrow tipped with black feathers struck his chest before the boom had died.

A moment of calm, quicker than a heartbeat, stilled the street.

With a roar, the tilk charged toward the soldiers, carrying no weapons but their rage.

"No!" I fought against the arm that held me. "Stop them. You have to stop them!"

A clang of metal close by drew my gaze from the bloodshed on the street.

A pack of soldiers surged toward us, their weapons raised. Finn met them head on, parrying the blows of the pauns' weapons with his sword.

Bellowing, Emmet leapt into the fray, unsheathing the daggers at his hips.

"Stay here." Liam let go of me and ran toward the others, both hands raised.

Emmet ducked beneath a slicing sword, driving his blade into the throat of a soldier as Finn slashed through the belly of another.

"Get down!" Liam shouted.

Emmet and Finn dove, rolling away from the soldiers.

Liam opened his hands. A horde of stones hovered above his palms then shot toward the soldiers, striking a dozen of the beasts in the chest. But as the men fell, ten more stepped up behind them.

Emmet and Finn were already on their feet, diving back into the fight. Liam ran forward, drawing his own blade.

"Help me!" a voice shouted from the main street.

The soldiers had surrounded the tilk, cutting them down like they were no more than weeds. A boy broke free of the soldiers, clutching a wound in his side.

I started toward him, desperate to help stop the bleeding. An arrow struck him in the back of the neck. He didn't even scream as he fell toward the ground.

A hand grabbed my arm, whipping me around. A soldier with blood on his face seized my hair, flinging me into the mud as though I were no more than a doll. The fall knocked the air from my lungs, and mud blurred my vision.

He raised his sword, its point aimed at my gut.

"Please don't," I begged, my fingers fumbling as I reached for the blade hidden in my boot. "I'll do anything you want, just don't kill me."

The man smiled.

I closed my fingers around the hilt of my knife and yanked it free. It glinted in the sunlight for a split second before I drove the blade into the soldier's thigh.

He screamed, whether from pain or anger, I didn't know.

I pulled my knife free and aimed higher, stabbing just above his hip as his sword slashed for my neck.

I rolled to the side, wrenching my blade from his gut. Pain sliced through my back as I scrambled to my feet, my skirt heavy with mud.

A roar of rage came from behind me.

I set my teeth, determined not to scream as the soldier killed me. I spun to face him, but he was already dead with Emmet's dagger sticking out of his chest.

"Get up." Finn rode toward me, my horse beside him.

"But—"

"Now." Emmet shoved me toward my horse.

I fought against the weight of my mud-laden skirt, trying to get my foot into the stirrup.

Emmet lifted me, setting me stomach-first on the saddle as he had done when I was too little to climb up by myself.

By the time I had gotten astride, Liam and Finn were mounted on their horses beside me, facing the soldiers on the main street.

"We have to help them." The words tore at my throat.

"There's no one to help." Finn kicked his horse and rode away from the Massacre of Marten.

47

I wished for a storm during that horrible ride back to the mountains. I wished the sky would open and rain would wash away the blood and dirt that covered me. But the sky seemed as determined as I not to shed a tear.

I didn't speak in the hours it took to reach the forest, or stop to tend to the others' wounds or let them look after mine. Our injuries were not as dangerous as being out in the open.

Dusk had come by the time we reached the canopy of trees. The forest smelled of new life. No one had told the woods of the death that surrounded us.

"It's my fault." My voice crackled as I spoke. "It wasn't the gods who killed the beast, it was me. I started it, and now those people are dead."

A heavy burden beyond grief weighed on my entire being.

"It's not your fault." Emmet guided his horse to ride next to mine. "The soldiers didn't come to town seeking vengeance for a murder. They came to stop a man from spreading hope. Hope is more dangerous to the Guilds than we could ever be."

"It started with me," I said.

Finn passed me a waterskin. "Don't think like that. Unarmed

men who run against swords—they're already dead. We saw them choose the end of their torment. They had a moment of freedom, one choice that was theirs alone. Many would be willing to die for that."

"More will before the end of it." Liam didn't look back. He kept riding in front of us, guiding us to safety in the mountains. "But we have to keep fighting. If we stop, there won't be any hope left at all."

48

Hope and freedom. The words pounded in my head for weeks, burning themselves into my memories of the Massacre at Marten. The blood washed away, the wounds healed, but hope and freedom—they carried me into the darkness that lay ahead.

Ena's journey continues in Mountain and Ash. *Read on for a sneak preview.*

THE GUILDS ARE NOT HER ONLY ENEMY.

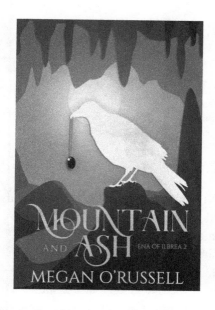

Continue reading for a sneak peek of *Mountain and Ash*.

1

"Look at me." I took the child's face in my hands, blocking her view of everything but my eyes. "Look at me, love. Don't look at anything but me."

Her tear-filled gaze found my face.

"Good girl." I smiled.

A banging echoed from the street, but I couldn't tell the distance. The next house over, maybe the one beside that—my heart raced too fast for me to be sure.

"You are the bravest little girl in the world," I said. "Did you know that?"

She took a shuddering breath but didn't answer.

"You are so brave, you can do anything. I promise you can." I picked the child up. She weighed nothing in my arms. "Do you know what we do when we're brave?"

The girl looked over my shoulder toward the corner of the room.

"No, look at me." I balanced her on one hip, using my free hand to block the side of her vision. "When we are very brave, we look into the darkness, and we say, *I am not afraid.*"

A woman screamed in the distance.

The child gripped the front of my bodice in her little hands.

"We do not scream, we do not cry." I moved closer to the window. "We stare into the shadows and whisper, *I am not afraid.* Say it. Say, *I am not afraid.*"

Her lips wobbled as a fresh batch of tears glistened on her cheeks.

"Say, *I am not afraid.*" I slid the window open.

The crash of splintering wood carried from the street.

The child didn't look away from my eyes.

"Say, *I am not afraid.* Come on." I wiped the tears from her cheeks. "*I am not afraid.*"

"I am not afraid." Her voice cracked as she spoke with me. "I am not afraid."

"You are the bravest girl in the whole world," I whispered in her ear. "You will not scream when you're scared. Only whisper, *I am not afraid.*"

"I'm not afraid."

"Good girl." I held her out the window and let go.

She didn't scream as she fell, but a gasp came from the corner of the room.

"What have you done?" The woman cowering deep in the shadows shook with quiet sobs.

"What's best for your daughter," I said.

A bang came from close by, but the floor didn't rattle. The soldiers hadn't reached this house.

"Do you want to join her or not?" I said. "We're out of time. You have to choose."

"I..." The woman stepped toward the window. "I have five children. I have a home and a shop."

"May you find peace with the choice you've made." I lifted my skirt and climbed onto the windowsill.

"Please"—the woman grabbed my arm—"she's my baby."

"Not anymore. You have four children. Your baby does not exist."

"She needs me."

I took the mother's face in my hands as I had done with the child's. "She will never know fear again. She will not know pain or darkness. For the rest of your days, think of her in sunlit fields, running through bright spring flowers. You have given her endless peace, and she will always be thankful."

The woman fell to her knees, coughing through the sobs that wracked her chest.

"Remember her laugh and her smell." I turned toward the starless night. "Remember that it is still your duty to protect her." I stepped from the window ledge and plummeted into the darkness.

The warm wind lifted my hair from my neck as I fell. I exhaled all the breath in my body, bending my knees as I landed in the wide bed of hay.

"Ena?" Finn leapt up onto the front seat of the wagon. "Are you hurt?"

"Go." I scrambled through the hay, fighting my way to the front of the cart. "Is she under?"

"Didn't make a peep." Finn clicked the horse to walk. "I've seen grown men crumble at what that five-year-old faced silently."

"She's strong." I climbed into the seat beside Finn, brushing the hay from my skirt. "She'll make it."

"Of course she will. She's got us looking out for her." Finn steered the cart out of the alley behind the houses and onto the rut-covered thoroughfare of the tiny chivving town called Wilton.

"Halt." A soldier stepped in front of our cart.

"Whoa." Finn reined in the horse. "Happy to stop for you, sir. Is there something I can help you with?"

I clung to Finn, sliding my hand beneath his to coat to grip the hilt of his knife.

"We're searching for a sorcerer hidden in this village," the soldier said.

Four men in black uniforms stepped out of the shadows to surround our wagon.

"Sorcerer?" Finn said.

"Like magic?" I asked. "By the Guilds, you've got to find them. Are we safe? Is the sorcerer going to try to kill us?"

Two of the soldiers climbed into the back of our wagon.

"Do you really need to search our wagon?" Finn asked.

"Who cares about where they're searching?" I swatted Finn on the arm with my free hand. "We've got to get out of here. Unless the sorcerer is on the road. Oh, by the Guilds, do you know which way the sorcerer ran?"

The soldiers dug through the hay in our cart, tossing it out onto the dirt road.

"Hush, my love." Finn wrapped an arm around my waist.

"What if they're waiting in the dark?" Fat tears slid down my cheeks. "What if they're lurking by the road, waiting to attack? I told you I didn't want to leave home. My mother warned me of all the horrors that wait in the world."

"You're fine, my love." Finn wiped the tears from my cheeks. "I promise, I will not let any harm come to you." He brushed his lips against mine.

I pulled myself closer to him, letting my chest press against his as I parted his lips with my tongue.

"Hey." A soldier smacked his hand against our wagon.

"Sorry," Finn said.

"Sorry." I pulled away from him, tucking his blade under my skirt.

"The wagon's empty." A soldier hopped down from the back of the cart.

"Move on then."

The men stepped aside to let us pass.

"Thank you." Finn bowed his head. "Thank you for reminding

me there are some things in Ilbrea that are worth protecting." He laid his hand on my thigh.

"You are such a wonderful man." I leaned in to kiss Finn again.

"Get out of here before we have to take you in for indecency." The soldier had a smirk on his face as he waved us on.

"Sorry about that." Finn clicked for the horse to walk. "Have a lovely evening."

I clung tightly to his arm as the wagon rattled forward, smiling at the soldiers and listening for the sniffles of a small child coming from below.

2

It was well into the night by the time we'd gotten far enough away from Wilton to risk sleep.

Finn stopped by a stand of trees, cooing lovingly to our horse as he unhooked her from the cart.

"You are such a good girl." Finn patted the horse. "Such a pretty, kind girl."

"Should I be jealous of the horse, my love?" I hopped down from my seat, taking one last look around before heading to the back of the wagon.

"Never," Finn said. "There is nothing in this world that comes close to my adoration of you."

"Careful, you might make a girl blush." I ran my fingers along the back of the cart, searching for the latch to our hidey hole.

I slipped the metal aside and lifted the three long boards that made up the center of the cart. The compartment below was wide enough to fit two adults if they lay side by side, and just deep enough to leave a few inches of space above a person's nose.

I held my breath as I squinted into the shadows. I'd come up with a hundred different things to say to comfort the child and a dozen apologies for having locked her in the dark.

The child lay in the corner, clinging to a folded up blanket.

"You're all right now," I whispered as I climbed into the compartment. "Let's get you someplace more comfortable to sleep."

The child didn't move.

"You can come out now." I knelt beside her.

She didn't stir.

My heart skittered against my ribs as I laid my fingers on the child's throat. She gave a shuddering sigh and nestled her face into the blanket.

"Oh, thank the gods." I ran my hands over my face.

"She all right?" Finn peered in from the back of the wagon.

"Sleeping." I lifted her, cradling her to my chest. "I wonder how long it took her to drift off."

"Hopefully not too long." Finn reached for the child.

Part of me didn't want to hand her over. I'd taken the girl from her mother. I should be the one clutching her in my arms until we could leave her someplace where she wasn't in any danger. But her safe haven was still very far away.

She would be passed from hand to hand a dozen times before she'd truly be free of the Guilds. Finn and I were just one tiny cog in the massive clockwork that would ferry her south to a place where she would never need to be afraid again.

"Come on." Finn held his arms higher. "The sooner we get to sleep, the happier I'll be."

"Try not to wake her."

It didn't take long for us to get the tent up, a circle of stones placed around us, and the bedrolls down. I tucked the child in, and she still didn't fuss. Finn and I slept on either side of her, each with a weapon tucked beneath our heads. I stared at the canvas of the tent for a long while, waiting for sleep to come. I drifted into darkness, clutching the stone pendant around my neck.

Order your copy of Mountain and Ash *to continue the story.*

ESCAPE INTO ADVENTURE

Thank you for reading *Ember and Stone*. If you enjoyed the book, please consider leaving a review to help other readers find Ena's story.

Ena's journey began before she joined the Black Bloods. Learn more about her life in Harane in *Wrath and Wing*.

Join Megan O'Russell's Readers Community to receive a free copy of *Wrath and Wing*, the prequel novella to *Ember and Stone*. You can sign up by following this link: https://www.meganorussell.com/wrath-newsletter

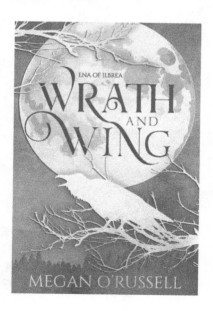

ABOUT THE AUTHOR

 Megan O'Russell is the author of several Young Adult series that invite readers to escape into worlds of adventure. From *Girl of Glass*, which blends dystopian darkness with the heart-pounding danger of vampires, to *Ena of Ilbrea*, which draws readers into an epic world of magic and assassins.

With the *Girl of Glass* series, *The Tethering* series, *The Chronicles of Maggie Trent*, *The Tale of Bryant Adams*, the *Ena of Ilbrea* series, and several more projects planned for 2020, there are always exciting new books on the horizon. To be the first to hear about new releases, free short stories, and giveaways, sign up for Megan's newsletter by visiting the following:

https://www.meganorussell.com/book-signup.

Originally from Upstate New York, Megan is a professional musical theatre performer whose work has taken her across North America. Her chronic wanderlust has led her from Alaska to Thailand and many places in between. Wanting to travel has fostered Megan's love of books that allow her to visit countless new worlds from her favorite reading nook. Megan is also a lyricist and playwright. Information on her theatrical works can be found at RussellCompositions.com.

She would be thrilled to chat with you on Facebook or

Twitter @MeganORussell, elated if you'd visit her website MeganORussell.com, and over the moon if you'd like the pictures of her adventures on Instagram @ORussellMegan.

ALSO BY MEGAN O'RUSSELL

The Girl of Glass Series
Girl of Glass
Boy of Blood
Night of Never
Son of Sun

The Tale of Bryant Adams
How I Magically Messed Up My Life in Four Freakin' Days
Seven Things Not to Do When Everyone's Trying to Kill You
Three Simple Steps to Wizarding Domination

The Tethering Series
The Tethering
The Siren's Realm
The Dragon Unbound
The Blood Heir

The Chronicles of Maggie Trent
The Girl Without Magic
The Girl Locked With Gold
The Girl Cloaked in Shadow

Ena of Ilbrea
Wrath and Wing
Ember and Stone
Mountain and Ash

Ice and Sky

Feather and Flame

Guilds of Ilbrea

Inker and Crown